NOTHING TO LOSE

NOTHING TO LOSE

A Novel

Mike Holst

From The Author of A Long Way Back

iUniverse, Inc.
New York Bloomington Shanghai

NOTHING TO LOSE

iUniverse books may be ordered through booksellers or by contacting:

iUniverse
1663 Liberty Drive
Bloomington, IN 47403
www.iuniverse.com
1-800-Authors (1-800-288-4677)

Because of the dynamic nature of the Internet, any Web addresses or links contained in this book may have changed since publication and may no longer be valid.

This is a work of fiction. All of the characters, names, incidents, organizations, and dialogue in this novel are either the products of the author's imagination or are used fictitiously.

ISBN: 978-0-595-51432-8 (pbk)
ISBN: 978-0-595-61897-2 (ebk)

Printed in the United States of America

This book is dedicated to my son Greg, who gave so much of his time and talents to being a devoted police officer. Like so many of them, he lived the job to its fullest until the job nearly consumed him. The job may be over for him, but the pride he feels will live on forever in his heart, and mine.

FOREWORD

This story is about the untold side of the life of a police officer and his family. All too often we see only the officer that has been hired to protect us, and we forget that they, like all of us, have loves and dislikes, spouses and kids, friends and family. We don't realize that police officers don't have a job that is easy to leave behind them at the end of the day. That they shed that stoic protector image and all their armor to go home and take on a new look as mothers and fathers, husbands and wives, friends and lovers. A time when they sometimes strive hard to put some normalcy back in their lives.

You will see a side of police work that exists, yet no one talks about. It is a look at the politics at the top of the department, and the undying camaraderie between the officers. The dedication to the job of ridding our cities and neighborhoods of crime, and the vicious people they deal with, as well as the criminals who often have no regard for human life and suffering.

This is also the story of an officer who made the supreme sacrifice and about the heartbreak that followed in its aftermath for his family. Those fears that every police officer's spouse lives with will come to life in this story as you have never imagined. This story is a poignant reminder of what can happen, and too often does happen.

And it is the story of a wife who takes over where the laws that were meant to protect her let her down, and how she takes on a role that sickens her in order to find some kind of justice. She finds that to get to the right people, like police officers, she has to get in the gutter with them.

In real life we can't always control the outcome of adversity such as this, but in the world of fictional literature we do have the means and the liberty of making it right. Here is how one woman tried to do just that.

Mike Holst

ACKNOWLEDGEMENTS

This book would not have been possible without the work of Donna Nelson, my editor extraordinaire, or without the love and support of Kitty, who looked over my shoulder each step of the way. A special thanks to all of the police officers I have known in my years of public safety, especially those in Brooklyn Park and Champlin, Minnesota.

A POLICE OFFICER'S PRAYER

Lord I ask for courage

Courage to face and
Conquer my own fears …

Courage to take me
Where others will not go …

I ask for strength

Strength of body to protect others
And strength of spirit to lead others …

I ask for dedication

Dedication to my job, to do it well
Dedication to my community
To keep it safe …

Give me Lord, concern
For others who trust me
And compassion for those who need me …

And please Lord

Through it all
Be at my side …

—Author Unknown

-I-

Beth rolled over in bed and looked at the red numbers on the digital alarm clock through her half-closed sleepy eyes. It seemed like it had been only a few hours ago that she had curled up next to Mick and tried to forget all of the bad things that had happened the day before. He always felt so good to spoon with, and she loved to soak up some of that body heat he was always radiating, especially in the middle of winter, and especially in Minnesota. There was a sense of comfort beyond the warmth of his body however; it was the security of knowing he was lying there beside her. He was her rock, her protector and her comforter.

But right now was no time to be nostalgic. The clock read 7:14 a.m. and, she needed to get out of bed and back into reality. Mick had been gone for over an hour, his spot in the bed now cold, and Sarah had to get up and have her hair fixed for school. And Beth needed to shower, fix her own hair, and go over some assignments she had made for her fourth grade class.

"Sarah, get up and get your teeth brushed, honey. We are running late again," she said as she passed Sarah's bedroom doorway on her way to the kitchen. Beth poured a cup of lukewarm coffee that Mick had left for her, and punched the microwave to 100 seconds.

Then it was back to Sarah's bedroom for a second call. The little red-haired girl was sitting on the edge of the bed holding her holiday teddy bear and rubbing her eyes with the back of her hand.

"Sarah lets go!" Beth's voice had raised an octave. "Get in the bathroom, and please put on some clean underpants. Come on … move, child, move." She patted Sarah on the butt as she herded the still half-asleep little girl into the bathroom.

While Sarah was brushing her teeth, Beth brushed out her long red hair and put it in a ponytail, snapping a red clip in place to hold it, and then swiped her face with a warm soapy washcloth before taking her back into the bedroom.

"Put on that outfit on the chair, pumpkin, and then get downstairs. Mommy's sorry we're late again." She bent over and kissed her daughters forehead, which brought a sleepy smile. Sarah had yet to make a sound.

Beth rushed back to the kitchen, poured some juice and tossed a Pop Tart in the toaster. "Not very nutritious, but oh, so delicious." She laughed at her little poem.

Mother and daughter met on the steps as she was going back upstairs. "Drink your juice, honey. Your pop tart is in the toaster. Then get out to the corner. You have five minutes till the bus gets here." Beth pulled the drapes back just enough to peek outside while she kicked her pajama bottoms off. It was cloudy but not snowing and it looked mild enough, because the streets were still wet and not frozen. Some kids were already at the corner waiting for the bus, shrieking and laughing while they threw snowballs at each other.

Beth slipped her nightshirt off and headed for the shower, stopping at the top of the steps to yell at Sarah to get going, but there was no answer. She had already left.

Mick's wet towel still lay draped over the back of the toilet stool and she threw it on the floor as she sat down to relieve herself. She was staring at his dirty boxers on the floor in front of her. Beth picked up his dirty clothes and threw them with the towel thinking, *Good old Mick, such a neat freak.*

The shower felt good and some day she was going to have the luxury of just standing in there until the water ran cold and let it wash all of her troubles away. She ran her hands over her breasts as she washed, feeling for lumps … a habit she had formed since her mom died of breast cancer two years ago. All she found was a hickie on the side of her breast from Mick, and she smiled, remembering their love-making session of the night before. They were undeniably good together, and Mick knew all the right moves to pleasure her. They had been married for thirteen years and he had had a lot of practice.

Thirteen years of marriage, and thirteen years on the police force for Mick. Beth had still been in college when they got married, and for the last nine years she had been teaching fourth grade at White Oak Elementary. She took part of one year off to have Sarah eight years ago, but other than that had never missed a day.

Suddenly as if a hypnotist had snapped his fingers bringing her out of a deep trance, she realized she had been in the shower way too long and grabbed her towel from the rack. After quickly drying herself, she wrapped it around hers body, and went back to the bedroom. She quickly put on panties, a bra, some gray slacks, a white sweater and those gold ring earrings Mick had gotten her for her birthday.

A mess of uncollected thoughts were racing through her mind *Brush out my hair and I can do the makeup in the car. My shoes. My shoes. Where? In the kitchen where I kicked them off last night. Where did I leave my briefcase? That's right. It's in the car, right where I left it.*

Beth grabbed her coffee out of the microwave, a banana from the counter and went out the side door, hitting the garage door opener as she went. Damn, she was getting good at this. She would look at those assignments at school.

Mick Motrin loved being a cop. From the time he had been a small child he had told everyone he wanted to be a policeman. But what kid didn't? The big difference with Mick was it wasn't just a dream; he had actually become one. Right out of high school he had gone to college and received his degree in criminal justice.

Mick was a big strapping guy with the kind of a goofy smile that almost made you think he was always up to no good. He loved to laugh, and he loved to make Beth laugh. Their world was a playground to Mick, and he was the playground leader. But when things got serious, as they often do in police work, that impish grin would fade and a look of grim determination would take over. He would run his hand through those curly black locks, and say, "Let's get it on."

He stayed after work each night to work out in the physical training room, and it showed. His stomach was flat and his arms rippled with muscles. He could still run five miles without exerting himself much. He looked good and he loved looking good. Nothing looked worse than a cop with a big paunch hanging over his gun belt, and Mick would be the first to tell you that.

Three years ago, after ten years on the streets, Mick had changed course and gone into investigation. Not that he didn't like the streets … he did, but he just wanted to learn it all. He wanted to be all that he could be. He had been shot at, spit on, and cursed at. He had been in fights with people who had ripped his uniform halfway off, and had gone home many nights with bruises and welts, but always he came back for more, and more determined than ever.

He came back for more because there were times when he could help an old lady breathe until the ambulance got there, or take a wandering toddler back to its mother. He had delivered a baby once, and swum in a freezing river to pull a young boy to safety. He had stuck his finger into a bullet hole in a teenager's body to stop the blood flow and cried when the boy died in his arms. Yes, Sergeant Mick Mortin was a cop's cop.

Mick's partner in investigation was Larry Sorenson. Larry, unlike Mick, was small and wiry. Larry, or Lars, as Mick called him, was the brains of the operation. He was patient and thoughtful like his partner, but he was also a genius at investigation. He missed very little at a crime scene, and he and Mick had become as close as brothers.

Lars was also gay, a secret he had shared with only one person—Mick—and the topic had never again been discussed after it had first been disclosed. Larry loved classical music, or 'that longhaired shit," as Mick called it. He had an apartment in the northeast section of town where he had lived with his dad for many years, but recently his dad had gone into a rest home, so now, for the first time, he was alone.

Larry was often with Mick on their days off and they went running or duck hunting up-state, or he would come over and watch Sarah when Mick and Beth wanted to just get away for an evening. Beth had also grown to think of him as a close friend, and she shared his secret, unbeknownst to Larry, as Mick had sworn her to secrecy.

Today was like any other day in homicide. Larry had been down in the coroner's office getting a report, and Mick was working on finishing up some reports. There were only two other people in the office, and they both were on the phone when Mick's phone rang.

"Motrin here. Homicide."

"Sergeant Motrin, this is Lieutenant Collier. We are on the scene of what looks to me to be a double drug-related killing. Can you break free and get down here? I couldn't find your supervisor anywhere."

"Naw, he's down at the coroner's office with Larry, but they should be back any minute. What say I head your way? Where are you at?"

"Just north on Morgan and Broadway. You'll see the cars."

Mick drove out of the compound behind the station and headed west on Broadway. There had been a rash of killings on the north side in the last few months, and they had very few leads. This would make numbers five and six.

He keyed the mike on the car radio and asked for unit 471, his supervisor's car. He and Larry should be done by now.

"Wicks here," the call was answered.

"Hey, Captain, this is Motrin, is Larry with you?" Mick swerved to avoid a jaywalker who had run out from between two cars. "Hey," he yelled, "use the crosswalk. Do you want to get run over?"

"Yes, he is," said Wicks. "We've been monitoring your situation and we'll be there in about five."

Mick turned the corner onto Morgan and gazed into a sea of squad cars and an ambulance. An officer in the middle of the street held up his hand and Mick lowered the driver's window.

"Hey, Mick, how you doing?" The man in the street stuck his outstretched hand through the open window.

"Kowalski, how you been? Still freezing your butt off on the old beat?"

"Yeah, Sarg, but I like the area. Never a dull moment. Hey, Sarg, I think they want you out back in the alley."

Mick swung the unmarked car around, and drove down half a block. Another officer stood in the middle of the alley blocking his entrance, but Mick flashed his badge out the window and she stepped aside. She pointed and said, "Three houses up and on the left." He drove ahead and stopped the car, trying to park off the beaten track as much as possible. He could already see somebody's foot horizontal under the garage door, which was hanging suspended a few inches above the apron.

A paramedic walked out of the garage's service door, followed by a fire fighter. Both of them were talking and shaking their heads, but they were too far away for Mick to hear what they were saying. He could hear tires rolling behind him, however, and he turned and looked as Larry got out of the car.

"There won't be anybody left living on this side of town if they don't quit shooting each other," Larry said sarcastically, as he caught up with Mick. The two men walked up to the garage and stood in the service doorway. The floor was littered with blood-soaked gauze pads and discarded latex gloves.

One police officer and the lieutenant stood leaning against the far wall. "Hey, we finally can go," the lieutenant said.

"Not until you tell us what you know about this," Larry said.

"Not much, Larry. Squad 414 answered the call about fifteen minutes ago. It came in as 'several gunshots out back'. The woman in the house, who's still in there with another officer, called it in. She's a real mess. Can't make heads or tails out of her gibberish."

Mick walked back outside and noticed a few drops of blood on the sidewalk. He put a red evidence flag alongside of them. There were also two shell casings and he marked those, too, then went back to the garage where Larry was examining the body closest to the door. One of the victims appeared to be of Asian decent and the other was Hispanic.

The Asian man appeared to have been shot twice in the back, high up, almost in the neck. The other man looked like he had been shot once in the throat and once in the face. Both shots had come from the front. He had a 38-caliber revolver still in his hand with one empty shell in it. The other man had a forty-five automatic stuck in the front of his pants but it didn't appeared to have been fired.

"Let's get the lab boys down here," said Larry, "and then you better go in and talk to the woman in the house."

"Gotcha," said Mick. "Hey, Lars, there's some stuff outside the door here. I marked it for you."

-2-

Sarah walked down to her mother's classroom at the end of the school day, quietly slipping in the back door of the room. Beth often tutored special needs kids for an hour each night, so Sarah would stay with her mom instead of riding the bus home.

Tonight she had just two students, and Beth was working with them on their English studies. Both children had emigrated from Viet Nam a year ago with their parents, and right now she had given them a writing exercise to do.

Sarah sat in the back of the classroom so as not to be a disruption and worked on her schoolwork. Beth looked fondly at her little girl, bent over the desk and working so seriously. Sarah was a perfectionist and Beth was proud of her. She was also beautiful and petite, with delicate features, soft blue eyes and reddish hair that was almost auburn. Sarah was quiet and inquisitive, always trying to find out why things were as they were. She was also the center lobe in her daddy's heart.

Beth turned and looked out the window to the parking lot that had been full of cars earlier and was now almost empty. A couple of stray dogs ran around in circles on the asphalt chasing a paper cup blown by the wind. The sun was already going down behind the houses across the street. Although it was spring, the long days of summer were still a ways off. One solitary school bus waited by the curb in front of the school with its door open. The elderly bus driver was sitting on the step reading the morning paper and smoking a cigarette.

One of the two students, a small very thin boy named Xian, said quietly, "Mrs. Motrin, what is this?"

Beth turned her attention back to him. His delicate finger pointed to a word on the paper he was reading and she bent over to read it. "That word is 'delegate', Xian. It means a couple of things, but in your sentence it means a person who has been appointed or elected to represent other people. Okay?" She rustled his hair and he smiled timidly.

A look at her watch told her she had ten more minutes before class would be over. Beth straightened up her desk and locked the center drawer. It was the only drawer she cared about because it had her records in it.

Just then the phone on top of her desk rang and it startled her. She grabbed it before it disrupted her students. It was Mick.

"Bethy, look I'm sorry, honey. I know we were going to go to Sarah's piano lesson together and then out to supper, but we have another bad case and I'm going to be tied up late. I'll tell you more when I get home. Ok?"

"Ok. Mick. Be careful." She had grown used to these kinds of interruptions since he had gone into investigation. Crime had no schedule.

"Tell Sarah I'm sorry. Love you, honey." The line went dead.

"Well, guys, that does it for today. For tomorrow, I want both of you to write me a short essay about your families. Tell me about your bothers and sisters. Tell me about your parents and where you live. Then we will look at how your writing is progressing."

Xian asked softly, "What is progressing?"

Beth laughed. "It means moving along, getting better. Thank you for asking." The two students left and Beth went back to Sarah, who was still working with her head down. "Let's go, pumpkin. It's been a long day, but we have a piano lesson don't we?" She was fixing Sarah's hair as she talked.

"Mommy, can we go to McDonald's after the piano lesson? I don't want to go to that restaurant where daddy always wants to go."

Beth smiled, "Well you're in luck, my little daughter, because your daddy just bombed out on our dinner date and now we can go wherever we want."

They heard sirens coming at them as they left the parking lot and Beth checked her mirrors and pulled over just in time to let a huge fire truck roar by. The sirens always made her think of Mick's job and how dangerous it was. Why couldn't she have married an accountant? She laughed at the thought and visualized Mick in an overcoat with glasses, holding an attaché case and smoking a pipe. Naw. It didn't fit no matter how hard she thought.

Sarah's lesson was at the Stewart School of Music downtown. Beth parked the car in a ramp and they scurried along the sidewalk, trying to dodge all of the people. It was dark out now, but the city was well lit with hundreds of neon lights and signs humming in the cool night air. Beth was holding Sarah's hand tightly as the little girl ran to keep up with her mother's fast pace. A police officer blew his whistle and held his arm outward, pointing to them to stay where they were, and they waited impatiently to cross the street.

Parents weren't allowed in the room with the students, so while Sarah was having her lesson, Beth opened her briefcase and took out some papers to correct. She had to use her time wisely because she had so little of it. It seemed like only minutes and Sarah came out clutching, her lesson book.

"How did it go?" Beth asked.

"Ok," Sarah answered.

McDonalds wasn't crowded, as it was seven-thirty and most of the supper crowd had already left. Sarah ate some chicken nuggets, Beth had a salad, and they shared a chocolate shake.

An unkempt man in a gray sweatshirt kept looking at Beth over the top of his newspaper and it made her nervous. She went around to Sarah's side of the booth so she didn't have to see him. "Scoot over honey and let me sit by you. And finish up your nuggets so we can leave." The man was gone when they finished eating and they hurried to the car and headed home. Beth was thinking about how the little animals in the forest spent their entire lives on guard to keep from becoming prey and thought it was getting to be that way with humans, also.

It was after eight when they finally got home. Beth made Sarah get in the tub and then she sat down in the living room and dialed Mick's cell phone. Her call went to the message center. Discouraged, Beth threw the phone on the other end of the couch and sat brooding. Most husbands were home with their families at this time of the evening.

She walked to the kitchen and cleaned some clutter from the table, then stood looking out the window over the sink as she washed a few dishes and continued her sulk. She was looking across the two yards into the neighbor's family room and could see Jessie, and Doug, her husband, curled up on the couch watching television. What she wouldn't give to be on the couch with Mick doing that right now.

"Mom, I'm clean." Sarah was standing in the doorway in her pajamas, her wet hair dripping onto the floor and her pajama top.

Beth took her by the hand and they went back upstairs. She finished drying Sarah's hair and brushed it out. Then she tucked her in bed. Most nights Mick or she would read to Sarah, but not tonight. She just wanted to take a hot bath and go to bed.

While the tub was filling she undressed in the bedroom and put on a fluffy white terry cloth robe. Her 'evening attire' she called it. Mick had given it to her for Christmas and she lived in it. It was the essence of comfort. Beth went back down-stairs to the kitchen and poured herself a glass of wine but spilled some on the table. She grabbed a washcloth from the sink to wipe it up, and something at the neighbors' house caught her eye. Jessie and Doug were now on the floor together, on the rug under a blanket, and they were making love. They had doused the lights but the television was still on, showing them in shadow. Beth was almost embarrassed that she had seen them. The sight of them in the middle of their lovemaking made her again want Mick. Disheartened, she took her wine and went back up to her bath.

Mick opened the back door carefully so as not to make any noise. It was after midnight and Larry and he had just finished up at the scene of the murders. Now they were waiting for the coroner's report. He was beyond tired, and right now all he could think of was a hot shower and bed. He just wanted to snuggle up next to Beth and sleep as he had never slept before.

Beth didn't stir as he slid into bed. He could smell the sweet bath salts she had used in the tub and the shampoo in her hair. He reached to touch her shoulder and she turned over, lying half on top of him. For a second her breathing became more rapid and he thought she was waking up. Then her arms went around his neck, and she slipped back into a deep sleep.

Maybe it was the wine that made her sleep so sound, or maybe it was just the warm bath. In either case, Mick was gone when she woke up. It was Saturday but there were no days off in homicide, she knew. She lay and stared at the ceiling for a while gathering her thoughts and planning her day, but it seemed to be a waste of time. Might as well get up and get some laundry done.

Beth shut Sarah's door as she walked by, noting that her child was sprawled sideways in the bed, but still sleeping soundly. Filling the coffee pot with water and gazing out the window, she could not help but think again about her neighbors making love on the rug last night. The room was empty now. What kind of a voyeur was she becoming? Beth took the water and walked over to the coffee maker across the room and that's when she saw that a single red rose had been left in the middle of the table, and a note from a yellow legal pad lay next to it.

"Dear Bethy," it said, *"I will be back by early afternoon. Please forgive me for last night and accept my invitation for supper at Mocirines tonight. Larry says he will watch Sarah. I Love you, sweetheart. Mick."*

Beth sat down at the table and held the note to her breast, smiling. Mick knew just how to push her buttons and make everything right. Oh, how she loved that sly dog.

The perking of the coffee pot covered the sound of small footsteps shuffling across the floor, but she turned and Sarah crawled up on her lap. "You are getting too big for this," Beth said, as she leaned down and kissed the top of her head. "What do you want for breakfast?"

"Pancakes! Pancakes with whipped cream, Mom. Please." She bounced off Beth's lap and took her place across from her at the table.

"Pancakes with whipped cream it is, and coming right up, my dear." Beth poured some coffee and started digging around in the cupboard for the pancake mix.

The morgue smelled like morgues always smell—a mixture of formaldehyde, the coppery odor of blood, and the sour smell of death. Mick was taking notes as Doctor Kenneth Kramer went over what he was finding out about the two dead men in the autopsy.

So far they knew that the Hispanic man was Benny Ricardo. He was the husband of the babbling woman in the house yesterday, and the father of two small children. He drove a cab for a living, but it had long been suspected that he delivered more than people. He and his wife were both heavy drug users.

The other man had not been identified yet. He carried no identification. He had a tattoo on his right forearm that was a symbol for an Asian gang that had been operating in the neighborhood for some time, much to the dislike of another gang that had been there first. He had over three thousand dollars in cash on him and a small amount of crack cocaine.

"Mick, both of the bullet wounds in this man have ragged entrance wounds, almost like shrapnel. Did the bullets go through something else first?" Dr. Kramer was looking over the top of his surgical mask.

"I think they went through him first." Mick pointed to the body of the Asian man lying across the room. "We only found two shell casings at the scene. Both of them were from a 44 magnum. That gun has enough power to kill four people if you line them up."

"Well, it will take a few days to get the lab results, but I will get them up to you or Larry as soon as we get them."

"I guess, Doc, that what I am most interested in is those two small blood spots from the sidewalk that we turned in. Those were outside the garage, and if I don't miss my hunch, I think there was a third victim there. We have an alert out right now to the hospitals in the area to watch for a gunshot victim, but I don't think it was a major wound." He pointed at the two bodies. "If you could just eliminate those samples as being from either one of these guys, it would help a lot."

"We can do that right away. Let me call the lab. That should only take a few minutes if there is a tech on duty."

Larry had walked back in the office just a minute before Mick arrived and the two partners got hot coffee and sat down to discuss where they were with the case.

"You know what I hate about these cases, Lars? We have a couple of druggies here that got wasted over some turf war or something. The real victims are those two little kids back in that house with their addicted mother. She's so strung out on this shit that she will be out pedaling her ass before his body even works up a good stink."

"Yeah, it's a damn jungle out there in the addicts' world," Larry came back. "But the thing that bothers me the most is that even if, or when, we find the guy that did this, five more will take his place."

The blood they had found outside the door was someone else's, just as Mick had thought. Both men were killed with the same bullet, also just like he thought. He got one good slug out of the deal for ballistics. It was stuck in Benny's sinus cavity. The shot that killed him, though, was the one to the throat. It took out his carotid artery and he had bled out in minutes.

"Funny he was able to get a shot off at all with wounds like that," Mick said. "But remember that he was looking in that direction. He might have even gotten a shot off before it hit."

"Let's get out of here," Larry said. "It's Saturday. I'll be over to your place tonight by five or so. What kind of pizza does Sarah like? I'll bring one along."

"Just cheese, Lars. She's a picky eater."

"I'll pick up a kid's movie too. Got to keep up the 'good old Uncle Larry' image."

Beth heard his car come up the drive and ran to the window to watch for Mick. He walked back down to the mailbox before he came up to the house. It was only forty-five degrees outside and there he was in a short sleeved shirt. But he looked so good. She was waiting for him behind the door and jumped on his back when he came in, but he didn't seem especially surprised. Mick spun her around, his hands on her bottom. He had that impish grin on his face and kissed her softly on the lips.

"Some cop you are," Beth said. "Any crook behind that door would have you right by the short hairs, buddy boy."

"You can have me right now," said Mick, "short hairs and all." He dropped her on her butt on the kitchen table.

"Not right now," she said laughing and kissing his nose, "but your chances are pretty good tonight, my handsome man." Beth pushed him away and slid off the table.

Beth was still in her robe with her hair in big curlers when Mick came in the door for the second time later that afternoon. He had run a couple of errands with Sarah, and she was eating the last of a soft serve cone.

She opened her robe and flashed him playfully, before running upstairs to dress. He had seen Beth in her underwear countless times before, but tonight was special and she ran for the bedroom and locked the door. "Bethy? Whatcha doing?" Mick called up the stairs. "Playing hide and seek?"

She heard Sarah giggle at her dads' comments. "I'll be down in a minute, Mick." She had bought a black sheath a while back that had driven Mick nuts the first time he saw her in it. It was a special-occasion dress, and tonight was going to be a special occasion, not just supper. Tonight they were going to have a serious discussion about having another child, something Mick hadn't been too cool about in the past, but she was not going to delay this conversation any longer.

She finished brushing out her hair and slipped the black sheath over her head. It showed just enough cleavage to be sexy but not enough to be provocative. The hem was mid-thigh and she did have nice legs, if she had to say so herself.

"Bethy," he was rattling the door to get in.

She reached over and unlocked it. Mick stood staring at her almost as if she were a stranger and then slowly walked over and put his hands on her. He was holding her at arm's length, his hands on the sides of her chest right behind her breasts. He didn't say a word, but that impish grin was coming. It started in the corner of his mouth and was halfway across his face when Beth spun loose from him. "No feeling me up before you feed me," she laughed. "You better get ready."

The back door rattled and Larry came in the kitchen his arms full with a hot pizza, two movies, and a quart of orange soda. "Hey! Hey," he hollered, "where's that goofy kid I'm supposed to watch?"

Sarah ran and gave him a big hug. "Pizza and pop," she screeched. "You're the best, Uncle Larry,"

"You guys drink all of that and you will both wet the bed," Mick said with a wink.

"Sarah, you can stay up until we get back, but no calling your friends. You understand?" Beth was giving her one of those lectures with a smile.

"Have a good time," Larry said and helped Beth with her coat while Mick answered the phone.

"Who was that?" she asked.

"Work," said Mick. "But it can wait."

Mocirines was busy, as they always were on Saturday night. You could smell the pasta and spices the moment you walked through the front door with its large ornate gold doorknockers. The tablecloths were soft checkered linen and the napkins were red. Baskets of fresh flowers were on every table. The cushy red carpet's pattern was so detailed that it almost made a person dizzy to look at it.

When the maitre d' seated Beth, his look told Mick, who was standing across the table, that he was impressed with the lady. He handed them a small appetizer menu and took their coats to check them.

They had been to Mocirines before, and they had never tired of its charm and old world cuisine. A minstrel worked his way from table to table, playing his violin as if he was seducing it. His eyes were closed as if he was in some kind of musical trance.

For a few minutes they just soaked in the atmosphere, and then the waiter was back for their appetizer order. Mick ordered garlic toast, bread sticks, and a bottle of chardonnay.

They talked about everything but his work. That subject was taboo, an unspoken given. At last, they were talking about Sarah, Mick's favorite subject of all, and Beth could wait no longer, and changed the subject. He had been led to the bait. It was time to strike. She had thought of how she would approach the subject, but then she just said it.

"Mick, I want to have a baby. I don't want Sarah to be an only child and she's fast approaching an age where a sibling wouldn't interest her. I know you grew up as an only child, and you haven't experienced what it's like to have a brother or sister, but its important, Mick." Beth was serious and Mick had said nothing yet.

He reached across the table and took her hands in his. "If I say yes, can we talk about football?"

Beth broke out laughing but her eyes were brimming with tears and she wiped them with her napkin. "I love you, Mick," she said almost too loudly and in front of the waiter, who was standing right behind her with their appetizers.

Her surprise and any embarrassment faded, though, as Mick said to the waiter, "Did you hear that, my friend? She loves me."

"You are a very lucky man," the waiter said while putting their appetizers down.

The main course was a huge platter of the spiciest spaghetti west of the Mississippi and a loaf of hot Italian bread right from the oven, bathed in garlic butter. They ate until they could hold no more, and then had the rest boxed up to take home as they finished their wine and lingered over coffee. Mocirines never rushed you. They used each table only once each evening and customers were free to stay as long as they liked.

As Mick settled up the bill on the way out and retrieved their coats, Beth tugged at his jacket sleeve. "Let's walk Mick. I don't want to go home yet." They strolled down Hennepin Avenue, Beth's arm hooked through Mick's, looking in the shop windows. A street cop directing traffic yelled, "How's it going, Sarge?" to Mick, and he waved back.

They stood on the Mississippi River Bridge in the cool spring air and watched the lights of the city reflecting off the slowly moving water far below them. There were still patches of ice in the out-of-the-way crevices and crannies, a grim reminder of the winter past. The gutters were littered with a winter's worth of cigarette butts, candy wrappers and sand. Quite a few other people were out enjoying the early spring evening, some with friends or lovers; others were just by themselves, alone with their thoughts. A jogger ran by, breathing hard, and an old man shuffled past with two little white dogs that yapped at everything. The city was very much alive tonight.

Mick led Beth down to a sidewalk that followed the riverbank and they strolled a few blocks north, just glad to be there with each other and saying nothing while they walked. It was dark and out of the way, but she felt safe with him. Finally they turned around and walked back to where they had started from and decided to call it a night. They were both cold, and Beth cuddled next to Mick on the way home while the car slowly warmed up.

There was only a light on in the living room when they got there and the house was quiet except for the television and Larry's snoring. Sarah was sleeping on the floor in front of him on top of her pillow.

Mick and Beth said good night to Larry out on the steps, and then Mick came back and carried Sarah upstairs. She was getting too big to carry, but she would always be his little girl. He tucked her in and kissed her goodnight, lingering for just a moment to admire her. She looked so angelic, so perfect.

When he came into the bedroom, Beth was already in bed and judging by the underwear on the chair, she was not wearing much.

Mick shut off the light and undressed, sitting on his side of the bed. When he slid under the covers Beth moved over to him and he could feel her nakedness. She was on her stomach lying half on top of him, her breasts pressing into his chest. His hands went to her back, and then to her butt, and he pulled her all the way of top of him, one cheek in each hand.

They kissed and explored each other until neither of them could wait any longer. Beth sat up for a moment straddling Mick and leaning over him. Mick kissed her nipples softly and she slid down his body and took him in.

If lovemaking were graded the way Beth graded her students papers, an A-plus would have been in order that night. Exhausted now, they lay spent in each other's arms. Mick kissed the side of her neck tenderly, not looking for anything more, just little bites of satisfaction. "When are you going to go off the pill?" he asked.

"Yesterday," she giggled.

Mick was up first in the morning and when Beth came downstairs he was cooking breakfast, while Sarah sat at the table reading the funnies from the Sunday paper.

She was ready to eat, with a fork in one hand and her napkin in the other. Beth hugged him and kissed the back of his neck while Sarah yelled, "Yuk! Where are my pancakes?"

-3-

That afternoon they drove to the country to see Beth's father. Walt lived about fifty miles north of the metropolitan area, still in the same old house he had been in for over forty years. It was the house Beth and her sister had been raised in, and the house their mother had died in.

After Beth's mom died, Walt had closed off the upstairs, but the downstairs was still like it had been the day she had died. At one time it had been a busy diary farm, but Walt had sold off most of the land. He kept only a patch of woods of about twenty acres, located directly behind the house.

It felt good to be out of the city and back in the country, even if it was for just an afternoon. Mick had been born and raised in the city, but he loved the great outdoors. Beth was, and would always be, a country girl at heart. Maybe it was the quiet, and maybe it was the friendliness of knowing all your neighbors and most everyone you saw. If someone around here stared at you in a restaurant too long, you just stuck your tongue out at them and laughed.

Patches of white snow could still be seen in the shady spots in the woods, but green grass was already pushing its way up in the ditches and sunny spots. Several deer grazing on the tender shoots of grass at the side of the road watched them pass by. Sarah's eyes opened wide and filled with excitement and she pressed her nose up against the car window when she saw the deer. She almost cried when they passed the carcass of a deer that had had a collision with a vehicle.

Walt Robbins was waiting for them on the porch when they pulled up. Beth had told him they would arrive around noon and it was just a few minutes after. She ran to hug her dad but stepped to the side so Sarah could jump into her grandpa's arms first. He spun her around and then set her down and took Mick's outstretched hand.

"Good to see you all," he said. "You know I love it here, but since your Mom died it does get lonely. Just me and old Rascal here now." Rascal, the old black Lab, thumped his tail on the porch floor but didn't get up. Sarah petted his head cautiously. She didn't have much experience with dogs.

"Let's go inside," Walt said, "it's chilly out here. Bethy, I put a chicken in the oven a couple of hours ago. Maybe you want to make some of those dumplings like Mom used to make. I never could make the damn things right."

Beth laughed. "Okay, Dad," she said, reaching up to tossle the old man's white hair. Despite the fact he had shrunk a little with age, Walt still stood over six feet tall. His hands were rough and gnarled, the hands of a man who had worked hard all of his life tilling the earth and taking care of livestock. The skin on the back of his neck was a leathery, dark brown and deeply lined from the sun and those long hours he spent on the tractor. But his eyes, those vivid, dark blue eyes, still sparkled with life.

"You know, Dad, I have never tasted food that tastes as good as it does in this house," Beth said as they all sat around the old dining room table.

"Amen to that," said Mick. "Hey, do you still have that old four wheeler, Walt?"

"I do, Mick, and it could use some time on it. Want to take it out?"

"Well, I thought maybe Sarah and I could go for a ride after dinner, if that's okay?"

"Yes, Yes. It will give Beth and me some time to talk, and I have some things of her mother's that I want her to go through, anyhow."

The battery was dead, but it had a pull-start and Mick had the four-wheeler running in a few minutes. He had brought Sarah's bicycle helmet and now fastened her chinstrap and put her on the back of the big red machine. Then getting on in front of her, he took off alongside the woods behind the house on an old field road.

When they got to the end of the woods, Sarah was cold, so Mick stopped and put her in front of him. They had come out on a small hill in an alfalfa field, and in the middle of it a large buck deer stood staring at them. He had not shed his antlers yet for spring, and the rack on top of his head was huge and menacing. He was chewing slowly as he watched them; seemingly unafraid and, his dark black eyes were unblinking. Mick had cut the engine and they sat in silence watching him until something spooked him, and he trotted away, looking over his shoulder at them.

"Was he afraid of us, Daddy?" Sarah asked.

"That's how he got to be so old, sweetheart, being cautious. Do you remember the dead deer that was lying by the road? That was a foolish deer, Sarah, and that's what happens when you are not careful."

She nodded her little head slowly. She had understood. Mick could not see her face, just the back of her helmet, but he knew she had just learned a lesson. It was his goal to teach her all he could about life.

By the time they returned to the house, Beth had a box full of things ready to take back with them. The fresh air had tuckered Sarah out and she fell asleep on the couch with Rascal while Mick, Beth, and Walt drank coffee and reminisced. They made plans for Walt to come to the Twin Cities for a few days for a visit and an appointment with a foot doctor to get some work done in about three weeks.

It was starting to get dark when Beth said, "Well, Dad, we better get going. We both have to work tomorrow, and Sarah has school."

Walt nodded his head slowly. He was sad to see them go, but he was glad they had come. They said their goodbyes and left.

The ride back was quiet and uneventful. It seemed that as they drove toward the glow of the city lights, they both wished for the peace and quiet they had left behind them.

"Hey Mick!" Larry was excited as he came into the office the next morning and threw his coat on a chair. "You know that notice we sent out to the area hospitals to be on the lookout for a gun-shot victim? Well, we just got a call from the Riverton police asking if we were still looking for somebody."

"Where the hell is Riverton?" Mick asked, with a puzzled look on his face.

"It's about forty miles south of here, down on the Minnesota-Wisconsin border. It's a small town of about twenty thousand, but they do have a good hospital and that's where our boy showed up."

Mick was listening intently now. He stood up and moved to sit on the front of his desk, one hand on his knee, the other rubbing the back of his neck. "Tell me more," he said.

"Let's get Captain Wicks in here so we don't have to go over this twice," Larry said and went down the hall to get him. He was back in a few seconds. "He wants to do this in his office."

Dan Wicks was a thirty-year veteran of the police department. The walls of his office were decorated with numerous pictures of him taken with different city officials during his years of service. He had received several awards and accommodations which he displayed proudly. He had been the head of Homicide for four years now, and his desk looked like every letter and memo he had gotten in those four years was still on top of it.

Dan was waiting for them, leaning back in his chair, his hands locked behind his head. "Hi, Mick. How the hell do you stay so slim? Don't you eat?" Then without waiting for an answer he said. "Okay, Larry what have you got?"

"The Riverton Police Department called this morning and said they had a gunshot victim show up yesterday at their hospital. It was suspicious to them for a couple of reasons."

Wicks held his hand up to interrupt. "Had they seen the flyer you guys sent out?"

"No," Larry said. "They're outside the area we sent it to, but one of the doctors there reads our local paper, and he got suspicious and called our office. Anyway this guy shows up shot in the thigh, and his story is that he was cleaning his gun, and it went off accidentally. This doctor, he isn't buying that. The wound is old, and the entry point is in the side of his leg, not the top. X-ray shows the bullet was lodged in his femur. The guy is dying without help so he gets to work patching him up. The other thing that got the doctor thinking is this ... the guy and his partner are adamant that he is not staying in the hospital. 'Just patch him up, and let him go,' he says."

Larry stopped to take a drink of his coffee. "I mean, this guy is seriously injured. They had to give him blood, for Christ's sake. Well, they take him into surgery and then when the guy wakes up, his buddy takes him out to the car and they're gone. They paid cash for everything and it was nearly six thousand bucks. I mean cash, not a check."

"Damn," Mick said, "If only we had—"

"No, wait, Mick," Larry interrupted, "it gets better. The doctor saves the bullet. He also has enough of the guy's DNA to clone him, and I'm betting it matches those blood drops at the scene we were at the other day. But here's the real pisser, my friends. While the guy was knocked out in surgery they took his picture, and Riverton police just E-mailed it to me."

Larry handed the picture to Mick first.

Mick looked up at him and said, "Sanchez, Raul Sanchez." He handed the picture to Wicks.

Wicks looked at the picture and handed it back to Larry. "I take it you know this guy."

"We do," said Mick. "He's the youngest of the four Sanchez brothers."

As soon as they could, Larry and Mick were on their way to Riverton Police to pick up the slug, and the DNA sample. They had also issued an all-points bulletin for all departments to pick up and hold Raul Sanchez for questioning.

The Sanchez brothers had been a thorn in the police department's side for some time now. They controlled a great deal of the drug business on the north side of the city, and didn't take kindly to competitors. Although, if true, this would be the first time the police knew that they had actually murdered someone.

It took less than eight hours for ballistics to determine that the slug that came out of Raul Sanchez's leg came from the cabby's revolver. It took three days to find out that the blood drops outside the garage on the sidewalk and Raul Sanchez's blood, were one and the same.

-4-

Beth was still not sure she had convinced Mick to make a baby. Outside of last Saturday evening he had not come near her, even though she had snuck in the shower with him last night. He had been surprised and they laughed and scrubbed each other's backs, but nothing else had happened. There had been a time when all she had to do was bend over and he was ready to go. Something was bothering him and if it was his work, she was getting her fill of it.

Her fourth grade class was busy right now taking a spelling test. The words had been handed out to them spelled incorrectly and their job was to correct them. Beth was staring at Benjamin Sinclair in the front row. If she had a baby boy she wanted him to grow up to look just like Benjamin, black curly hair, olive skin and a grin just like Mick's. Come to think of it, he looked like Mick. Then her mind snapped back to reality. *She wasn't pregnant and she was teaching school, so pay attention.*

There was a soft knock on the door and before she could walk over to it, it opened part way.

"Beth, hi." It was Laurie Norden. Laurie taught 2nd grade, but not Sarah's class. She and Beth had become very good friends over the years. Laurie was everything Beth wasn't when it came to looks. Her nose was too big and her chest was flat. She wore thick glasses and had a habit of showing way too many teeth when she laughed. But she had always been there when Beth needed her, as had Beth been for her.

"I was just wondering if you were going to be at the parents' meeting tonight. I know you usually are, but just checking." They were standing in the classroom door talking and Laurie waved at another teacher who was walking by.

"Sure, Laurie I'll be there. Maybe we could go out for a sandwich right after work. I didn't have any lunch and my knees are knocking from hunger."

"Sounds good to me. See you then, Beth." Laurie quietly closed the door. Mick was coming by to pick up Sarah, so she had everything taken care of. They had one of these parents' meetings every other month. They were well attended and she hated to miss one of them. Tonight she was to lead a discussion on students' study habits at home.

Beth was back at her favorite window watching the parking area for Mick's arrival. It had been a mild day out despite the fact it was cloudy, and most of the kids milling about outside had shed their spring jackets. Three white boys were right under her window, teasing a chubby black girl. Beth resisted the impulse to rap on the window and ask them to stop. It was wrong, but it was also life at work, and they needed to work these things out by themselves.

She had dismissed her last class of the day and tonight there would be no tutoring. Sarah had come down to her mother's classroom and was sitting behind her desk coloring a picture. A glance at the clock on the wall said 4:35, and Mick had said he would be here by 4:30.

Her door opened again and it was Laurie. "Hi, Laurie, I'm just waiting for Mick to show up and take Sarah, and then we can get out of here. Sit down and take a load off your feet."

"Think I'm that fat?" Laurie came back at her laughing. If there was one thing Laurie was not, it was fat. She was lucky if she weighed ninty pounds.

Beth laughed politely but had no comment. She was back at the window, nervously tearing a Kleenex up in small pieces and stuffing it in her sweater pocket.

Laurie pulled a chair up in front of Beth's desk and was watching Sarah who was bent over, seriously coloring in a book. The ringing of the phone made them all jump and Beth walked quickly back to her desk to answer it, but Sarah had picked it up and was holding it out to her.

"Bethy," Mick said. He never called her Bethy unless something was wrong or he wanted something.

"Yes, Mick, where are you?" Beth's voice left no doubt she was irritated.

"Look, honey, I 'm not going to make it. We put an all-points bulletin out on this guy yesterday and we just got a break. One of our snitches gave us his location and we are on our way down there to bring him in. Bethy, I know this is disappointing to you and I wish it was different, but I ..."

"Mick, you do what you have to do." Her voice was as cold as a January night as she hung up the phone.

Immediately she regretted it. Laurie was pretending that she hadn't heard anything, and Sarah had paid no attention to the conversation. *I never even said good-bye to him,* Beth thought. *What if he got hurt? How would I feel then? Maybe I could call him back on his cell phone,* she thought, but then decided not to. That would only make things worse. She needed to settle down a bit before she said something else bad.

She would just have to keep Sarah with her. Beth thought of skipping the meeting but no, damn it, she had important things in her life, too.

"Well, Sarah, that was your daddy and he is on an important assignment tonight, so you are going to stay with Mommy, I guess."

"I'm sorry," Laurie said. "Something just come up?"

"Laurie, when you're married to a cop something always comes up." She sounded disgusted. "I'm sorry," Beth, said, "I shouldn't be like that. Let's go eat. Where do you want to eat, pumpkin?" She asked Sarah as they went out the door.

Raul Sanchez was not staying with the rest of his family. He was in an apartment on the near north side. His brothers had taken him there right from the hospital in Riverton. He was still in tough shape physically, but he had hit the coke hard, and the drug was doing a good job of covering his pain.

Normally the four brothers were inseparable, riding around the north side in their copper-colored Lincoln Navigator. But for now Raul was lying low while he healed, and his brothers were taking care of his part of the business. At least that had been the plan until Cocoa found out where he was.

Cocoa Harrison worked in the tobacco shop that was beneath the apartment Raul was staying in, and he had been a police informant for some time now. In exchange for his information, the police turned a blind eye toward the small amount of drugs he sold out of the tobacco shop. The fact that he was on probation on federal drug charges made his cooperation even more imperative.

Cocoa hated the Sanchez brothers. They had come in and tried to destroy his business, and Raul had beaten Cocoa severely one hot July night last summer right here on the sidewalk, and right in front of his store and his wife. It was Cicely, his wife, who saw Raul being helped up the stairs to the apartment above. She could not wait to tell Cocoa, and Cocoa could not wait to tell the cops, who in turn told him to keep his eyes open.

It was almost fool-hardy for Raul to stay in the same building with Cocoa, but that was the Sanchez's plan. They figured the police would never look there. They knew the heat was on since the Riverton Police had let the cat out of the bag and it was in the papers. Raul had an overgrown bodyguard named Nemo to protect him, and his girl friend to keep him warm. The wound was healing nicely, and he had all of the pain relief he could want. Almost a kilo of it.

There were two squads going down on the bust, with four uniformed cops and Mick and Larry in their unmarked car. They had talked about having a S.W.A.T team take it down, but it seemed too easy for that, so they dismissed the idea. He was one guy and he was injured. How tough could it be?

They parked all the cars at the other end of the block. Larry and two of the uniforms came in the front and Mick and the other two uniforms were in back. There was no other way out. They waited until everybody was in position, and then simultaneously took the stairs.

Nemo, the bodyguard upstairs, had seen them out front, and was already screaming for everybody to get out the back. There was a porch on the back of the building with the stairs coming down through the wooden deck to the parking lot below.

Meanwhile, the big bodyguard was watching for the police to come up the front and was ready for them. But the front stairs had a landing part way up and there was some cover there. His first shot hit the uniformed cop diving for cover on the landing in the foot. The other cop and Larry returned fire and the bodyguard retreated back inside. All three officers backed off immediately, realizing they were in a bad situation.

Raul heard the gunfire and took it to mean that the cops were coming up the front stairs. This only hastened his flight into the two officers who were waiting for him under the steps below. He was limping badly, carrying an Uzi in one hand and the .45 automatic that he had killed with before in the other.

"Raul, put your hands where we can see them and throw down the guns," Mick hollered at him from behind a car where he had taken cover.

Mick was answered with a spray of bullets from the Uzi. One of the two uniformed officers under the stairs moved, and Raul saw him. He sent a burst of lead from the Uzi between the step risers, striking one officer in the chest and knocking him backwards into the other.

That was the opening Mick needed. He stepped out from behind the car and fired three shots from his nine-millimeter Smith and Wesson automatic. Two of them entered Raul's chest, one on top of the other. The other took part of his right elbow off and the Uzi went flying, clattering to the pavement below.

Raul toppled forward but he did not go far. He was lying face down on the steps, one of his feet still caught between the steps above him, his blood pouring through the steps into the gray snow piled below.

The uniformed cop who had been hit in his bulletproof vest was coughing violently, but yelled that he was ok. Mick asked the other one to watch the door at the top while he called for an ambulance and more backup.

Larry and the other two officers out front had stayed under the canopy above the store windows, watching the stairs. A crowd had gathered and the officers yelled at the people to stay back, but for the most part they paid little attention. More squads poured into the area, and more police took up positions, with Larry barking orders. All was quiet from upstairs. Larry had tried to raise Mick twice on the radio when he had heard the shooting in the back of the building. He got no response, but then he heard Mick's call for an ambulance, and now Mick was calling him.

"Go ahead, Mick. Are you guys alright?"

"We're ok, Larry. What's the situation out there?"

"Well, we took fire from someone. It wasn't the guy we came here for, though, and he's retreated back inside."

"The one we came for is in custody, Lars. I think it ended kind of bad for him. Better get a supervisor down here and work your way around to the back, if you can. I'm going to walk down the alley a ways. I have to get away from this."

Larry walked around the block and came up the alley from the other direction. Mick and several officers were sitting in a white suburban with the doors open. A paramedic was combing some glass out of Mick's hair and swabbing a cut by his eye. His pants were torn and his knee was showing through, but it wasn't cut or scraped.

"Mick, what happened?" Larry was squatting in front of him, his hands on Mick's knees.

"It was him or us, Lars. He opened up on us with an Uzi and an automatic."

"Where is he now?" Larry asked.

"Right where he fell," said Mick.

It was getting dark and the night was strangely quiet. A S.W.A.T Team had taken over the scene down the block and the voice of somebody over a bullhorn could be heard asking the others to come out and turn themselves in. Raul's body was still on the steps where he had fallen. Because the bodyguard and possibly others were still above them in the apartment, it could not be removed. The blood had stopped flowing from his wounds a long time ago. It drained down into the snow below the steps, and then came out of the bottom of the snow pile, filtered to a much lighter color. From there it drained into the middle of the alley where it became part of an oily puddle.

Deputy Chief Prebisco, the supervisor in charge, came and asked Mick for his firearm and told him he was to report back to the precinct for debriefing. As of right now, he was on administrative leave. Mick rode back with Captain Wicks, who had come from home to be with his officers.

Mick's hands were shaking and his eyes showed all of the extreme anxiety he was feeling, darting from object to object almost like a frightened animal. It might have been from being shot at, and it might have been from the experience of taking another man's life. Time would tell.

The debriefing was short and he was told to go home. They had taken some blood samples from him but the talking could wait until later. Larry drove him home, as he was in no condition to do so himself, and Mick stared out the side window as they rode, thinking. How many times in the thirteen years that he had been on the force had he, like so many cops, bragged about taking someone out if it came to that? Right now he wished he had never made that statement, and he prayed to God it would never happen again.

Larry stopped in the driveway and walked around the car, opening the door for Mick as he might for a date. Mick stepped out and stood for moment looking at Larry, and then they briefly hugged. There were tears in Mick's eyes, and he spoke for the first time. "Call me tomorrow, Lars."

He tried to be quiet going in as it was after midnight and the house was dark. Mick left his shoes by the door and walked up the stairs without turning on a light, feeling his way along. He stopped to look in Sarah's room, but for only a second. Sarah was sleeping on her back, her bedside lamp still on, and turned down low. She rubbed her nose but didn't awaken, and Mick didn't go in. Right now he needed Beth.

Beth was sleeping on her side, her back to Mick's side of the bed. Just the very top of her head was showing above the covers. He walked softly to the bed and then knelt beside it next to her, something he had not done since he was small and his mother made him say his prayers. Slowly he pulled the cover down so he could see her face.

Beth must have sensed someone was there and was startled when she awoke, but Mick put his hand on the side of her head and said, "Shh, Bethy, it's me."

She touched his face and it was wet. "Mick, what's wrong?" she asked. He was crying. Mick never cried. In all of the years she had known him, she had never seen him cry. She pulled herself up on one elbow and turned the lamp on. In the dim light she saw the bandage on his eye and all of the anguish on his face.

"You're hurt! Oh, my God, Mick, you're hurt, and I am so sorry I hung up on you, darling. I feel so bad." Beth had slid down next to him and they both knelt beside the bed holding each other. She was in her robe despite having been under the covers. She always wore it when she was feeling insecure. He held her away from him and looked into her eyes. She was crying now, too, but had no idea why.

"Bethy, it's not what you think. I shot a man tonight."

Beth's hands went to her face and she gasped as she sat down on the floor, her legs curled under her. "How, Mick? No, don't tell me. I don't want to know. You're safe and that's all that's important to me." She went back into his arms.

Mick picked her up as if she were a child and laid her on the bed. He lay down beside her and held her tight. They didn't need to talk right now. There would be plenty of time for that later. Right now he just needed to hold her.

-5-

Mick was awake, up and about long before Beth was. He had slept very little, but seemed to have gotten it out of his system and settled down somewhat. Sarah was sitting at the kitchen table in her pajamas, waiting patiently for her pancakes, but alas, they were out of pancake mix.

"Not a problem," said Mick. "We're going to I. Hop for breakfast, pumpkin. Get your clothes on, little girl, and wake your mother."

"Can't make it," Beth yelled from the upstairs bedroom. "Have an appointment with my hairdresser, but you guys go and have fun."

She watched the car backing out of the driveway. Through the windshield she could see that Sarah was talking a mile a minute and Mick was laughing at her. Beth was relieved that he was better. He had scared the hell out of her last night. He had never acted like that in all of the years she had known him. They still hadn't talked about it, but it could wait. It was Saturday, and Mick was on administrative leave and home for a while. Something good had come of this after all.

She took off her white terry robe for the first time since last evening and was standing nude by the bed. She had had other plans last night, but they had gone by the wayside. Beth was feeling bad about the phone incident with Mick and a little makeup sex would have taken care of a couple of things. It would have worked just fine for making a baby, and at the same time let him know she wasn't mad at him. But things had gone sour, hadn't they? Maybe tonight would be better. It was a mile walk to the hairdresser. "*I better get in the shower,*" she thought.

Beth was next in line for Teresa, who was her hairdresser of choice. She took a chair and picked up the morning paper. She scanned the front page and nothing looked important, so she dug around for the metro section. Beth seldom read the paper because it was usually just bad-news stories from one end to the other. They didn't get it at home because Mick said he could read it at work and she just didn't have time to read it.

The print wasn't that big, but the article jumped out and hit her right between the eyes. ***"Local Drug Dealer Gunned Down in Fight With Police."*** The article went on to talk about the gunfight that had erupted when Raul Sanchez had resisted arrest yesterday. ***"He was wanted for questioning in the deaths of two other men in North Minneapolis late last week. A man and a woman were taken into custody by a police S.W.A.T. team without incident. Sergeant Mick Motrin, a thirteen-year veteran of the force, has been placed on administrative leave pending an internal investigation for shooting Sanchez. Officer Eric Prescott was treated at the local hospital for a gunshot wound and released."***

"Beth, I'm ready for you." Teresa announced. Beth continued looking at the paper for another minute and then Teresa called again. "Beth? Ready to go?"

Beth folded the paper and stuck it inside her coat sleeve. "There is something else I wanted to read in there," she explained, with a forced smile, as she made her way to the chair.

The shop was busy this morning, as it always was on Saturdays. "Same style, same color, Beth?" Teresa spun her around so they were face to face. Beth had tinted her normal auburn hair a little lighter the last time she had been here, not to change color as much as to hide the few gray hairs that were sneaking in. Mick had no gray hair, and she wasn't going to have any, either

"Yes, let's just keep it the same, but cut it a little shorter than you have been." Teresa turned her back around so she was facing the mirrored wall, and Beth noticed she was getting lines by her eyes and it almost seemed like her eyelids were drooping more. *Oh God*, she thought, *she didn't want to think about getting old already.*

"How are Sarah and Mick?" Theresa asked.

"Ah—good," Beth replied. "They went out to I Hop for pancakes this morning."

"I wish my husband would take as much interest in the kids," Theresa said.
"Mick is a good father," Beth replied. "I just wish he had a different job."

"He's a cop, right?" Theresa peeked around Beth's head while standing behind her with a comb and a scissor in her hand. "I thought you told me that."

"Hey, you know what, before I go today let me make an appointment for Sarah. She needs to get her hair cut, too." *Anything to change the subject,* Beth thought.

Theresa smiled and said, "It will be fun to see her again. She is just a little duplicate of you, Beth. You guys look so much alike."

In a short while Theresa was done and Beth went over to sit under the dryer, retrieving the newspaper from her coat sleeve on the way. She resumed reading again.

"Raul Sanchez was the youngest of four Sanchez brothers. He had been in trouble with the law several times and had a long record. Raul was suspected in the shooting deaths of two local men in a drug deal gone bad. Homicide detectives received a tip on his location, an apartment in North Minneapolis where he was believed to be recuperating from a previous gun-shot wound.

Inspector Motrin was treated for cuts and bruises and released.

His supervisor, Captain Dan Wicks, said the shooting of Sanchez by Mortin was justified and that it should send a message to the drug dealers and gang members that if you want to resort to gunplay with the police, you will end up like Raul Sanchez. Dead."

"He told me he shot a man last night. He never said he killed a man." She was talking to herself but it seemed almost audible, and Beth turned around to see if anyone had heard her. *No wonder he was so upset last night.* She thought *I need to call Larry. He was there. Maybe he knows the whole story.* She was getting upset herself, now. She fumbled in her purse for her cell phone and punched in Larry's number, but all she got was his recorder.

The dryer clicked off and Theresa came over and combed her hair out, turning her around so she could see in the mirror. "How's that?" She asked.

"I like it," Beth said, primping a little while handing Theresa her credit card. She signed the slip and pressed a five-dollar tip into Theresa's hand, suddenly realizing that she was still holding the newspaper.

"Whoops, better not steal your paper," she said, and handed it to Theresa who laid it on the counter next to the till. She watched Beth walk out and down the sidewalk.

She had forgotten Sarah's appointment. Theresa thought. *Oh well, she'll call. She was a little strange today for some reason. Not herself at all, and what's with this newspaper? She never reads the paper in here.* Then Theresa saw the article.

Mick and Sarah were still not home when Beth got there and she thought they must be shopping. She had had time to think things out a little on the walk home and decided she would just ask Mick to sit down and talk about it. *No more damn secrets,* she thought.

She dumped out the laundry hamper and started sorting the clothes. Mick's tan khaki's that he wore yesterday were right on top. They were spattered with blood and the knee was torn out. His white shirt was under the pants and it, too, was bloody. She set them aside and started a load of wash as she heard the garage door going up. Mick and Sarah were back.

"Mom, wait until you see what dad bought me!" Sarah was more excited than Beth had seen her in along time. "What is it and where is it?"

"Dad's bringing her," she said.

Before Beth could figure out what "her" meant, the door opened and Mick came in with something in his arms. Something reddish brown and furry.

"Mick, that had better not be a dog," Beth said somberly.

"Not yet," he said. "But it will grow into one someday." He handed the puppy to Sarah who ran in the living room with it.

"Sarah, don't go in there with your puppy," Mick said. "Remember what I told you about her needing to be house trained."

"No, Sarah, you stay in there for a few minutes," Beth told her. "Your dad and I have something to discuss. Mick," she said in a lower voice, "we had an agreement that there would be no dogs and—you get that grin off your face right now! Right now, Mick Motrin."

Mick walked over and grabbed Beth in a big bear hug. "I love your hair," he said kissing her softly. His hands were down on her butt and now he was kissing her neck.

"Look, I talked to your dad last week, and if it doesn't work out he said we could bring it out there. Besides I want our baby boy to grow up with a dog."

"What baby boy, Mick? Did you buy one of those too?"

"No, but I'm going to start working real hard at getting one."

She was defeated. Bending down to pick up the puppy, she could see the look of anticipation on Mick's and Sarah's faces. It licked her face with its little pink tongue, and she nuzzled its soft fur. Then she set the puppy back down and said, "We'll give it a try," at which both Sarah and Mick let out a big hooray, and the puppy peed on the floor.

Larry came over around four and Beth asked him to stay for supper. Mick was cooking steak on the grill, which he had set up on the driveway outside the garage. There had been no talk at all about last night with Mick, so Beth waited for him to go outside again to turn his steaks and then asked Larry what had happened.

"It was bad, Beth" was all he would say, "but if you want to talk about it later we can. Just not tonight. How's Mick doing?"

."Well, Larry, if you had asked me last night I would have said horseshit."

He could detect the anger in her voice.

"I've never seen him so upset. But today he seems to have forgotten."

"I hope he does," Larry said. "I hope he does."

On Sunday morning Mick and Beth slept late. Their lovemaking had gone on into the wee hours of the morning. He made coffee and came back upstairs with two steaming cups. The events from the day before seemed to be forgotten, and they talked about the future.

Santanelos Funeral Home was set on a small hill on twenty acres of land in the southern part of the city. It catered mostly to the affluent, but it was also the funeral home of choice for the Hispanic community, at least those who could afford it.

The building was a bright white structure which resembled an old southern plantation house. Gothic-styled columns extended across the front and supported the massive roof of the verandah, ensuring that it was always dry and always shady. It was a nice place for friends and mourners to gather and socialize. The two-lane cobblestone driveway came off the street and curved to a wider parking area at the front of the building, then narrowed again and completed its semi-circle back to the street. All along the drive were streetlights with coachmen lanterns on them, and under each light there was a bench. The main parking area, however, was in the back where it could not be seen from the street, and you could enter on the side of the building or continue around to the front. Scattered snow banks were visible in spots that were shaded, the remnants of a long winter. There was a lot of green grass showing through, however, looking out of place with the surrounding neighborhood. It was almost as if it had been growing all winter long under the snow cover, but actually was the result of a cosmetic turf spraying job last fall.

Tonight the parking lot was full and several black limousines were parked in front. The Sanchez family was very influential, and they were sparing no expense for their son and brother.

Just inside the huge oak front doors of the building there was a large circular gathering area where the family stood greeting those who had come to pay their respects. Raul's mother Rosemary and his three brothers, Diego, Manny, and the family leader George, survived Raul. George Senior, the family patriarch, had been killed in a shooting several years earlier that had gone unsolved, but had been vindicated by the family. One way or another, they always got even.

Raul was laid out in a small chapel to the left of the entrance, and a Catholic Priest was leading a few people, including his sobbing mother, in prayers. The funeral mass would be held here tomorrow in the chapel, but only the immediate family would attend, according to Momma Rosemary. Two of the three brothers remained outside the doors to the chapel, greeting people as they came and went. George walked outside to talk with two men who had gotten out of a limo with Illinois plates on it. They were all smoking cigars and seemed to be involved in a very serious conversation.

On Monday morning, a cold, clear, crisp Minnesota day, young Raul was laid to rest next to his father. His mother and brothers took turns kissing the polished oak casket and laying roses on its top. It was then lowered slowly into the ground, his mother sobbing softly, while his brothers remained stone-faced and stoic. The four of them stood there for a short while in silence and then Momma, in a voice only they could hear, said to her sons. "I will not rest until the man who did this is in the ground." They did not reply, but they did understand.

That same morning Mick was to meet with the people from Internal Affairs to tell his side of the story. Officially he was off duty until the investigation was complete, and this was part of the process that he had to go through. Larry and the other four officers involved had already told their stories. Mick was the last to give his statement.

The Internal Affairs board would not be the one determining what had happened, or whether the shooting of Raul was justifiable. That investigation was being done by an outside agency. This was only being done to satisfy everybody that proper protocol had been followed.

There were five people on the panel. Three of them were police officers from the department. There was also a city council member, and one civilian. Mick was questioned about everything that led up to the call that day. It was hard to be specific on some answers without jeopardizing the on-going investigation, but he did his best and the questioning was over in about an hour. They promised their results in a day or two

After the questioning, Mick went over to the office because Captain Wicks had asked him to come in and see him. He was sitting at his desk reading when Mick stepped inside the office

"Oh, hi, Mick. Enjoying your vacation?" Wicks quipped. He seemed to be in a chipper mood despite the situation.

"Some vacation," Mick said. "I've been here all morning answering questions."

"County boys talk to you yet?" Wicks asked.

"No. Just our own people. The county is the outside agency?" Mick questioned with a frown.

"Yup. They handle most cases involving a shooting, Mick. The reason I asked you to come in is that I wanted to ask you a question. Sit down." He motioned to a chair. Mick sat tentatively and crossed his legs. For some reason he was never comfortable in the Captain's office.

"Why didn't you guys call the S.W.A.T. team on this? You knew that you were dealing with the Sanchez brothers and that in itself should have raised a red flag."

Wicks had gotten up from behind his desk and was standing by the window looking outside, but he turned now to look at Mick for his answer. "It was your call, Mick. Right?"

Mick fidgeted in his chair. He was not used to being put on the spot like this. "Yes, it was my call. Look, Captain. When we got the tip from a snitch—wait let me start over. The information we received was that Raul was staying at this apartment with his girlfriend. We knew he was hurt, but we didn't know he had a bodyguard. We had a car sit on the place for over eight hours and they didn't see anybody coming or going. We called in two squads to assist, and that is our usual procedure in these kinds of arrests."

"These kinds of arrests?" asked Wick's. "This man was suspected of killing two people. This man was no common car thief."

"Captain, if we called the S.W.A.T. team every time we had to arrest someone who was considered dangerous—."

Wicks held his hand up to stop him from talking. "Mick, you know what I'm talking about here, so don't argue with me. I think you were wrong, and I am sure Internal Affairs is going to agree. Right now the word is out on the streets that you—". Wicks, clearly exasperated now, had gotten into an area he wished he hadn't. "I'm not going to say anymore on this Mick. I just wanted you to know where I stand on it. I think you guys were awful lucky to come out of that with only one small injury to one officer. By the way, how are you doing, yourself? Do you need to talk with someone about this?"

"Like who?" Mick asked, angry about the dressing down he had just taken.

"We have medical people we use to help people get over traumatic situations like this. I know what it's like, Mick. I have been there more than once." He dug in his desk drawer and came out with a business card. "Here's a card. If you want to talk to these people, just go. I don't need to know about it and it is confidential."

There was nothing left to say, and Mick felt he'd better leave before he started to argue. "Is that all, Captain?"

"Take care, Mick I'm glad you're okay, and hopefully this all will blow over in a few days and you can get back to work." Wicks came over and shook his hand and patted him on the shoulder.

It seemed funny to walk out of the precinct knowing you were who was being investigated. Mick was the one who usually did the investigating. Spring was coming early to the city and a few more days like this, and all of the snow and ice would be gone. As soon as he got home he was going to go for a long run. He couldn't wait for that puppy to get big enough to run with him.

-6-

Beth and Laurie were in the teachers lounge and they had a case of the giggles. Laurie was telling Beth about an incident she had had in her classroom when she unexpectedly had passed some gas.

"I don't know what I ate, Beth, but so help me, when I came to school this morning I had the worst gas. I even had to step outside in the hall a couple of times because I though I was going to burst. There was no holding it in. Won't that have been a hoot if old Sniffle Puss came by when I was out farting in the hallway?"

They were both laughing hard now. Old Sniffle Puss was the principal, Mr. Cameron, who was always snuffling his nose instead of blowing it.

"Well, anyway, the kids and I were working on writing letters of the alphabet. I was at the black board and they were at their desks when I got another gas attack. My God, Beth, I have never had anything like it." Beth was now laughing so hard at Laurie's antics that tears are rolling down her cheeks.

"I decided I'd been in the hallway one time too many, so I thought if I was careful I could sneak it out and no one would be the wiser." By now they both had to stop they were laughing so hard.

Laurie continued although she was having trouble talking and other people at the other end of the room were looking their way. "It was no sneaker, Beth. You could have heard it in your room if you had been listening. Now Wilson, you know that little fat black kid who is always getting in trouble?" Beth nodded her head. She was biting her lip to keep from coming unglued. "Well, Wilson is right in the front row and he looks up and says. "Whoa, teacher. You let a fart.""

Beth had buried her face in her hands on the tabletop laughing. Two other teachers came in and one said, "Something's must be funny," and Beth and Laurie both broke out again. They sat wiping their eyes and Beth said, "I can't wait to tell Mick this."

"You better not," Laurie said, "but speaking of Mick, did I see his name in the paper in connection with some shooting?"

Beth went from laughing to somber in an instant. "Look, Laurie I can't talk about that. Mick isn't supposed to, either. Hey, did I tell you we got a puppy?"

Mick put on his running clothes in a hurry. He was a man with a mission and he was on his way. It was time to vent his frustrations out on the sidewalks, running himself into a state of near exhaustion. He loved to jog to stay fit, but it also was a great outlet for his stress.

He stopped long enough to let the puppy out in the back yard to relieve itself as they kept it in a pet carrier in the house when no one was home. Sarah had gotten very attached to Brandy, which was the name she picked out for it. It had cried for a couple nights until they had put it in Sarah's bedroom, and then everything seemed to be all right.

It was about a mile from their house to the Mississippi river and then there was a running path that went on for several miles. Mick loved to run along the river. He usually carried a small fanny pack strapped to his stomach with his badge and a small thirty-eight caliber Smith and Wesson Automatic in it, but today he was not in the mood to be a cop, so he left the gun locked in the garage in a locker.

It took him only six or seven minutes to get to the river and then he turned and headed south on the path. There were a lot of other runners today and a few walkers enjoying the spring weather. Mick ran with his head down, weaving in and out of the other people on the path. Down below, the river was flowing fast and furious, and a tugboat, pushing a barge full of coal upstream was making slow progress against the current, its diesel engine working hard, belching black smoke into the afternoon sky. Its prop was causing even more turbulence in the brown dirty water than the weather was.

Mick could not get the anger to subside. The more he ran, the more he felt he was getting the shaft. Yes, he had killed a man who was trying to kill him—and possibly others, and yes it did bother him. No one liked to kill someone. But right now the fact that he had to go through this without the support of his supervisors was just too much. Maybe he would go back on the streets. Maybe he would look for some other kind of work. Some kind of work where he was appreciated.

He had run as far south as the Ford Dam and now he stood for a few minutes and looked at the water spilling over the concrete below him. The water made a kind of back wash and down below there were logs and debris whirling around in front of the dam. The debris would push up against the base of the dam and then be sucked under, only to reappear again down stream, and make the trip right back to the dam.

That's what life was feeling like to him right now.... sucked under by all of the rules and regulations, and then fighting his way to the top, only to be sucked under again someday. There was no getting away from the politics he decided. It was time to go home.

He walked the mile from the river back to the street where he lived, just cooling down, both physically and mentally. He stopped in the street in front of the house for a second and looked at his watch. Beth would be home in a little bit and then everything would be all right. She always made everything all right. Mick went into the house, called the office and talked to Larry. He was still working on paperwork from the investigation.

"Mick, I heard the County investigation is going to come out against us on this whole thing," Larry told him. "I talked with one of their investigators this morning, and they think the whole thing could have been handled better. They know you were justified in doing what you did to Sanchez, but they don't think it should have ever come to that. They think we had him cornered and that we never gave them a chance to surrender. They are saying no phone call was made, no attempt to contact him at all."

"You know, Lars, I got my ass reamed from Wicks this morning on the same thing. What ever happens.... it was my decision, and I want you to stay clear of it."

"We're partners, Mick. I can't do that."

"It was my decision to go after him, not yours. You and I both know we never had the chance to talk to them. They started shooting, first at you and—Oh fuck it, Larry, what's the use? There's nothing we can do about it."

It was quiet for a moment, neither man saying anything, and then Larry said, "We took Cocoa into protective custody this morning. Word is out that the Sanchez's and their supporters fingered him as the snitch. Word is also out, Mick, that you are a marked man. Please be careful."

"Thanks, Larry," Mick said. "Is the department doing anything to keep me safe?"

"It's being organized as we speak," Larry replied.

"Talk to you later," said Mick and hung up the phone. He sat down at the kitchen table, mulling over all that had been said. He was looking through the window at a couple of kids just coming home from school, stomping in a puddle and trying to get each other wet. He reached up and pulled the curtains shut, then went out to the locker in the garage and retrieved his .38 and took it with him upstairs to the bedroom.

In the bathroom, Mick showered away his sweat and put on a clean pair of jeans and a tee shirt. He made up the bed and picked up his dirty clothes. He might as well do something now that he wasn't working, he thought. Stuffing the .38 in the back of his pants, he went downstairs just as Beth and Sarah were coming in.

Beth had some bags with some fast food, and said, "Sit down and eat, Mick." Motioning to the table, she sat across from him.

"You know, honey," Mick said, "I've been thinking.... it's been a long winter and we deserve a vacation. You have a week off coming up for spring break, and I thought we could go somewhere warm and relax."

Beth stopped eating, her fork balanced in her hand halfway to her mouth. Even Sarah had looked up from arranging her french-fries in the shape of a fort.

"Keep talking, Mick," Beth said. "I want to hear all of this. Mick Motrin wants to leave his job and take a vacation. Well, lordy, lordy. I can't believe my little ears," she said in her best southern drawl. "Is this the man who has not taken a vacation in seven years?"

Her mocking had set him back for a second, but he recovered. "I have a lot of vacation time coming, and I just thought.... well, I just want to get away for a while, Beth," he said somberly.

Beth was sorry now she had mocked him, as she suddenly realized that he was serious and that something wasn't right. She set down her fork and pushed her chair out. Going around behind him, she put her arms around his neck and placed her head next to his.

"I will go anywhere, Mick, as long as it's with you. Let's call the travel service after supper and see if they have any specials. What's this?" she asked, looking down at the gun in the back of his jeans. "You need to carry that in the house?"

Mick, looking sheepish, didn't answer her.

They were on the phone with the travel service for over an hour, and in the end they decided that a week at Disney World in Orlando would be best. Sarah was ecstatic, and called her best friend to tell her where they were going.

Mick would need to get the time off work of course, but right now that didn't look like a problem. He was already on leave.

"You seem to be troubled," Beth said later. "Are there things happening that you aren't telling me about?" They were both on the couch, Beth with her head in Mick's lap, while Sarah talked on the phone in the kitchen. "I read the paper the other day, Mick. I know what happened at that shooting you were involved in." She could feel his body tighten as she said it.

He had been running his fingers through her hair but now stopped, letting his hand rest on top of her head. "Beth, you may have read about it, but you don't know the half of it."

"Then tell me, Mick. For Christ's, sake I am your wife," she sat up and was shouting. "I need you to share things that happen to you with me. You treat me like a roommate, not your wife." There were tears in her eyes and she moved to the far end of the couch and looked at him sadly. Sarah had hung up the phone and was standing in the doorway, a concerned look on her little face.

"Let's talk about our trip, Beth. You know, maybe we should bring your dad along."

Without answering, Beth just got up and walked upstairs to the bathroom and shut the door, clicking the lock. She pulled off her clothes and stepped into the shower. She was furious that he wouldn't confide in her, but she knew she had over reacted. Calling him a roommate had been bad. "Oh, God, I'm so sorry," she said softly to herself. She washed and shampooed her hair, then stepping out of the shower; she wrapped a towel around her head, and reached for her big white fluffy robe on the hook on the back of the door. She slipped it on and cinched the sash. She needed some comforting now, and not from Mick.

There is a street that borders the river in the southern part of the city, almost outside of the city limits. According to the sign at the intersection it was called Hall Street, but it was referred to as 'Millionaires Avenue' by almost everybody else. The street runs for about two miles, and some of the most impressive mansions ever built in the city are located there. Every house is unique, and as one walks along the sidewalk that runs between it and the river, he can get a short course in architecture. It was almost as if each builder tried to outdo the other back in the days when they were constructed.

Back in the thirties, forties, and fifties that street had been home to a lot of corporate people and politicians who ran the city, but as the neighborhoods around it decayed, most of them had moved out to the suburbs. Not that the area was not still nice. It was. The clientele had simply changed from bankers and politicians to rich people that few people were interested in.

In a huge brownstone mansion in the middle of the street lived the Sanchez family. The home dated to the early nineteen-hundreds and had once been owned by the William Hunter family. William Hunter was a man who had gone on from his banking business to become mayor and then governor of this fine state. George Sanchez Senior had bought the house some twenty years earlier and refurbished it, but many people still called it the Hunter Mansion.

George and Rosemary Sanchez had raised their four sons here cloaked in secrecy, until they had matured, or had at least grown up. Some still questioned how mature they were. Rosemary had done all that was within her power to keep the boys from leaving home, even going so far as to insist that George Jr. and his wife and child move back in with her after her husband died. His wife Maria and her mother-in-law had formed a quiet truce, and Maria stayed upstairs for the most part, paying little attention to the family business.

The cigar and exotic tobacco import business had been legitimate for many years, but when times got hard they had branched out and 'diversified', as George, Senior used to call it. Diversified into drugs and money laundering. George Jr. was the chairman of the board, the kingpin of the organization and his mother's favorite son. She trusted George, and only him, to run the operation. Almost two-thirds of the drug traffic that came into the city was under the direct control of the Sanchez family It had been that way for the last ten years when George's father, George Senior, had first organized it.

It was a cutthroat business at best. George Senior had fallen to assassins from Chicago, and his sons lived in constant fear of being next. Small rival gangs were always starting up, and it was a never-ending battle to persuade them to quit the business. In some cases they simply had to be eliminated, although the family rarely got involved in this, preferring to hire the work done. That is, until Raul got carried away and ended up dead.

A black Buick Electra with an Avis sticker on the back sat in the drive in the front of the house this morning. The lessee had flown in from Chicago to do a little business. Almost all of the drugs that flowed into the area came out of Chicago, and the Sanchez Company was their main wholesaler.

George, Diego and the two men from Chicago sat in a smoky room that used to be a library when more educated people had lived there. It was still a nice room, and most of the shelving was still there, but now instead of holding books, it was loaded down with collector's items—vases, model ships and cars, and an almost endless array of pictures of the family decorated the walls.

The men sat in overstuffed black leather chairs at one end of an unusually long ornate oak table. Windows looked down on a huge manicured lawn that was bordered by the street and sidewalk, with the river beyond. The lawn was only partially green right now, still coming out of its winter dormancy. Colorful awnings covered the windows so it was always shaded and darker than one would expect in the room.

A thick man with a face like a thug sat silently at the table. The other man who did all of the talking was named Joseph Altero, and he was not happy right now. "This operation is running at about fifty percent from where it was five years ago. We've gone to great lengths to make sure that you've always had all of the supplies you needed, and we've spent a great deal of money to maintain that, and now you reward us by cutting your orders in half."

Altero walked to the window and looked out at a couple of joggers running by on the street. "George, I know the market has not dried up, so either your competitors are driving you out of business or you are getting supplies from someone else."

George, who also rose and walked to the window had a pained expression on his face as he turned to look at Altero. A day ago he had buried his little brother, and now the drug lords were here putting the squeeze on him.

"Look, Joe, you know damn well we buy from no one but you. But you're right about one thing. Everybody and his brother is trying to get into the business. We tried last week to stop a couple of them, and my brother is dead and in the ground right now because of it."

"Your brother is dead because he went off half-cocked and the cops were wise to him. I thought the Sanchezes were smarter than that. But that's not what I came here to talk about. You need to increase your business, and soon. I'm not in a position to sit on this shit. Right now I'm going to increase your orders by twenty five percent and you're going to pay for it up front. It's either that or you are out of business, and that will not be pretty, George."

Rosemary Sanchez had come into the room, drinking Scotch from a brandy snifter. She sat down at the far end of the table away from the men and smiled. "Trouble, boys?" she asked.

"No trouble, Momma," said George. "Have you met our friends from Chicago?"

"We were just leaving," said Altero. "Nice to meet you, Ma'am." Both men got up put on their coats and left by a side door that would take them around the house to their car.

"Bastards," said George as the door closed.

"Trouble?" asked Momma again.

"'No, Momma. We just need to get back into our groove."

Mrs. Sanchez got up and walked around behind George and put a hand on his shoulder as he turned to face her. "I have always stayed out of the business, my son, and right now I trust you to do what is right for the family. But my heart is still broken in a hundred pieces with the death of my baby, and you need to think about what you are going to do about that."

"Manny's looking into it as we speak," said George. "Don't worry, Momma. They will pay, but we need to be patient."

-7-

The plane ride to Orlando was a new experience for Sarah, and she sat by the window and looked at the landscape below. Beth sat next to her and Mick was on the aisle. Larry had taken Brandy for the week, and Laurie was coming over to water Beth's plants and pick up the mail.

This morning before they left they had gone to Mass at St Ann's for the second week in a row. It felt good to both of them to have a little outside help with their problems.

Right now Mick was in deep thought with his eyes closed and his hands clasped in his lap. There was a hint of that Motrin grin in the corner of his mouth, making Beth suspicious of what he was thinking about.

"Mom, look ... there's a river! And look ... I can see boats on it." Sarah had her nose pressed to the window.

"Those are barges, Sarah. They are probably filled with grain or something like that. They look kind of small from way up here, don't they?" Sarah didn't answer but continued to be mesmerized by the scenery below.

Mick had a slight look of contentment on his face and Beth wasn't sure if he was relaxed or watching the young couple across the aisle who had done everything but copulate since they had taken off. Right now the guy had his hand on her leg and she was squirming around like she wanted him to stop, but on the other hand didn't.

"Mick, what are you doing?" Beth asked. "Are you relaxing or getting your eyes full?"

"Full of what?" Mick asked, sitting up and looking around. Beth nodded at the couple across the isle, but just then a flight attendant stopped to talk to the young lovers and they both sat up straight in their seats and nodded their heads to whatever they had been told to do or not to do.

"Missed it," said Mick. "What was happening?"

"Yeah, sure you did. Some detective you are," said Beth.

The flight attendants came around with the soda and peanuts and Mick chatted with one of them about the plane, remarking that it had an almost new-car smell to it.

"That's because it is new," the attendant said. "This is only its second flight."

"Hope they got the bugs out of it," Mick laughed.

The rest of the flight was uneventful. There was a little turbulence over Georgia and they had to put their seat belts on for a few minutes, but Mick and Beth had both experienced much worse things than that in air travel. Sarah had looked a little nervous, but she quickly got over it with a few comforting words from Beth.

At last the pilot set the flaps and the plane made a slow, gentle descent to the runway and touched down with the familiar screech of rubber. They were seated in the back of the plane so they were almost the last to get off, but they weren't in any hurry and sat in their seats until almost everybody was gone.

After retrieving their luggage they walked out of the terminal and waited for the shuttle to take them to their rental car. It was nearly eighty degrees and the sun felt good. Mick was loaded down with suitcases, but he still managed to get a hand loose to pinch Beth's butt as the mini-bus pulled up for budget cars. Beth slapped his hand, but her smile told the real story.

Manny Sanchez had sat across from the 6th precinct in a cabstand all morning with the picture he had cut out of the paper of Sergeant Mick Motrin. Manny was in a blue and white cab, wearing a white tee shirt and blue jeans. He had a black baseball cap on backwards and had a gold earring in his left ear. He figured he looked the part of a hack driver pretty well. If he was discovered, he was breaking no laws. He had no gun or drugs on him.

The cabstand was right in front of St. Teresa's Hospital. A small patch of lawn separated it from the front doors of the huge eight-story building. Manny had borrowed the cab for the day from a customer of his in exchange for enough cocaine to keep the guy high for a couple of days. A lot of cabbies hung out here when business was slow.

St Teresa's was the main trauma hospital for the north side of the city, and there were very few days when gunshot victims did not make their way in either by ambulance or just by walking through the front doors. A lot of them in need of arresting were patched up and sent right across the street to the sixth precinct, as the hospital and the cops had a working agreement.

There were no windows in the precinct, at least none that he could see into. Neither could the cops see out, as the openings consisted of glass blocks. Most of the front of the building was just lots of gray brick, which Manny thought made it kind of dull-looking.

A small sign said **4th Precinct.** The uniformed Officers parked at the back of the building where the parking compound was fenced in with chain link topped with barbed wire. Numerous black and white squad cars stood in neat rows. Manny couldn't see them, but he wasn't interested in them, anyway. He was more interested in the plain-clothes officers who used the front entrance and parked across the street, and to the left, in another small lot that they shared with the ambulance drivers from St. Teresa's

Investigation and administrative offices were on the upper floor of the police station. The building had been built into a hillside, so the second story opened to the street and the lower level opened onto the back parking lot. Larry had gone in the front entrance this morning. Manny had no picture of Larry, although he knew that Larry had been at the scene when Raul was gunned down. He also knew that he and Mick were partners, that they worked the day shift and that he was working today and was driving a brown Ford sedan with the numbers 217 on the trunk lid. Funny what you could piece together from people and news stories. The car was in the lot right now, where it had been since Manny got there this morning. The police were not the only ones who had their snitches.

About three in the afternoon, Larry decided to call it a day and slipped on his overcoat and sunglasses and walked out into the mild afternoon air. He had spent the entire day in the office working on evidence for an upcoming court trial, and he was tired of looking at the computer. He missed Mick a lot, and would be glad when he got back. The County had cleared Mick of any wrongdoing in the shooting, ruling it a justifiable homicide. He had been released from administrative leave to go back on duty as soon he got back from vacation.

Tonight Larry was just going to go home and watch a movie he had rented two days ago and still had not seen. But first he would stop at Mick and Beth's to pick up the puppy chow that Mick had forgotten to bring over with the dog.

Larry was cautious, but it seemed like any other day, with a few cabs at the stand and an ambulance backing up to the emergency entrance of the hospital, it's backup horn giving off a steady beep-beep. He put the brown sedan in gear and started for home, oblivious to the cab that had pulled out seconds after he did.

Larry was not the one Manny wanted right now, but he felt that if he followed him, maybe he would find out where he lived. That might come in handy someday.

He knew Mick was not there today. He had called for him from the cab saying he was a reporter from the Journal and was told that he was not available and they were not sure when he would be back. When he asked for Larry he was switched through to homicide, but he hung up before Larry's phone could ring. The receptionist had just figured it had been a bad connection and let it go at that. Policy said that those kinds of calls should be traced on caller I.D, but that was too much effort for her.

Manny followed Larry, staying back about two blocks, blending in with traffic. Larry scanned his rearview mirror from time to time, but he had no reason to be overly suspicious today. At Central and Toledo Street, Manny was not paying attention, and ran a red light, almost causing a collision, but he still had Larry's car in sight. Larry had heard the tires screech and looked in the mirrors but saw nothing unusual.

The brown police sedan had pulled out onto the West River Parkway, but just a few blocks down it made a quick right turn and pulled into the driveway of a white and blue rambler with a white picket fence around the yard. Manny drove past and circled the block until he could see between the houses. By this time Larry was coming back out of the house, got in the car and drove back the way he had come.

Manny was on a dead end street, and by the time he turned around and got back out on the street in front of Mick and Beth's there was no sign of Larry. He sat at the corner, pounding his hand on the steering wheel.

I wonder why he stopped there, he thought. Turning to look through the back window of the cab, he stared at the house again for a few seconds. A car behind him honked his horn and Manny waved it around him. He smiled and waved at the old man in the car and then put the cab in gear and backed over to the curb and got out. Manny walked down the sidewalk and when he got to the driveway stopped and opened the mailbox. There was only one letter in it, but it was addressed to Mick Motrin. He took it with him and ran back to the cab and squealed away from the curb. He didn't know where Mick was, but now he knew where he lived.

Mick, Beth and Sarah, drove the freeway from the airport to Disney World as if the trip itself was the first adventure ride of their vacation. Mick had rented a red Chrysler convertible, and when they picked it up at the rental lot the top was already down for them. The back seat was full of their luggage, except for a small corner where Sarah sat, her long hair blowing in the warm Florida wind which whistled by their heads as they drove.

They were not staying in Disney World itself. They had not been lucky enough on short notice to get accommodations in the park. Where they were staying was about three miles away from the gates, and was one of the nicer inns around the area. It had its own restaurant and a huge wave pool surrounded by palm trees, and a sandy beach area that was meant to mimic the ocean. There was also a driving range for the golf enthusiast right next door.

"Let's just move here and get it over with," Beth said as they stood on their own little balcony overlooking the water park below them.

"Hey, Dad, let's go," Sarah said. Mick and Beth both turned to see their daughter in her swimsuit.

"Hey, you little squirt; can you wait until we get unpacked?" Mick picked her up and flung her on the bed.

"I'm unpacked," Sarah said, "let's go."

The warm sun was such a drastic change from Minnesota that Mick and Beth couldn't wait to stretch out on some lounge chairs and soak some of it up. It was not that it didn't get nice in Minnesota, but it was never like this at the end of March.

Sarah played in the water with Mick for a while and then made friends with another little girl about her age, so Mick joined Beth on the beach. They took turns swabbing each other with sunscreen. Beth's fair skin already had a pinkish hue on her shoulders, but you could not go back to Minnesota without a tan.

After a few hours it was time for a nice relaxing supper, and then they were going to hit the sheets early, because they wanted to be at Disney World by eight the next morning. The restaurant was full even though it was going on eight p.m., but the turnover was fast, and within ten minutes they were seated and ordering.

Mick shared a chicken basket with Sarah, while Beth had some crab cakes and bread sticks. Maybe it was jet lag or maybe it was just the end of a day which had had so much packed into it, but no one really seemed hungry.

Back in the room, Sarah was asleep within minutes, tired out from all of her swimming and playing. It had been a long day for all of them and Mick sat at the table and poured over the brochures, trying to plan their day tomorrow. Outside, the last bit of sunlight flickered on the horizon and then was gone.

Beth took a long, hot bath in the Jacuzzi tub, letting the bubbles massage her aches away. The management even provided body oils and bath salts, and a candle in a dish completed the setting. She was finally starting to relax after the flight and the drive, almost falling asleep in the tub. She came out of the bathroom wrapped in a big bath towel even though she had brought a robe in with her, and got right under the covers. Mick washed up and when he came out of the bathroom the towel was on the floor next to the bed.

Beth was on her side facing him when he got into bed and for a while they just held each other, kissing and talking softly. The kissing and talking soon progressed to touching, and when the touching became something even more sensuous, neither of them could hold back any longer. Beth looked back over her shoulder but Sarah hadn't stirred. The only light in the room came from a street light in the water park below them through the partially open drapes.

At home, in the privacy of their room, the sky was the limit when it came to lovemaking. In the early years of their marriage they had pushed that limit, but not for quite a while. Now here, with Sarah sleeping not more than a few feet away from them, they kept it toned down a little. For Beth it had the effect of almost teasing her, making her want him more than she had in a long, long time. She had always been the aggressive one.

"What about Sarah?" Mick asked quietly, raising his head part way up and checking on her. Beth put her forefinger across his lips.

"She's sleeping. Don't stop what you are doing, Mick, please." Beth was whispering almost in a hiss. She wanted to just sit up and grind herself into him, but at last, even in the slow motion they had to maintain, she crossed over into that sublime rapture she had been working towards. It came in wave after wave. She could feel Mick's release too, and then she felt nothing but peaceful bliss and fell asleep exhausted.

Beth woke up halfway through the night, and, putting on her pajamas, sat looking out the window at a now deserted water park. She could make out the lights of Disney World just a few miles off in the darkness. It appeared as a soft glow in the night. She had waited a long time for a vacation like this. She looked over at Sarah and almost giggled when she thought about what they had done tonight. She remembered a night just after they were married when she and Mick had made love on the couch while her folks slept right around the corner. It had been a night to remember and so was this.

Larry sat at his desk and looked at the letter from Captain Wicks. He had read it twice and still could not believe it. It was short and to the point: **"Effective March 23rd, Sgt. Mick Motrin will no longer be the lead homicide investigator. The position has been transferred to Detective Larry Sorenson.—Capt. Wicks."**

Why would they demote Mick when he wasn't even here to defend himself, Larry wondered. Why would they demote him at all? He hadn't done anything wrong. And who said he even wanted to be lead investigator? There had been no discussions with him. Larry picked up his phone and called Wicks' number. "Captain, can I see you?"

"Sure, Larry," Wicks replied. "I was expecting your call."

The door to Wicks' office was closed but Larry opened it without knocking and walked in. Captain Wicks was on the phone but he pointed to a chair in front of his desk. "Let me call you back in a little bit," he said to the person on the other end of the line.

Wicks was talking to Larry the moment he hung the phone up. He had seen the disturbed look in Larry's eyes and the copy of the memo in his hands. He knew he wasn't here to talk about the weather. "Look, Larry," he said, "I know why you're here, and I know exactly what you're going to say. But my hands are tied in this whole thing. After the Deputy Chief saw the report from the county he demanded that I do something about it. For Christ's sake, Larry, they wanted me to bust Mick and take away his stripes. This was a concession on their part."

"A concession to what?" asked Larry. "Mick has done nothing wrong. You weren't there. We had no reason to expect that there'd be trouble. We've always used SWAT when there's a hostage situation or someone has threatened to shoot it out. But this didn't call for it."

"Look, Larry, do you want the job or not?" Wicks was getting upset now and his voice had raised. "I know you and Mick have been good friends for a long time now, and I thought this would be the way to not hurt either of you more than I had to. Now, if you don't want the job, I can find someone else. Like Kastansa."

"You would give this job to Walt Kastansa?" Larry looked bewildered. Walt Kastansa had been a thorn in Mick's and Larry's side for all of the years they had worked with him, almost four years now. He was a suck-ass who was ninety percent politician and ten percent cop. He was despised by everyone on the force except those at the very top, who he kissed up to each and every day. Larry stood wringing his hands while Wicks stood and came around his desk. He put his hand on Larry's shoulder.

"Look, Larry, nothing you or I can say or do is going to change this. I think having to do this while Mick isn't here stinks, but again, I have nothing to say about that. They wanted it done today. I believe what Mick did was questionable, but hindsight is always easy, and those who pull the strings like to use it a lot. Let's let it go and hope Mick understands."

Larry was defeated. Wicks had a compelling argument. If he went farther up the ladder they could both be back walking a beat. And a part of him thought that maybe that wouldn't be so bad right now.

"Who all got copies of this?" Larry asked holding up the memo in his hand.

"Just you and Mick. I mailed Mick's so he'd get it when he got back from vacation. No one else will know until he knows, unless you tell someone."

"Can I be the one to tell him?" Larry asked.

"I'd appreciate it if you did," said Wicks. "You better see him before he reads his mail."

Larry went back to his office and grabbed his hat and coat. He had a date with Cocoa and they were going to talk about the Sanchez family a little more. It was the last week in March but it felt like the last week in April. It sure had been an early spring, He exited out on the freeway and headed west. Cocoa was in protective custody in a jail in a suburban community, and Larry had a bus ticket for him when he got there.

The Pleasant Heights Police Department sat in a complex of municipal buildings just off the freeway. Pleasant Heights was a small bedroom community of about twenty thousand people northwest of the metropolitan area. Larry parked his squad in front and went inside to the receptionist counter and explained that he needed to see the day shift supervisor. He showed her his badge and she showed him a nice smile. A uniformed officer with sergeant's stripes came to meet Larry. He had been briefed that he was coming, and he took him right to Cocoa.

Cocoa was mad. He could not understand why he had to leave town, and no amount of Larry's reasoning with him was going to change that." Man, you'd think I was the fucking criminal here. I try to help you guys out, and then you shoot off your fucking mouths and now I'm the bad guy with the Sanchez boys. I'm the one sitting in the goddamn jail."

"No one said anything about you saying anything to us," Larry explained. "This is just a precaution we'd like to take until we can find out a little bit more about what's going on with them. It's just for a few weeks."

"What about my business?" Cocoa asked.

"Which business would that be, Cocoa? The Tobacco shop you use as a front, or the drug business you run out of the tobacco shop."

"Hey, man. I don't run no fucking tobacco…. I mean, I don't run no drug business. Where you get that shit?"

Larry smiled and snapped Cocoa in the forehead with his forefinger. "Right now, my little black friend, it is my job to see that you stay in business, what ever that is, so why don't you come with me and we will let you pack a bag so you can go on vacation for a while."

It was quiet ride down to the tobacco shop. This was Larry's first time back here since the shooting, and it made him nervous. He stayed out front while Cocoa went in and packed. Cocoa had said to just give him a couple of minutes. Larry sat in the car looking at all of the pipe tobacco and cigars that were advertised in the windows. The store was open for business, so someone must be running it. He could see people inside. Two kids were sitting on the curb with a slingshot, shooting eggs at the cars as they went by but Larry ignored it. He stared at the stairs on the side of the building where all of the shooting had started the other day. A bad memory it was. He just wanted to get out of there.

It had been over ten minutes when Larry decided he'd waited long enough, so he got out of the car and walked into the shop, which had living quarters in the back. A young, very thin black girl in white jeans and a red blouse was behind the counter. She had a red bandana tied around her head. The red blouse was unbuttoned far enough down the front to show that there wasn't any bra under it, and that she had nothing to put in a bra if there had been one.

"Where's Cocoa?" Larry asked. "Who are you?"

"Cocoa's wife," she said." He went in back." She pointed to the door in the rear of the shop. "Who are you?"

"A friend," was all Larry said. He pulled out his service revolver from his shoulder holster and held it down by his leg while he stepped side-ways through the door. "Cocoa, where are you," he asked? There was no answer. Larry was in a living room of sorts. It was small with very little furniture. A couch was pulled out into a bed. At the other end of the room was another door and when Larry opened it, he was looking at a small empty kitchen, an empty bathroom, and a door to the alley which was wide open.

Larry ran into the alley but it was empty. He went back out the front the way he had come in. The girl at the counter followed him with her big brown eyes, but said nothing. Larry keyed his hand-held radio. "Give me a marked squad to this location," Larry told the dispatcher, and followed up with the address.

They searched the neighborhood for another hour but found no sign of Cocoa. Larry headed back to the precinct. *How I am going to explain this*, he wondered. Maybe Kastansa was going to get the job, after all.

-8-

Manny and George sat at the table with the letter Manny had stolen in front of them. They had both read it and saw that the department was disciplining Mick. That was not going to be enough to satisfy them, however, and they had their own form of discipline in mind. If there was one thing the Sanchez brothers did not hire out, it was getting even with their enemies. Diego would be back from Chicago in the morning, and he wanted to be a part of this. He was the ruthless one, a born killer, and had it not been for George he would be in prison by now. He had made a lot of enemies for the Sanchez family over the years, but George had always made it right. This time, however he could come along, but George would be the one getting even.

The word they had was that Mick worked days, so the safest way to take him down was to come in like a thief in the night. Manny was going to do a couple of drive-bys of the Motrin home tonight, and if it looked good, they would go in tomorrow night. They were not sure how much family Mick had, but if they got in the way they would have to go, also. There could be no witnesses.

"You remember when we took care of that Rodriguez shithead?" Manny said to George. "I shot that son-of-a-bitch right between the eyes and his pig of a wife never even woke up. So I shot her too. This baby is so quiet." Manny was holding his H&K 9 millimeter up to his cheek and sighting down the barrel. It had been fitted with a European silencer that made it as quiet as a splat gun. He had only used it twice before, both times for revenge killings.

From the time Mick, Beth and Sarah had gone through the gates into the Magic Kingdom, they were overwhelmed by Disney World. There was literally too much to see, and there was not enough time to do it all. Their schedule called for them to spend three days there, and then they were going to drive over to St. Petersburg to see a friend of Beth's that she had roomed with in college and hadn't seen since.

Sarah wanted to go into every shop and ride on every ride and attraction. They ate until they thought they would burst and even Beth, who was religious about eating properly, threw caution to the winds.

The weather could not have been nicer, not a cloud in the sky and the temperatures were in the high seventies. By the end of the day they were exhausted, and only a promise to Sarah that she could go in the wave pool as soon as they got back to the hotel persuaded her to leave Disney World. Beth was too tired to go in the pool so she stayed up on the balcony while Mick and Sarah splashed and played in the water below.

Done in the pool, Mick was now sitting at the small table in their room looking over plans for tomorrow, while Beth washed Sarah's hair, trying to get the sand and chlorine out of it. They just had to do this more often, he thought. Life was too short, and Sarah was growing up too fast. He thought about them having another baby and how that would give them a few more years to enjoy their kids.

Mick wandered over to the bed, tired himself, and lay down, turning the television on to a sports channel. A stockcar race from Daytona was on and the announcer was trying to give all of the details of who had run into whom in a twenty-car pileup. Mick was wearing only his swim trunks. The cars going around and around the track lulled his eyes closed and when Mick awoke, it was three o'clock in the morning and Beth was sleeping with Sarah. Her arm was still lying over her as if she was protecting her. The television was off. There was a night light on in the bathroom and with the door open it showed just enough light on the bed that he could make out their faces as they slept. Sarah was a carbon copy of her mother; the same features, the same color hair. They even held their mouths the same when they slept.

He used the bathroom and then laying back down on his side continued to watch his girls. Mick was contented, but also thankful. He had been truly blessed.

On Monday evening the house had been dark each time Manny had driven by, and that confused him. This was not a busy neighborhood and he didn't want to be seen hanging around. He would make one more pass in about a half hour, and if no one was home then they might have to rethink their plans. Maybe Mick was staying someplace safe for a while.

Laurie was nervous about being out after dark, but she been over to a friend's house and thought she would stop by to pick up the mail and check the house for Beth on her way home. She didn't have a key, only the garage door opener that Beth had left her. When the big door went up she figured, why not, and parked inside just as Manny drove slowly by.

He went down and circled the block and came back. Laurie was watering plants in the kitchen and he could see her going back and forth, but not Mick. But he figured he had to be in there someplace, as there were two cars in the garage. He picked up his cell phone from the seat and called George.

"Looks like they're home, all right, George. Let's plan on tomorrow night."

"Sounds good," George said. "And quit using my name over the phone," he scolded as he disconnected.

Manny threw his phone on the floor of the car. I can never do anything right for that asshole, he thought. No matter how hard I try he finds fault with it. Manny took off for downtown. He had a party to go to, and besides, he had just enjoyed a little snort of powder and was feeling pretty loose. Maybe if he were lucky he would get lucky. Manny was, and had always been, the playboy in the family.

Larry had thought about calling Mick about the changes at work, but then thought better of it. Why ruin his vacation? He went down there to get away from this crap. Larry had stopped at the house and picked up some more stuff for the dog. The little shit was driving him nuts. He had finally relented and let her in bed with him because it seemed to be the only way to pacify the pup. Still he had to admit it was nice to have a companion. He just wished he had one that didn't pee on the floor, although she was getting better about going to the door and whining. The only bad thing was that Larry didn't have a fenced yard so he had to go out with the pup, and it was cold at night.

He sorted through the mail that Laurie left on the kitchen table but didn't find any letter from Captain Wicks. Maybe Laurie hadn't brought that one in. He looked in the mailbox to make sure, but it was empty. Larry hated to call Laurie and ask her. It would appear that he was being nosey. And maybe he was. Things had settled down at work a little and it was time to move on. Hopefully Mick would take the changes in the right spirit, and hopefully he wouldn't resent Larry being the boss. They had been friends too long for that. There had been another murder last night on the south side that did not appear to be gang or drug related, and right now they were looking for the victim's husband. Larry and two other detectives had worked all day on it today and were pretty confident they had identified the right suspect. For now he was tired and it was time to call it a day.

Momma had cooked a big supper for her three sons in honor of tonight's mission. Normally there was a cook, but tonight she had been given the night off, and George had told his wife that he had a meeting to go to and not to wait up for him. He had brought supper upstairs for her and their daughter Melanie who was two, although there was a kitchen up there if she wanted to use it. Maria and Melanie were like prisoners in Momma's house, but Maria minded her own business and George had promised her that in just a year or so they would move out and get their own place.

George sat on one end of the table and Momma at the other. A large silver candelabrum with three white tapers sitting in the middle of the table provided the only light. Adding to the eerie darkness, the three men appeared all dressed in black pants and black turtle neck sweaters, all of them strangely quiet. A picture of Raul stood next to the candelabra, and Momma was putting on an Academy Award winning performance with her crying and theatrics.

George talked softly as he went over the plans for the night. "Manny, you are to stay outside to watch our backs." he said, and Manny's face fell a little as once again he was being cast in a somewhat insignificant role. George continued, "If there is a dog, we need to take it out right away before it can make trouble. We don't know much about the layout of the house, but with the window pattern, it appears there are only two bedrooms and a bathroom upstairs. We'll enter through the service door in the back of the garage. The stairway to the upstairs is right around the corner from the kitchen."

Manny had done a good job of laying out the place for them and George, seeing his disappointment at not having a more significant role, thanked him for that.

If there was an alarm, they would just leave immediately. "Don't touch anything. You will have gloves on but everything must remain exactly as we found it. Now, the car we are using is a stolen, and we need to ditch it as soon as we're done and are sure we're in the clear. Momma will be waiting on 42nd street just a few blocks away to pick us up."

It was now eleven p.m. They would leave at two a.m., which gave them three hours to have a couple of drinks and think about Raul and what the police had done to him. They left the dining room and were now sitting in the den where a big-screen television was running muted and they could only guess at what David Letterman was saying. Momma dabbed at her eyes while Deigo leaned back in a leather recliner and tried to take a nap. Manny was just standing at the window overlooking the wide front lawn and thinking. He was going to go on his own pretty quick. He had made that decision tonight. He would never be successful with George giving him orders and watching his every move. George was watching Manny and thinking how much he distrusted him.

At five minutes after two they left in the stolen Chrysler minivan. The car had smoked windows and you could not see in the back seat at all. Manny was alone up front driving. The red glow of his cigarette was all that showed as it dangled from the corner of his mouth.

George and Deigo sat way in the back in the third row seat, George's fingers nervously tapping the barrel of the H&K wrapped in a towel in his lap. Diego stared straight ahead as if he was hypnotized. He was very subservient and would do what ever George asked, although he wished that he could do the killing.

They drove slowly by the house first. It was dark, as was every other house on the street. The neighborhood seemed deathly quiet. A cat wandered across the street and Manny swerved to try and hit it, but it scampered away. He laughed out loud and said. "Fucking cat was too fast for me." He laughed again.

George said nothing, but a look of disgust which Manny could not see in the rear-view mirror crossed his face. "Park in the driveway," he told Manny.

Both men exited quickly and walked around the garage to the back. No interior lights came on in the van because Diego had smashed them out before they left.

With the tip of his knife, Diego slipped the strike back on the lock and they were in the garage quickly. "I thought Manny said there were two cars," George whispered. He hesitated for a second, and then tried the kitchen door. It was unlocked. They walked quietly through the kitchen, going straight for the stairs. The only sounds in the house were that of the refrigerator running and the ticking of a clock somewhere in the living room. The only light came from the glow of the read-outs on the microwave and the stove.

As they had assumed earlier from the placement of the windows, one bedroom was to the right at the top of the stairs, with the other across from it on the left, while the bathroom lay straight ahead. The shades were up in the bedroom and the light coming in from the street light showed George an empty bed. The red shining letters from the digital clock said two thirty-three. Diego had gone to the other bedroom and he now came back around the staircase and whispered that it was also unoccupied. They were in an empty house.

"Let's get out of here," George said his hand on the wall by the bedroom doorway to orient himself in the near darkness. Diego was already heading for the stairs when George's hand slipped across the light switch, and for a moment the lamps in the bedroom came on. Realizing what he had done, he quickly flipped the switch back off, but not before Bonita Crowley, the seventy nine year-old widow who lived across the street and had gotten up from bed to go to the bathroom, saw the flash of light.

She had been reaching for her own light switch in the bathroom when it happened. She hesitated for a moment, then turned on the light and sat down on the stool. Just as she started to relieve herself she heard a car backing out of the driveway across the street. She stood back up and peered out the window. It was hard to see with the light on in the room, but she knew the Motrin's were not supposed to be home. A silver van was pulling away.

Maybe, she thought, it was the lady who Beth said would be coming to take care of the mail. They had talked at the mailbox last week, Beth explaining where they were going and how long they would be gone. But Bonita had seen the woman there taking the mail in earlier tonight and she didn't have a van, and heck, it was the middle of the night. She sat back down on the stool, thinking that maybe she was just seeing things.

On the way back through the kitchen, George had seen the pile of unopened mail on the kitchen table. He handed the H&K to Deigo while he sorted through the letters with the aid of a penlight he had brought along. Most of the mail was addressed to Mick Motrin or to "Mr. and Mrs." So they where in the right place, all right. But the postmarks showed it was several days' worth of mail. They just weren't here. "Who the hell did Manny think he saw?" he whispered to Diego.

They sped away from the house and met up with their mother. Manny lit some paper on fire and stuffed it under the front seat as they left the silver van and walked across the street to where she was waiting. She had already gotten into the back seat of the Lincoln Navigator she had driven over there to meet them.

"The house was empty, Momma," George said as Manny pulled quickly away from the curb. "But don't worry, we'll find them." Rosemary's face was filled with disappointment, and George hugged her and kissed her cheek.

As they left the gates of Disney World, Mick, Beth, and Sarah stopped to look back and reflect on their three magically-filled days of fun. They had not seen it all, but they would be back to try again. It was getting dark and the park was getting ready to close for the evening. Some of the shops were already closing up on their way out.

Tonight would be their last night at the hotel, as they would be hitting the road first thing in the morning for St. Petersburg. Beth's friend Darla and her husband Rich's place was their destination. It would be good to see Darla, Beth thought. It had been a long time. In school they'd been like sisters, and they'd been roommates in college.

It was too late to go swimming once more, but the way it looked, Sarah wasn't interested, anyway, as she fell asleep in the back seat before they could drive the three miles back. She was sitting, or really kind of hanging, from her seat belt and shoulder harness, her chin on her chest and a Mickey Mouse bobble-head doll still clutched in her hand. She had chocolate on her blouse and mustard on her face. Beth reached over the seat and unhooked Sarah's seat belt and laid her down on the seat amid a pile of packages. It was dangerous to be unbelted, but she looked so uncomfortable. They had a couple of errands to run, mailing post-cards to friends and getting gasoline, before they went back. Mick was deep in thought, oblivious to what Beth was doing.

It was raining softly the next morning when they woke up, and it looked like it had rained most of the night. In the west the sky was blue, and that was the way they would be heading.

Beth woke to the smell of coffee and Sarah's chatter. Sarah and Mick were sitting at the table playing checkers and Sarah was arguing about something Mick had done, and he was responding by teasing her and laughing at her.

It was already eight a.m., and they needed to be on the road in the next hour to be in St. Petersburg by late afternoon.

"Why don't you get the car packed and I'll take a quick shower," Beth said. By the time she was out of the bathroom, everything was gone and Mick and Sarah were standing down by the car waiting for her.

-9-

Although they had failed to accomplish anything in their nighttime adventure, George and Diego were not much disappointed. For the sake of their mother they wished they had been successful in their mission, but these kinds of things took time to accomplish unless you wanted to get reckless and get caught.

As for Manny, he didn't give a shit one way or another. He was high on dope most of the time, and spent most of his evenings downtown raising hell. That worried George and he knew there was going to be a confrontation between him and Manny soon. But George in his own methodical way was taking things one at a time.

They had already had one conversation about whom Manny had thought he had seen in that house. George was sure it wasn't Mick Motrin or his wife, but Manny said whoever it was had parked in the garage like they belonged there, and had been in the house for quite some time.

"Just something else you don't believe me about," said Manny. "Maybe you should do your own damn snooping, big brother. I really don't give a rat's ass if that cop is dead or not. It ain't going to bring Raul back." George had grabbed him and held him against the wall for a second on this one, but calmed down and let him go.

The other thing that bothered George was that Diego had left his shoes in the stolen van. He claimed he had stepped in dog shit on the way back to the van that night.

"I didn't want to get shit in Momma's car," he said, "and what the hell, George, Manny burned the damn car, didn't he?"

George was going to Chicago in the morning for a few days. "We'll try again when I get back," he said.

The Motrin's drove the freeway surrounded by Florida sunshine, and the closer they came to the gulf, the more they could smell the salty air and feel the humidity. It was as if it had rained only a few minutes before, the way the moisture hung in the air.

The road kill patrol hadn't been out on the freeway for a few days, and Interstate Four seemed to be a battle ground with dead armadillos, snakes, possums and even a few deer and alligators. Mick wondered what it would be like to hit a two hundred pound alligator at sixty miles an hour. He remembered a joke he had heard back in Minnesota about 'why did the chicken cross the road?' The answer was, 'to show the raccoon that it was possible.'

They went through a lot of small towns and hamlets that seemed to be nothing more than row upon row of manufactured homes and trailer houses ... winter homes for the snowbirds that came down from up north to wait out the cold months. Maybe some day that would include him and Beth.

Darla and Rich lived about thirty miles north of St. Petersburg in a little town called Halverston that was right on the gulf. Mick skirted the outside of Tampa, came into St. Petersburg and headed north on State Highway19. The road wove in and out from the gulf, giving them glimpses of the water until they were about ten miles from their destination, and then it slipped into another little town on the gulf shoreline.

It was just before suppertime and it had been a long day of driving, so they stopped to eat at a seafood restaurant. Sarah was still tuckered out from her days at Disney World and she slept a good part of the way, despite the fact that Mick had put the top down on the convertible. He was like a kid with a new toy with this car.

"My God, look at us," Beth said. "We're all sunburned. We're as red as lobsters. I need to get some Noxzema for Sarah." They were in luck, as there was a Wal-Mart right across from the restaurant and Beth walked over while Mick and Sarah went out onto the pier behind the business to look at the water. They were stopped at the entrance by a local police officer who was moonlighting for the restaurant. The pier was for customers only, and it was his job to keep others off. Mick explained that they were customers, that as soon as his wife got back they would be eating, and then struck up a conversation about him being a cop, too.

When Beth returned Sarah was playing in the sand, disgusted with Mick's long conversation with the police officer. Beth stood her up and brushed her off, giving Mick a scowl for letting her get dirty. "Mick, let's go. We're hungry," she said. Mick shook hands with the cop, said goodbye, and joined his family to go inside the establishment.

"Who was that?" Beth asked. "Did you know him?"

"I don't need to know him, Beth. Why are you questioning me? We're cops.

Beth just gave him a disgusted look. Was there no getting away from it? She wondered.

The café was open to the breezes on all sides; it was almost like eating in a pic-nic pavilion only fancier, with a lot of fishnets, boating paraphernalia and pic-tures decorating the walls between the windows and ceiling. Each table sat under a white ceiling fan that spun lazily in the evening air. Beth looked around, care-fully taking it all in, and thinking that Ernest Hemmingway had to be here some-place.

The food was as fancy as the ambience, with a price tag to match. It was brought up from the kitchen located somewhere below them, giving the impres-sion that it came right from the sea. Beth fretted about having to leave most of Sarah's meal there because she didn't want to eat and they had paid eighteen dol-lars for it. Mick had the biggest lobster she had ever seen, and she had her favor-ite, shrimp salad, and a margarita to calm herself down. She was being a little bitchy, and she didn't know why.

There was a small band in the corner playing some kind of calypso music. They were colorful, and peppered their act with lots of jokes and antics. Beth had mellowed a little from the alcohol and Mick hated to leave, but they needed to get on the road. One hour later and sixty-three dollars lighter they were on the way to Darla's.

Darla and Rich lived in a white rambler in a nice area of older homes. Their house was back farther from the road than the houses around it and had a long driveway that looked like it was covered with sea shells, but that were really some kind of white rocks.

All Mick knew about Rich was that he was a criminal lawyer and worked for the public defender's office in the local county. Just the kind of guy a cop loves to spend a couple of days with, thought Mick. Beth had told him they had two chil-dren, a boy named Darren who was about Sarah's age, and a four-year-old daugh-ter named Mandy.

Darla almost ran from the house as Mick stopped, and grabbed and hugged Beth the moment they got out of the car. Both women were overcome with emotion and gave way to tears. They were truly happy to see each other, and Mick and Sarah stood by awkwardly, holding hands and waiting to be introduced.

A moment later, Darla turned from Beth and walked toward them, wiping her eyes with the back of her hand. "This must be Sarah," she said. "Oh, sweetheart, you are so pretty, and just the picture of your Momma all over again." Darla's speech was heavy with a southern drawl, something Beth was not used to, as they were both from Minnesota originally. Sarah just hung onto Mick's hand shyly.

"And this is Mick." Darla opened her arms for him with a big hug. Darla was tiny … less than five feet tall and slight of build, and Mick felt like he was hugging a child.

"Hi, Darla," he said. "Nice to meet you."

"Well, you all just have to come in and make yourselves comfortable. Rich is working late, but the kids are in the back yard playing in the pool, and just waiting for Sarah. They have done nothing but talk about her coming all day."

Rich came home a few minutes later and Darla introduced him to Mick. The two men walked out back, each with a beer to watch the kids in the pool. Rich had gone for the beer the minute he got in the house, and it was obvious to all that he had had a few drinks before he got there.

Rich was as big as Darla was small, and the years had added a significant roll around his waist, which made him seen even bigger. He was congenial, though, and after watching the kids in the water for a while, suggested to Mick that they both join them.

Mick and Rich standing side by side in swimming trunks was like a 'before and after' picture ad for a health club. Rich in a swimming suit was even fatter than he had looked fully dressed, and especially standing next to Mick, who had a stomach like a washboard.

Darla said to Beth, "Mick sure looks good."

Beth just smiled and replied." He likes to stay fit in his line of work. Don't tell him that though, or he'll get a big head." They both laughed.

It was getting dark and both men got out of the pool and headed for the gazebo next to the house, while Beth and Darla got the kids settled down for the night.

"Your yard is like a park", Beth said. She and Darla had joined the men in the gazebo. "When we left Minnesota, the ground was still covered with snow in some places, and here we are sitting outside in seventy-some degrees."

"I do miss Minnesota," Darla replied. "The weather here is nice, but we get a lot of rain and the bugs seem to come from everywhere sometimes. I think the Minnesota winters go a long way to help control the bugs."

Rich, who was a native Floridian gave Darla a disappointed look.

Mick, realizing the tension, said "Except the mosquitoes. Minnesota calls them its native bird." They all laughed.

Around midnight, after exhausting a dozen topics, Mick and Rich, who was now about a .20, referring to his alcohol content, decided to call it a night. Darla showed Mick to the bedroom he and Beth would be using, which was obviously hers and Rich's.

"Beth and I are going to stay up and talk for a while," she explained. They had paused for a second in the doorway passing each other, and she placed her hand on Mick's bicep to hold his attention and just as quickly she pulled it back and held it to her chest. It had been a long time since she had touched a man who felt like that.

Mick sat on the end of the bed and looked around the room. One wall was decorated with diplomas and legal books. There was a picture of Darla and Rich from a few years ago, and several pounds back for Rich. The furniture in the room was beautiful and looked very expensive. Exhausted, Mick striped off his wet swimming trunks, took a shower and went to bed.

George's trip to Chicago had been a disaster. He'd gone to ask for some reconsideration of the threats that had been made against the family business for not selling enough drugs. He wanted to explain that the competition was rising in the drug trade and how, as in any business, there were ups and downs. But all of his talk had fallen on deaf ears. These people were ruthless. They told him that no matter what the problems were, they were his and not theirs. That there were ways to control the competition, and that was part of the business.

"It's also what had got my younger brother killed," George explained, but knew he was wasting his breath. He walked out into the cool Chicago air and stood watching the people hurrying back and forth on State Street. Most of these people were making an honest living, and he wished he were, too. He had a wife and a child he needed to think of, but the trouble was it had been so long since he had made an honest living, he wasn't sure he could anymore.

He had a few hours to waste before he caught a flight back, and no friends in this town to speak of. Maybe he would just catch a cab out to O'Hare and eat in one of the airport restaurants. He had made a decision. There were a few loose ends George needed to clear up and then he was going to find a better way to make a living. He would help his brothers get revenge on that cop who had killed Raul. Not that he hated the cop that much; it was just that he had promised Momma he would. Then Diego could take over and put up with Manny's crap.

George had killed before and it had always left a bad taste in his mouth. He wasn't made like Diego, who loved the thrill of the hunt.

Mick woke to the sound of loud voices, and lying in bed, he tried to figure out where they were coming from. The digital clock on the nightstand said seven fifty-five, and he couldn't believe he had slept this late. His left arm was asleep and pinned under Beth who for some reason had snuggled all night.

Mick slowly pulled his arm loose and sat on the edge of the bed trying to rub some feeling back into it. The voices had stopped but now he heard a car start up and back hastily down the driveway. He pulled the drapes apart just enough to look out and saw Darla walking back to the house. She was crying and holding her robe sleeve up to her face to hide it.

Mick lay back down. The plan for today was that they would leave after lunch and head back to Orlando. Tomorrow they were going to take a bus over to the Space Center and tour the grounds. Saturday they would be going to Sea World, and then they'd be catching a late flight Saturday night to go back home.

Beth had opened one eye to look at him.

"Hi, sleepy head," he smiled.

She leaned her head on his chest. "Mick, let's get going early today. I want to leave as soon as Sarah's up." She was talking so softly he could hardly hear her.

"What brought this on?" asked Mick. "Why the rush?"

"We can talk about it on the road," she said. "It would be uncomfortable to talk about it here. It's not about you, dear, and I'm sorry I was mean to you yesterday."

Sarah was up and at the table with her new-found friends when Mick came out to the kitchen, and Darla was making pancakes for all of them.

"Well, that was a good night's sleep in a great bed," Mick quipped. "I wish my wife had stayed on her side."

Darla turned from the stove, smiling. "Good morning Mick, I'm glad you slept well. How about some pancakes?"

"Naw, just some coffee, please. Beth and I aren't much for breakfast. She's in the shower right now, but she'll be right out." He squeezed Sarah's shoulder as he sat down beside her.

Darla handed Mick a steamy cup of coffee. Their eyes met for a moment and Mick could see that all was not well. Police officers learn to read body language almost as well as they do written language. For just a second he took her hand and squeezed it softly. Her hand was frail and cold.

Beth came into the kitchen carrying the suitcase. "We have to go right after breakfast, Darla. I wish we could stay longer, but we can't." Hurt showed in her eyes but Darla didn't protest. She knew why Beth felt they had to leave.

An hour later they were on the road again after hugs, tears and goodbyes. They promised to write to each other, but the last thing that Beth said to Darla got Mick's attention the most.

"Be strong, and I will pray for you and the kids."

Darla's eyes overflowed with tears and she hugged Beth for a long moment before abruptly turning and walking back into the house.

It was another beautiful day, but Mick kept the top up on the car this time. Sarah's nose was already peeling and Beth had sun-burned the top of her head right through her hair. They drove south, retracing their steps back to the interstate. It was quiet in the car and the traffic was flowing smoothly. Sarah was playing with an electronic game Mick had bought her, and Beth seemed to want to be alone with her thoughts.

Mick finally broke the ice by asking Beth if there was trouble between Rich and Darla.

"You might say that," Beth answered. "We were up until three a.m talking about it. I wish there was something I could do to help her, but I don't know what that would be. Years ago when we were in school we shared everything, and I guess we tried to get back to that last night and it ... it."—Beth was close to tears and out of words. She unhooked her seatbelt, and moving over, snuggled against Mick.

Mick put his arm around her and held her tight.

"Rich has drunk or snorted away everything they own. But the worst thing is that he has also been unfaithful and abusive to her. She showed me her bruises last night, Mick, and it was awful."

"I can't believe he could find other women who would think he was attractive," Mick said. "My God, he looks like the Pillsbury Dough Boy, and Darla is pretty in her little, petite way."

"She wants to move back to Minnesota and leave him, but she has no money. Her parents still live north of the Twin Cities and would welcome her back, but Rich told her he would hunt her down and make her sorry. How can she protect herself from him, Mick?"

"She has to make the first move and divorce the jerk, Beth. There's not much anybody can do for her until that happens. If he's being rough with her now, she can get a restraining order, but she'll have to get the courts involved. It's a tough situation, and she has to think of the kids."

Beth snuggled a little closer. "I love you so much Mick, for loving me."

"I do love you, sweetheart." Mick bent down and kissed her forehead. The car drifted onto the shoulder of the road and threw up a spray of gravel, followed by a horn blast behind them.

Sarah yelled. "Hey, you messed up my game, drive nice. Dad, Mom hasn't got her seatbelt on. Why do I have to wear one?"

Mick and Beth broke out laughing and Beth slid back to her side of the car and buckled herself back in.

"Sorry, Sarah," Mick said "Beth, you get your seatbelt on right now," he scolded.

Beth pouted and flashed her skirt up, giving him a look at her panties, which made Mick almost run off the road again, and Beth shrieked with laughter.

It was six-thirty when they pulled back into Orlando. They were staying at the hotel they had been at before, but in a different room.

The day at the Space Center was fun for Mick, but Beth and Sarah were bored. They all enjoyed the following day at Sea World, however. Sarah got to pet a dolphin and feed the seals, and there was another Florida cloudburst late in the afternoon, but it didn't last long ... just long enough for them to dive into a restaurant and enjoy some more seafood.

It seemed like their trip had just begun and already it was time to go home, but they were tired and home was going to feel good.

"This was the best time I've had in a long time, Mick," Beth said. They had just dropped off the car at the rental agency, and were waiting for the shuttle to the airport.

"I think we learned something about enjoying life while we can," Mick said. "Let's go home and plan next year's vacation."

"It might take a year to pay for this one," Beth said.

Sarah slept all the way home, her head in Beth's lap. It was dark outside the window of the plane and there was nothing to see. Mick amused himself reading a book he had bought at the airport. Beth just relaxed, but she couldn't quit thinking about Darla.

Larry was waiting for them at the airport. "My God, look at the sunburned faces," he said. He didn't know when he was going to tell Mick about the changes at work. He'd asked Captain Wicks to send out another letter but he'd refused. Larry had a copy of the memo he'd gotten in his pocket and maybe that's how he would break the news when they got home. But for now, he scooped up Sarah and spun her around. "Hey, pumpkin, how come you never sent Uncle Larry a card?" Sarah just giggled. To her, Larry really was her uncle.

Larry kissed Beth on the cheek and took her luggage from her. They crossed the street to the parking garage and headed home. Although it was thirty degrees colder than Florida it was still nice to be back in the city. Larry avoided talking about work and instead kept them busy talking about their vacation.

At the house Beth chased Sarah upstairs to get into the tub, leaving her and Mick alone with Larry.

"Mick, I don't know how to tell you this, but there have been some changes at work," Larry finally said. "They had to do something, Mick, even if it was wrong, and they did." He handed him the memo. He didn't mention the letter that had been sent out, believing it was lost in the mail. Mick read the memo and then sat down at the kitchen table, handing the paper to Beth, who was standing by the sink. For a long moment nobody said anything, and then Mick turned to Larry, who was now sitting across from him.

"My first reaction is to be hurt, Larry, but knowing the political crap we put up with this isn't that much of a surprise. I've thought a lot about what happened, and maybe I didn't use the best judgment, but if I had to do it over, I doubt I'd do anything different. I'll go to my grave regretting that I had to kill someone, and I hope I never have to do it again. You just don't know how bad it feels, Larry. I'm glad they gave you the job. Can I still ride to work with you?"

Larry laughed and said. "If you don't criticize my driving." Mick, as the head of the department, had been given a take-home car, but now with him and Larry switching roles, the car would go to Larry.

"Let's go on from here, my friend, and thank you for telling me now and not letting me find out at work Monday morning."

For Larry this was a great relief, and he and Mick hugged for a second before Larry said, "There is one more thing. I need to run home and get you that damn puppy that's turned my home into a disaster area." After saying that, he grabbed his jacket and slipped out the door.

Beth crumbled the copy of the memo that she was still holding and threw it in the trash as Sarah yelled, "Mom, I have soap in my eyes! Come up here!"

George and Manny were home, standing outside the house under the carport. Manny was getting ready to go raise hell for another night, but George wanted to talk to him before he left.

"Can you borrow that cab again?" he asked.

"Sure, as long as I give Marco a little nose candy, he'll give me anything."

"Well, look, let's be careful that Marco doesn't know what the hell you're doing with his cab. I need you to watch the police station again Monday morning and see if he's back. I don't want you in that neighborhood where Motrin lives anymore. That was probably a bad idea to start with. If we can catch him in the car some night, that'll probably be our best chance."

"Shit, man, why don't I just knock him off and get done with it?"

"You try that and I will knock you off, you dick head." George gave him a slap playfully on the back of the head. "Be careful out there," he said, and walked back in the house.

-IO-

Mick's first day back on the job went smoothly and the other detectives seemed to be enthusiastic in welcoming him back. No one even mentioned the change in command, even though the general consensus was that Mick had gotten screwed. Larry and Mick changed nameplates early in the day, but otherwise everything else was the same.

Captain Wicks was out of town on business and not there to talk with, but he had left a voice mail for Mick welcoming him back and trying to explain why he had to do what he did. Mick listened to it and deleted it. It was behind him now.

It was Monday night when Mick noticed the foot print on the garage floor. Normally there would have been two cars in here, but now with Beth not home yet and no police car, the garage was empty and the track stood out like a sore thumb. It also struck a cord with something else Beth had found inside on the carpet going up the stairs. Dog poop. They had thought maybe Larry had accidentally done it. Beth had found it in several spots and just cleaned it up, but not before she chided Mick about his dog and cleaning up after it so people were not stepping in its crap.

Walking outside in the back he found the smashed poop pile with the same shoe imprint in it. Whoever had stepped in it was going into the garage, by the direction of the footprint. It was some kind of tennis shoe, and Larry didn't own any tennis shoes that Mick knew of. He'd often been kidded about his year-around penny loafers that he wore even when he was on a picnic. And it was too big to be Laurie's foot. And why would they have been out in the back yard anyway? Larry had the key to the front door, and Laurie only had the garage door opener for the big door.

Mick started raking up some leaves out in the front yard while he was waiting for Beth and Sarah to get home. Sarah had Brownies, which was an offshoot of the Girl Scouts, right after school, and Beth had gone grocery shopping.

It was a beautiful spring day, the first day in April, and the warm weather had brought a lot of people out of their homes to start on the yard work. This work was something Mick had left for Beth in the past, but now with a new attitude about not taking his job so seriously, he was going to start doing a few things around here. He even had plans to go down to Home Depot after supper with Beth to pick out a plan for a deck he wanted to build in the backyard.

Brandy was leashed to a small tree were Mick could watch her. She was trying to dig a hole under it and. Mick went over and put a rock in the hole to stop the dog's digging, but she just started digging along side of it, and Mick swatted her on the butt with the rake handle.

"Mick!" He had heard somebody calling his name and looked up to see Mrs. Crowley crossing the street. She had wet knees from kneeling in her flower garden and she was trying to get her muddy gloves off as she walked toward him.

"Mick, it's good to see you people are back. How was the vacation?"

"Oh, great, Bonnie, but it's good to get home, also, and sleep in our own bed. We had a great time, and Sarah really enjoyed Disney World."

Bonnie was doing her best to keep the puppy away from her as it was trying to take her gloves away until Mick swatted it again. "I'm not sure getting this dog for Sarah was such a good idea," he smiled. "She wrecks things faster than I can fix them up."

Bonny smiled back and ignored his comments about the dog. "I was going to come over and talk to you yesterday, but it got late and one thing led to another. You know, Mick, the strangest thing happened while you guys were gone. It was Tuesday night, or was it Wednesday? Oh, I'm not sure. But I had gotten up during the night to use the bathroom and you know my bathroom window faces your house."

Mick just nodded his head and pulled the puppy away from her.

"Well, anyway, I was walking into my bathroom when I saw your lights flash in your house. It was only for a second, just on and off, you know."

"Downstairs?" Mick asked.

"No, upstairs. I never thought to look in your driveway; I had to go to the bathroom pretty bad." She gave a nervous laugh. "A moment later after I had sat down to go potty, I heard a car start up, and when I got back over to the window this van backed out of your driveway and left."

"What color was the van?" Mick asked. "Did you see the driver?"

"I didn't see the driver, but the van looked like it was silver. The street light is right there, you know."

"Well, I'll look into it," Mick said. "And thank you so much for keeping an eye on the place. It's nice to have good neighbors."

Brandy was digging again, and Mick had had all he wanted of it. "I better get this puppy out of here while I still have a yard," he said. He picked up the dog and headed for the house, but not before he thanked Bonnie again and she went back across the street.

Mick was more than concerned. He was convinced somebody had been in the house, especially now with this new information from Mrs. Crowley.

Manny had seen Mick and Larry both come to work and go home on Monday. He followed them far enough that he knew they were going to Mick's place. He would watch them again tomorrow and the next day, just to make sure of their schedule.

Diego was also itching to get this over with and was trying to arrange for another stolen car. They would not fail this time. He had secured two AK .47s in Chicago his last trip down there. As soon as they were done with them they would be destroyed.

George was establishing an airtight alibi for all three of them. Right now the plan was to go on Friday afternoon, and if it didn't work out, they would do it the following Monday.

Mick didn't say anything to Beth about somebody being in the house while they were gone until they were in bed on Wednesday night. First thing that morning, he checked to see if any silver mini vans had been stolen in the last week or so. He knew for a fact that if they were looking for him they would not use their own car. The only silver mini van that was on the stolen list was found burned the same night Mrs. Crowley had seen one at Mick's house, and not very far away. They had been lucky because the fire department had been on its way back from a call when they found the smoking vehicle, so the car hadn't burned too badly. The crime lab had been through it and they were not able to get any prints, however. The only things found in the car were some soggy magazines that belonged to the owner and a pair of shoes that were not on the owner's list.

Because they were still smoldering when the fire department left the scene, they had left them laying in the gutter.

"Bethy, are you sleeping?" Mick asked.

"No, but I'm too tired tonight, Mick, if that's what you mean."

"That's good ... so am I. I just wanted you to know that I have some pretty conclusive proof that someone was in our house while we were gone."

"What! How?" Beth sat up and turned the lamp on.

"I think they came in the back of the garage. Why they did, I don't know. There's nothing missing that I know of, so it wasn't burglars. It had to be someone looking for something that wasn't here, and I think that something was me." Mick went on to tell her about the dog poop in the garage and Mrs. Crowley's conversation.

"Why would they want to hurt—Oh, Mick, you're not saying that the friends of the man you shot are looking for you! Oh, God, Mick, I'm scared." There was a touch of panic in her voice.

Mick pulled her over to him and held her tight. "I don't know, sweetheart, but it's possible it could be something like that. We just need to be cautious. I've notified the precinct supervisors over here and they're going to keep an extra eye out in the neighborhood for a while. In the meantime, I want you to keep the drapes pulled, the doors locked, and your eyes open."

Mick reached across her and turned off the lamp. They both lay down, still holding each other. Soon Mick was asleep. Beth got up and pulled on her white fluffy bathrobe and sat in a chair holding her knees to her chest and thinking for a long time.

By Thursday morning, Beth had gotten over her initial scare and stopped thinking about it, even though she had mentioned to Laurie that she felt as if they had been violated by someone entering the sanctity of their home. She also asked Laurie if she'd stepped in dog crap or had been in the back yard.

"Ish, no," was all that she said.

On Thursday night they went over to Home Depot and Mick ordered all of the lumber for their new deck. It would be delivered on Saturday morning. They also went out to supper at The Olive Garden. Beth loved their manicotti and Mick ordered a large spaghetti platter. The place was packed and they had to wait almost twenty minutes to be seated, but it was worth it.

When they got home Beth and Mick sat together on the couch after Sarah had gone to bed and talked about their week. Beth had been somewhat concerned about Mick's changes at work and how he was going to react to them, but he seemed to blow the whole thing off. Tonight he seemed to be more concerned about getting into her pants then anything else. He was sure doing his part in this whole baby-making scheme, Beth thought.

She put up with his advances on the couch for a while, but then, getting aroused herself, finally said, "Not here, upstairs," and hurried up to the bedroom.

Mick went to the bathroom and freshened up. When he got out Beth was lying on her side with the sheets pulled back. She was naked, facing Mick as he came in the room. She had the tip of the forefinger on her left hand poked seductively in the corner of her mouth and had just a hint of a smile on her face. He stood and looked at her with that coy little smile of his.

"Bethy, you are the most beautiful creature I have ever seen. I'll never tire of looking at you."

She rolled onto her back and held her arms open for him.

After they had finished making love, Beth lay in bed and thought how perfect she and Mick were for each other. After all of these years, the fires of romance still burned brightly. But it wasn't just about the sex. They just loved to be with each other. They were truly made for each other

-II-

The stolen car Deigo had delivered to him was a nineteen-eighty-seven Buick Electra. It was light blue in color and had a few nicks and dents, but not much rust. It had been taken from a used car lot that was going through chapter eleven and was not open for business at the moment. Diego had asked for something that would not be missed for a few days. It was amazing what you could get for a few snorts of cocaine.

The plan was for Manny to watch the police station in the morning and then Diego and George would show up in the late afternoon with the car and the guns. There had been an argument last night between George and Manny, as Manny could not see why they didn't just hire it done and be through with it.

"This is one thing, Manny, that you do not hire done," George lectured. "This is personal, and we need to avenge our brother's death. The only way we can accomplish that is by doing it ourselves." Manny didn't press the point, although he still didn't agree with him.

George had told his mother that this was the end of it for him. "As soon as this is accomplished, Momma, I'm going to move out and start a new life. The life expectancy in this business is just too short, and I have a family to start thinking about."

His mother had come around the table and cradled George's head in her arms, holding him to her bosom. "This is all you know, George. How will you do anything else? I want you to think long and hard about that, my son."

Beth called Mick around two in the afternoon and asked him to pick up Sarah on his way home. She had a meeting with parents after school and would not be home until late.

"It's I Hop for supper for us," was all Mick said. Sarah's favorite restaurant was I Hop, although if she had suggested a hot dog stand Mick would have taken her there.

"It will be after three," Mick said. "You know Larry has the car now, so he's the boss. I'm just along for the ride."

"We need to get a second car," said Beth.

"A truck," said Mick. "We need a bright red pickup with four-wheel drive and big muddy tires. Then on the weekends we can go up to your dads's and bounce around in the woods and swamps." He was playing with her now, and she didn't have time for it.

"You keep dreaming, dear, and don't be late to pick Sarah up. Love you."

"Love you too, Bethy." Mick hung up the phone. They weren't supposed to use the city cars for personal business, but what the hell, it was right on the way. It's not like it was costing anybody anything.

It had been a day in court for both Mick and Larry, and they were both feeling good about this particular case. It was a case that would probably go to the jury in a day or two. It had been a tricky one that involved a woman who had killed her abusive husband while he slept. She had refused to plea bargain the case because she was convinced she'd done the right thing. Both Mick and Larry tended to agree, and although not withholding evidence against her, they hadn't been very aggressive with the case. They both believed he got what he had coming.

Mick had on a light blue sport jacket and tan khaki slacks. He had a blue striped short sleeve shirt and no tie. Larry, more conservative, had worn a gray suit with a black tee shirt sweater under it. Both men were in good spirits as they pulled up to the school, looking forward to a nice weekend. The weather forecast was for more of the same, lots of sun and unseasonably warm temperatures. Mick was going to work on his deck and Larry was going to visit some friends for the day on Saturday.

Larry stayed in the car with the motor running while Mick ran inside to get Sarah. The school parking lot was nearly empty, with just a couple of skateboarders enjoying the nice April day and running their boards on the curbs around the parking lot.

The hallways in the school were deserted and Mick's footsteps made the only sound. They echoed off of the rows of steel lockers and he felt like he was in some kind of a sound chamber. Beth's classroom was four doors down on the right, and he could hear Beth and Laurie laughing before he got there. He didn't knock but walked right in, and both of them laughed even harder when they saw Mick.

"I must be the source of your amusement," he quipped.

"No, not at all," Laurie smiled. "But you did pop in at a funny time."

"Honey, I have a prescription at Snyder's. Would you mind picking it up on the way home?" Beth was playing with his lapel while she gave him a shy 'poor-little-me' look … one that Mick could never resist.

"Give me some money, because I'm broke." Mick kissed her on the forehead.

Laurie helped Sarah get her backpack zipped and she ran up to the front of the room to take her dad's hand.

"Have a good day, pumpkin?" Mick asked.

"I did, Daddy, and guess what.… Bonnie Clement is going to come to our house tomorrow night to sleep over. Mommy said it was ok."

"Well, you went right to the top with that one, didn't you, sweetheart? There are no objections from me."

Beth had wondered about having someone else's child in the house with things being the way they were right now, but had no way to tell Sarah no without lying. Something she just wouldn't do. Besides, it would be evening and Mick would be there, she reasoned.

Beth pressed a bill in his hand that she took from her purse. "Bring me back my change you cheapskate."

Mick smiled and said. "See you later." They walked out to the car, Sarah skipping along to her dad's long footsteps.

Manny and George were in the front seat and Diego was in the back as they pulled out of the hospital parking lot. The hospital sat up on a slight hill and there were actually three parking lots, each one terraced up from the other. They'd been sitting in the middle one in the last row where they had been watching Mick and Larry's car for a couple of hours.

"There they are," said Manny. "Why the hell don't we just whack them right now and get the hell out of here."

"Shoot them in front of the police station? You sure are a stupid bastard, Manny." George glared as he addressed him. "Just drive the fucking car and I'll decide when, ok?"

They followed Larry and Mick about three cars back and once at a red light lost sight of them, but that was all right, as they had a pretty good idea where they were going.

"There they are," said Diego. "They're going into that school parking lot." He was fingering the AK .47 lying across his lap. George had a similar one, but he had laid it on the floor at his feet.

Manny started to turn into the lot but George told him to circle the block.

"What's wrong with that place," asked Manny?

George didn't answer his question but said again in a sarcastic tone, "Go around the block, asshole."

After they circled the block they noticed only one man in the car so they elected to go around again. It was a big block and they hit traffic so it was nearly five minutes before they got back. George was hoping they'd be gone so they could forget this whole thing. He had lost all desire for killing.

As they came around the corner of the school, they saw that Larry and Mick were back in the car and Larry was backing out. Mick had put Sarah in the back seat and belted her in. She was short enough that her head didn't show above the window from the rear.

Manny pulled the blue sedan over to the curb, while Deigo slid down in the back seat so no one could see them. Larry and Mick headed up the street in the left-hand lane of the double-lane road. This confused Manny, as they needed to be in the right lane to turn a block ahead if they were going to Mick's house.

"Where the hell are they going now?" he asked.

"Just follow them," muttered George.

Half a block up from the school Larry turned left into a strip mall and parked in front of a Snyder Drug store. They had barely stopped when Mick emerged and ran into the building.

Diego was still lying on the seat when they turned in and parked in the row behind Mick and Larry, facing the street.

"The one we want went in the store," George said. "We'll take him as soon as he comes back out and is in the car. Shoot into the car only. I don't want anyone else hit. We'll have to shoot them both; we want no witnesses. Wait till they pull out and are side-ways to us, Diego. Manny, you back out the same time they do so we are broadside." The driveway between the cars was quite wide so two cars backing out at the same time was not of much concern. George put the rifle in his lap and clicked the safety off and Diego did likewise. George looked at Diego and saw that he was he was grinning from ear to ear. It was scary, even to George. How could someone enjoy this?

It seemed to take a long time and the men had their gazes frozen on the doors of the store, not paying much attention to the car. Had they looked, they would have seen Sarah bobbing around in the back seat and Larry leaning over the seat talking to her.

It was hot and George was drenched in sweat. It was running into his eyes and he wiped his face on his shirt-sleeve just as Mick came out and reached for the car door.

"Wait, Wait," he was saying to Manny. "Stay down, Diego, until I say, now."

Larry backed slowly out, unaware of the big Buick slowly backing out at the same time, then stopped the car to shift from reverse to forward. The car was facing left, the way it had come in. Manny was facing the other way.

"Now," George said, tapping Manny on the shoulder.

"Look out!" was all Mick had time to shout. He had seen the guns appear in the car windows. He turned to look at Sarah in the back seat just as the first volley of shots rang out. Larry hit the throttle but it was too late. The windows exploded out of the car. Larry's foot froze on the throttle and he plowed into a parked car, shoving it into the front of the building. He was now a full car length past the blue Buick, which hadn't moved yet.

George and Diego were now shooting through the back window and then the smoke rose from the rear tires as Manny hit the accelerator and headed into the parking lot and made a u turn. That brought them back alongside the police car but they were not shooting now. Their clips were empty. With a squeal of burning rubber, the Buick roared out into the street, almost causing an accident as they went. Tires still squealing, they sped off. Behind them in the lot the smell of gunpowder smoke mixed with the smell of burning rubber drifted lazily away. It was quiet inside of the police car, and strangely quiet outside.

Mick never knew what had hit him. The bullet had torn through in front of his right ear, exiting out the top of his head. Portions of bone and brain matter were splattered on the headliner of the car and were dripping down on Larry. Two more bullets had hit him in the shoulder and the chest but they mattered little. He slumped forward, his head face down on the dash, and died instantly, held in place by the seat belt and harness. A pool of blood collected in a depression in the dashboard under his face, and then ran down the front of it over the radio dial and onto the floor.

Larry had been hit once when they fired through the back window. The bullet hit him midway between the hips, after passing through the back of the seat cushion. It severed his spinal cord and he felt for a moment as if he had been electrocuted. He never lost consciousness, and when the Sanchez brothers came past him on their way out, he was looking right at Manny and Diego. The thing that was burned in his memory, however, was Manny shouting out of the window. "That's for Raul, assholes."

Sarah, who had been slumped down, sat up to see what had happened to her dad. A bullet fired by Diego through the back window tore through her neck, partially severing her carotid artery before going on to nick Larry. She lay over on the seat gasping for air. None of the Sanchezes saw her as they left.

Dr. Tom Nelson, who was a surgeon at St. Mark's Hospital six blocks away, was in the drug store when the shooting started. The pharmacist, Bernie Adams, was an old friend of his from college and they often talked. He had ducked down when one of the plate glass widows in the front of the store exploded in a million pieces. He was looking at the front doors, but no one came in.

Dr. Nelson waited a moment, and then crept to the front doors to look out. He had heard the collision with the cars and the tires squealing as Manny left the lot, but he was too late to see who did what.

The only witness outside appeared to be a young woman who was screaming and pointing inside the car, her face filled with terror. She had been parked next to Larry when he backed out and it was her car he had plowed into. She hadn't been hurt.

Dr. Nelson took only a moment to survey the scene and rushed to the car the woman was pointing to. He turned Mick's head to the side but his eyes were already dilated. Larry was slumped against the door moaning softly. Then Nelson's eyes went to the back seat where Sarah lay sprawled, with blood spurting from a red gash in her neck.

He reached for the door handle but it was locked and he had to reach inside Mick's door and push the electric lock. He unhooked Sarah's seat belt and laid her on her back, blood still gushing from her neck. At once his fingers expertly probed the wound and he found the severed artery and pinched it off. The bleeding stopped but he couldn't move. He could not let go of that artery.

Someone came up behind him and put his hand on Nelson's shoulder. It was Bernie, who had stopped long enough to call 911 and report gunshots.

"Bernie, get me some artery clips or something to pinch this off. Oh, and a cuff," Dr. Nelson was yelling. Sarah's blood was everywhere and the front of his white shirt was splattered. It seemed like forever until Bernie came back with a kit with some clips. A female clerk was right behind him with a blood pressure cuff, leaving it on the roof of the car as she turned away from the carnage. The young woman staggered away between two cars, her face ashen, and vomited.

Bernie had been a medic in the army in Vietnam, but it had been a long time ago. He moved to the driver's door to look at Larry, while Dr. Nelson worked on Sarah as the first squad car screeched to a halt.

A police officer ran to assist Nelson, a first aid kit in his hand. "Ambulance is ordered," the officer said, "and it should be here any minute."

"We may only have minutes," Doctor Nelson said. With the bleeding stopped he had tried to take Sarah's blood pressure but could not get a reading. Her breathing was very shallow.

He turned his attention to Mick and confirmed that he was gone. He next went around to assist Bernie with Larry, who still remained conscious. His vital signs were stable, so he went back to Sarah.

Bernie was unbuttoning Larry's coat to examine his wounds. There was a hole in the front of his pants just under his belt buckle, and a spot of blood about two inches in diameter surrounded the hole. Clipped to his belt was his badge.

"Officer! Officer, this man is a cop!" Bernie was trying to get the police officer that showed up to pay attention. He was still by the back door helping Doctor Nelson get a trach tube into Sarah, who now was barely breathing.

The officer came to the car door, leaned over the seat and looked at Larry's badge. Then he backed out of the car and went to Mick and laid him back onto the seat. He opened his sport coat and saw his badge, and at the same time he recognized Mick. He had worked with him several times. He ran to the back of the car and looked at the license plate. Then he saw the radio under the dash and the red light on the floor in the middle. It all came together, and he ran for his radio.

Just then a rescue squad pulled up and took over the care of Larry and Sarah. An IV was started in Sarah and fluids were soon dripping into her tiny arm. She was carried to the ambulance and laid on the stretcher. Dr. Nelson, who had identified himself to the men, stayed with her while they loaded Larry, also, and slid him in beside her. They were glad to have a doctor aboard. One of the paramedics stayed in the back with Dr. Nelson, while the other took the wheel, and with the siren blaring they sped toward the hospital.

Someone brought a blanket from another police car that showed up and covered the top half of Mick's body. Back at police headquarters supervisors had been notified and they were on their way. Only one witness could be found, as the lady who had been so traumatized in the car next to Mick and Larry's, had apparently left the scene.

The man, although shaken, did describe a light blue Buick sedan, and a bulletin went out to the cars on the streets.

The area was quickly cordoned off with yellow crime scene tape and little red flags were placed by all of the shell casings that littered the street.

About ten minutes later, Capt. Wicks was on the scene. He walked to the bullet-pocked car and lifted the blanket. For a moment he could not believe what he was looking at. Mick's eyes were now closed, but his face had taken on the ashen gray-blue color of death. His light blue shirt was drenched in blood, his gun strapped in its shoulder holster. Wicks reached down and ran his hand through Mick's hair and pulled it back covered with blood and bone splinters. He knelt beside the car in the glass, on the asphalt with tears running down his face. Another man in a suit helped him to his feet and they both went inside the drug store out of the public eye.

Beth was in her classroom meeting with the parents of one of her students. The window of the classroom was open to let in some fresh air.

"So many sirens," the man said as they all looked out the window. "This is a busy street," Beth explained. "There are always a lot of sirens."

-12-

Manny drove away from the scene as fast as he could without drawing attention to the fleeing car. He wasn't seeing well, as George had hit him with the butt of the rifle in the side of the face when he had yelled, "That's for Raul, assholes," out the window.

"You fucking idiot, Manny. Why didn't we just stop and you could have had your picture taken? The sooner I can get away from you assholes the better off I'm going to be." George slammed the dash in anger with heel of his hand.

Manny rubbed his swollen eye and was silent for a moment, and then he said, "They were both dead, George. What the hell difference did it make what I said?"

"You better hope to hell they were both dead, Manny. For your sake you better hope that's true, because if they weren't and you fucked up, I am personally going to take care of you."

"Hey, let's just get going and quit the bickering." Diego was sitting in the middle of the back seat smiling, and looking like he had just won a thousand dollar bet.

Neither Manny nor George answered him but George did hand him the AK .47 he had used. "Put them in that bag in the floor," he said.

Diego slid both guns into a cloth bag almost like a grain sack and tied the top. They pulled over to the curb behind Momma's Navigator. Diego and George got out and got in her car, but not before Diego slipped the guns under the back seat cushion and George told Manny. "You know what you're supposed to do. See if you can do something right. I'll pick you up in about an hour."

Manny drove north until he was in an old run down part of town and stopped at a salvage yard. He got out of the car and went in the office and a few minutes later a large black man on a forklift came and, driving the forks under the car picked it up and carried it away. It was headed for the shredders where it would be pulverized into scrap, no questions asked.

Momma and the boys were home and they were happy. They had gotten their revenge and now they needed to be home, when and if the cops came. But first, George needed to go pick up Manny, who was supposed to be waiting in a park, but had stopped for a bottle of beer and was sitting on a rock snorting coke.

Captain Wicks had composed himself enough to go back out to the car. As he looked inside the car once more at Mick's body he noticed the puddle of blood in the back seat. "Who was sitting there?" he asked the first officer who had arrived on the scene.

"A little girl about eight or nine years old. I think it was Mick's daughter, the way Larry was talking, but he was hurt pretty bad, so I'm not sure about that. He did ask about her several times."

"Which hospital did they go too?"

"Saint Mark's," said the cop.

Wicks went over to one of his investigators who had arrived on the scene. "I'm going to St. Mark's," he told him. "Have Mick's body transported as soon as possible to the county morgue. Otherwise you guys know what you have to do."

Wicks called the office on his way to the hospital to get Mick's home phone number. He had to talk to Beth as soon as possible. The phone rang three times at the house and then went to a recorder. He called his office again.

"Karen, look and see if there is a work number for Mick Motrin's wife. She teaches school somewhere."

He could hear the click of the computer keys as Karen, his secretary scanned the records. "Captain, try 563-6400. It's the school number, but I think most schools are out for the day."

"Thanks," Wicks said and pulled over to the curb to dial.

"Oak Elementary," a voice on the other end of the line answered.

"I need to talk to Beth Motrin," Wicks said.

"I'm sorry sir, she is in conferences right now and can not be interrupted."

"This is the police department and this is an emergency. Please get her." Wicks' voice left no doubt about the seriousness of the call. But what was he going to say to her, he wondered?

He would drive over and pick her up, he decided. He pulled over to the curb and made a U turn and headed for the school. *That's right,* he thought. *I don't want her driving all shook up like that. But I can't tell her her husband is dead while we're on the way to the hospital. But wait. They have chaplains and counselors there. These are people who are trained in giving out that kind of news. He would tell her about Sarah. Just Sarah for now. She was hurt. Yeah, that's right, she was hurt and they needed to get there right away.*

"This is Beth Motrin."

"Beth, this is Dan Wicks from the police department."

"Dan Wicks?" Beth asked "Oh! Captain Wicks." She had never heard his first name before. "Is something wrong?" Her voice had taken on some concern. She was alone in her classroom right now, but the next set of parents were coming down the hall.

"Beth, I'll be there in a minute. Can you meet me at the entrance?"

"Well, yes, but I do have an appointment. Can it wait a few minutes? This is my last conference of the—."

"Beth," Wicks interrupted. "This is important. Very Important."

Now she was scared. Beth grabbed her jacket and purse and while leaving her classroom met the next set of parents. "Please sit down anywhere," she told them. "I will be right back."

Wicks pulled up to the door at the very instant Beth walked out. The car was still rolling when he reached over and flipped open the door. His red light on the dash was going and that added to her unease. "Beth, please get in," he said. "There has been an incident and you need to go to the hospital."

He was already speeding out of the parking lot while Beth was sitting sideways on the front seat with one hand on the dash to steady herself, facing him.

"It's Mick, isn't it? He told me they were looking for him after that shooting. How bad is he hurt?" Beth's eyes were welling with tears now. They were four blocks from the hospital.

"Look, Beth, right now we are going to see your daughter. Sarah is her name, right?"

"Sarah! How did she get hurt? Were they in a car wreck?"

"No, Beth it was a drive by shooting and Sarah was in the car. A bullet or a bullet fragment hit her. We are not sure. But she was breathing fine when they left the scene in the ambulance." He was one block from the emergency entrance at the hospital.

"They shot my daughter? They shot an eight-year-old girl? Where is Mick? Is he at the hospital with her?" Beth was frantic. She was starting to shake and loose control.

Wicks did not answer her last question but pulled into the emergency entrance and parked. He ran around the car to open the door but Beth had already gotten out and was running for the entrance. He looked around and saw a security guard by the door and as he went by he said, "Police officer, Sir. Would you take care of my car?" He didn't wait for an answer but ran after Beth who was already in the emergency room lobby.

"My daughter!" Beth was half screaming and shouting. "Where is my daughter?"

Wicks caught up with her and grabbed her shoulders to try and calm her down but she would have no part of it. She wrenched herself loose from him and cried once more to the receptionist,"Where is she?"

Just then Doctor Nelson walked up to Beth. He had put on a clean smock over his bloody clothes but you could still see blood on his collar and tie.

"Please. I'm Doctor Nelson. I was with your daughter when they brought her in. Let's go back here where we can talk." He opened a door into a small room.

Wicks followed, although he wished right now he were anywhere else but where he was.

"Your daughter was hit by a bullet that just grazed her neck," Dr. Nelson said, but he wasn't sure Beth was even listening to him. She was walking around in little circles with her fists clenched yelling, "No! No! How can this be?"

"The wound in itself was not that bad, but she lost a lot of blood. She is in surgery right now. They need to get her transfused and—"

"Where is my husband?" Beth screamed. "Was he shot too? What are you not telling me?" She stopped moving and now was staring at Wicks, who was looking to the doctor for help.

"I am so very sorry, but your husband is dead," Dr. Nelson said. He reached for her hands but too late, and Beth collapsed on the floor in a heap. At first she was moaning and sobbing, her head buried in her arms, and then she looked up and screamed at Wicks. Her face was so contorted she looked like someone out of a horror movie. Tears and spittle ran down her anguished face.

"You knew he was dead when you picked me up and you never said a word to me about it!" Her purse had fallen open when she collapsed on the floor, and Wicks squatted, trying to pick up her things. She pushed at him and he fell over backwards. He made no attempt to get up, looking at her helplessly.

Another doctor came into the room and talked briefly in subdued tones with Dr. Nelson. It was Dr. Amanda Hurst, a neurosurgeon and neurologist at St. Mark's. She reached out to Beth, but Beth refused to be held or even touched by anyone.

Dr. Nelson spoke first. "Beth, this is the doctor who operated on Sarah, and she wants to take you up to see her now. She is in pediatrics in the intensive care unit."

The mention of Sarah's name brought Beth back a little and she allowed the doctor to take her hand and lead her to a bank of elevators. Dr. Nelson, Captain Wicks, and a hospital chaplain, who had just come in, followed cautiously.

The chaplain had a Bible in his hand, but for the moment he stayed back.

At the sixth floor the elevator stopped and they emerged into a brightly decorated hallway. The walls were alive with pictures of animals and clowns. It was visiting hours and people were walking in the hallway, some of them either pushing a child in a wheelchair or carrying a toddler. They went past rooms where people were laughing and one room in which someone was having a birthday party, to the end of the corridor where two wooden swinging doors that were stamped I.C.U. in big black letters. Underneath in smaller letters were instructions and restrictions for visitors.

The intensive care unit was shaped like a wagon wheel with the nurse's station in the center. A corridor went around the hub and then about a dozen rooms formed the outside of the wheel. The doors and the walls were almost all glass so each room could be observed from the nurses' station just by pirouetting around. About half of the rooms were dark, but one room had several nurses in it, and that's the one Dr. Hurst took Beth into.

The first thing Beth and the others heard was the whoosh of air from the ventilator. Dr. Nelson said something to one of the nurses and she nodded and left the room.

Sarah was lying on her back, her red hair splayed out over the pillow. Her eyes were closed and her hands were clenched in tiny fists. The white corrugated tube from the ventilator went to her throat, and her neck was covered with a patch of bandages.

Beth had stopped crying for the moment and now sat gingerly on the side of the bed and took Sarah's hands.

"She lost so much blood that it was touch and go for a while." Dr. Hurst was standing beside Beth with her arm around her. "The artery that was severed is one of two that feeds her brain. For a while she was not getting any blood to the right side of her brain but we have restored the flow. Now we need to pray that it wasn't interrupted too long."

Beth did not speak nor give any indication that she was listening to the Dr. She was just stared at her daughter as if it all was a bad dream, and began to sob quietly.

The nurse that had left returned with a white paper cup, and Dr. Nelson asked Beth to take the pills in the cup, but she shook her head. "Please," Dr. Hurst asked, but Beth refused. They brought her a chair and she sat beside the bed, just watching Sarah and sobbing.

Wicks had left, telling the nurses he would be back. He needed to find out what was happening with Larry. To do so he had to go down to the main floor to surgery where Dr. Nelson told him he had been operated on.

Larry was still in the recovery room but the surgeon who did the operation came out to talk to Wicks.

"He will recover," he said, "but he will never walk again." The bullet took about a half of an inch right out of his spinal cord. He'll be paralyzed from the hips on down. His vital signs are good, however," he added, almost as if that were good news.

"I need to talk with him as soon as you're sure he knows what is going on," Wicks said. "He may be the only witness we have."

"That shouldn't be more than an hour," the doctor said, and left the room.

Wicks took the elevator back up to the sixth floor and walked down the hall to I.C.U. again. Nothing had changed, except that the neurosurgeon was gone and the chaplain was now in the room, sitting on a chair, trying to talk to Beth, who was still crying uncontrollably, her face buried in the bed clothes. She was finding it hard to even breathe and gasping for air.

Wicks stayed outside the door but caught the chaplain's attention and pointed to the doctor, who was staring out the window deep in though, indicating that he wanted him to come out. The chaplain went over and said something to him and he turned and came out in the corridor.

"I need some help," Wicks said to the doctor. "Mick has parents, and I am sure there are other relatives that need to be notified. How is she doing?" He nodded toward Beth.

"She's in shock," he said. "We are going to try and get a bed in the room for her. She needs to stay with the girl for her own good as well as Sarah's. We did get her to take a shot and hopefully that will calm her down a little. I can't imagine what she is feeling," he said, with tears in his eyes.

"How is Sarah?" Wicks asked

"Not good," the Doctor said. "Her brain scan was almost flat. We'll know more in a couple of days. Sometimes some activity can return, but it's rare."

"That poor woman," Wicks murmured. He wanted to go to her and try to explain, and console, but there were no words that he knew of for a time like this and thought he might only make things worse.

He went back down to the floor Larry was on and waited for him to come out of recovery. He called the office and got emergency phone numbers for Larry, but the only numbers listed were Mick and Beth's and his sister's in Illinois.

He called the number of Larry's sister and got a recorder, but before he could give his entire message a woman picked up the phone and said hello.

"Are you Larry Sorenson's sister?" Wicks asked.

"Yes, this is Laura Borden. Is there a problem?" she asked.

"This is Captain Dan Wicks, Larry's supervisor at the police department. I hate to be the bearer of bad news, but your brother has been injured. He is stable right now but we could use your assistance in notifying any other family members."

"My husband and I will be right up," she said. "It's about a six hour drive. Are you sure he is all right?"

"Yes, come to St. Mark's Hospital. It's on Forty Second and Highland. Drive safely ... Larry is stable. Thank you." said Wicks. He didn't know what else to say.

There were getting to be too many irons in the fire, and Dan needed to get some help. He dialed the office and asked for Detective Ron Wagner to come to the hospital as soon as possible. Ron would be the next in command after Larry, so he would be the best one to interview him as soon as he came out of recovery.

At Oak School, the parents who had been waiting for Beth to return for their conference went down to the office after waiting almost a half an hour. The principal, Mr. Cameron, was puzzled about Beth's absence, as Janelle, his secretary, had not told him about the call from the police. He walked back down to her room with them, and seeing that Beth hadn't returned, apologized to the parents, turned off the lights and locked the door before taking them back to the office. "This is unlike Mrs. Motrin," he told them. "She is one of the most responsible teachers we have." He would talk to her on Monday morning. There had to be some kind of an explanation.

As he walked across the parking lot to his car he noticed Beth's car still parked where she normally parked. *That's strange,* he thought. He walked over and looked in the window but it was empty. For a second he thought that maybe he should call someone, but then he figured it was probably nothing. *I bet her and Laurie went out for a drink. They're always hanging around together. Time to go home,* he thought, it had been a long day.

-13-

The night nurse had checked on Sarah several times and each time Beth was still sitting in the chair, watching her and crying. They asked what they could do for her, whether they could get her water or something to eat, but she wanted nothing and just shook her head. Although they had made up the other bed in the room for her, Beth stayed in the chair next to her comatose daughter.

Her coat was open but still over her shoulders. Her purse was on the nightstand where Wicks had left it after retrieving all of the things she had spilled. Beth had no use for it. She wiped her nose and her tears on a paper towel she clutched in her hand, and remained that way throughout the night.

Sarah's condition did not change that night. Her vital signs were stable, but her brain function was barely registering. She could not breathe without the ventilator. She also had an IV hooked to her arm, and in the morning they would be putting in a feeding tube. This was explained to Beth by Dr. Hurst, but she gave no sign that she had understood what she was saying, or that she cared.

Early in the morning the sun broke over the horizon east of the hospital, facing the windows in Sarah's room. The traffic was picking up on the street out front and the sounds of food carts and doctors making rounds could be heard as the hospital came to life for another day. A new shift of nurses had taken over, and they had been briefed on Beth's situation but for the most part left her alone, as they just didn't know what to do for her, although they knew she had to be nearly in a state of exhaustion.

At exactly 9 a.m. Beth rose from the chair and pulled her coat back over her shoulders. She went into the bathroom in Sarah's room and when she came out her hair was combed and she had freshened up. Then she went to the desk outside of Sarah's room and told the nurse she would be leaving for a while. "If you need to reach me," she said, "here is my cell phone number," and she handed the woman the phone to read.

Beth walked to the elevators, and once on the ground floor walked out of the hospital and down the street, heading for Oak Elementary School. She walked briskly, not at all looking like someone who had been up for a day and a half and who had suffered the tragedy she had been through.

Her car was the only one in the parking lot. She started the engine and let it warm up a moment while she made a call to Dan Wicks at the number he had given her when he left last night.

"Dan, where is my husband's body?" she asked as soon as he answered the phone.

"Beth, where are you? Are you okay?"

"Dan, please tell me where Mick is?" With the mention of his name she started to sob but she stifled it as Dan answered.

"He's at the County Medical Examiners Office," he said. "They should be done with him soon. Beth, can I help you with the funeral arrangements? Can I come pick you up?" Her call had surprised and unnerved Dan, and right now he was nearly at a loss for words.

"If I need help, I will call," was all she said, and disconnected the phone. She put the car in gear and drove out of the parking lot, heading in the opposite direction from home. About six blocks down the street she turned into the Johnson Strom Funeral Home, parked the car and walked into the office.

An older woman with long silver hair got up from behind the desk and came out to greet Beth. "Hi, I am Muriel," she said. "How can I assist you?"

"I need to plan my husband's funeral," Beth told her.

Muriel fidgeted for a second as if she was undecided what to do next but then recovered and said, "Let me see if Mr. Strom is free."

Lester Strom had been a funeral director for over forty years, and had handled almost every kind of situation that one could come across in this business. He knew how to deal compassionately with distraught people. He was a big man with large hands and a full head of silver-gray hair. The years had been kind to him and he looked fifty-five instead of the sixty-eight he was. He enjoyed being kind to his clients and helping them in their time of need.

"I'm Les Strom," he introduced himself to Beth, who had remained standing while she waited.

Beth twisted a handkerchief nervously in her hands but otherwise was remarkably composed. "I need you to handle my husband's funeral," she said.

"You are …?" he asked. "I'm sorry I didn't get your name."

"Beth Motrin. My husband is—was Mick Motrin."

"Your husband was the police officer who was killed yesterday," he answered. Beth nodded her head.

"Can I get you some coffee, tea or juice?" he asked.

She nodded her head. "Coffee would be fine," she finally said. Muriel, who had been hovering nearby nodded to indicate that she had understood and left.

Lester brought out a pad of paper and went down the list of things that he needed to have answered: Where is your husband's body now? Will the funeral be in a church? Where would he be buried? What about a wake? Where? When? How would you like him dressed?

Beth answered all of his questions quietly and clearly while she looked down into her lap, afraid to meet his gaze. Afraid that she would lose the courage she had somehow summoned, and go to pieces, again.

Lester reached out to touch her arm, but she did not respond. She was numb from grief, and beyond feeling anything.

At last he said, "I think we have all of the information we need for now. We'll take care of everything for you and I'll call you tonight to confirm this, but first we need to take care of one other detail and that is for you to pick out a casket. Are you up to doing that now?"

"Yes," Beth answered quietly.

They went downstairs and into a large room with bright red carpeting where there were row upon row of caskets, all with price tags on them.

"I will leave you for a moment to make a selection," he said, and went into another office at the end of the room. When he came back out, Beth was standing by an oak casket with gold trim.

"I think he would like this one," she said softly.

Lester took both of her hands in his and, looking her straight in the eyes said, "I am so sorry for you and your family. I hope we can make this as painless as possible."

Beth started to cry and then shook it off long enough to thank him. "I really need to go," she said. "There are so many things to do."

He walked her to her car and asked again if she would be home later this afternoon.

"Call my cell," she answered. She opened the flip phone and showed him the number, and he copied it down. He stood in the lot and watched her drive off. He had seen so much grief in his life and it never got any easier but this death seemed especially sad.

Beth drove home and when she turned the corner, her driveway was blocked with a load of lumber. Mick's deck lumber had been delivered. She parked in the end of the driveway and walked tentatively up the drive. It was almost as if she was afraid to go in. Then she heard Brandy in the garage. She walked around to the back and opened the service door and Brandy exploded out of the garage. She had been locked up for over a day, and had made a mess inside the garage, but it could wait for another time. Right now she needed to make two phone calls. No three. She had to call Mick's folks. It was hard to think right now when she needed to cry and to sleep. But for now the crying was not going to wait any longer, and she collapsed at the kitchen table.

Beth was sobbing so hard she could hardly catch her breath. The sobbing went to a wail. Her chest hurt so much she could hardly catch her breath. There was no controlling it anymore. She was making sounds that she could not believe were coming form her. She beat the table top with her fists, knocking a porcelain cereal bowl to the floor and it exploded in many pieces. She kicked the pieces under the table.

After a few minutes she raised her head and listened. Was that the phone? Yes, that's what it was—the phone. Beth crossed the kitchen and lifted the receiver. It was her dad.

"Bethy, tell me it isn't true. I just saw it on the news."

"It's true Daddy, I was just going to call you. Please come and help me." She was sobbing again and trying to talk at the same time, but she was so distraught that Walt couldn't understand most of what she was saying.

"I'll be there in a couple of hours, sweetheart. Please take care of yourself until I get there."

"I will, Daddy. I will," she wailed and hung up the phone.

Beth slid down the cupboard and sat on the floor and the sobbing came again. If it was possible to cry your heart out, Beth was well on her way.

After about half an hour, she pulled herself to her feet. Brandy was scratching at the door so she let her in and then walked through the living room and went upstairs. The bed was still unmade, and Mick's boxers and undershirt were still on the floor beside it where he'd left them. She picked them up and held them to her face. She could smell his deodorant, his scent. Gone forever. She knew she would never smell Mick again.

She slid down beside the bed and another wave of grief worse than the last descended on her. She was praying now. *Dear God, bring him back. Please help Sarah. Please help me, Dear Lord,* she sobbed. *I'm all alone and don't know what to do. Oh, God, why did it have to happen? Why, God?*

Brandy come in and was licking her face and Beth pushed her away, then called her back and buried her head in the dog's fur while Brandy just stood there confused.

Beth stood up and looked in the mirror on the dresser. She was just about the most pathetic thing she had ever seen. Her hair was stringy and her makeup had run all over her face. Her nose was running.

Slowly she undressed until she had only her panties on then walked into the bathroom and turned on the shower. She would cry in there. It was cleaner that way. She sat on the floor of the shower sobbing and then realized she still had her panties on.

"I can't even think anymore," she said, throwing her wet underpants over the glass doors. She sat there until the shower water ran cold. Funny ... she had dreamed about doing that once, but never for this reason.

Beth stepped from the shower and after drying herself off, put on her white terry cloth robe. Her comforter. She wrapped her hair in another towel and went downstairs. Sitting on the couch she called the principal of the school. She had to stop crying long enough to make this call.

"Can I speak with Mr. Cameron?" Beth asked.

"Just a moment," the young voice said. "Dad!" Beth heard her yell. "Phone for you." A stereo was blaring heavy metal music in the background.

"Hello," he answered. It sounded almost like a question.

"Mr. Cameron, this is Beth Motrin, and I wanted to tell you what has—"

"Beth," he interrupted, "you have some parents to call and apologize to, my friend, after last night. I went down to your room and they were—"

It was Beth's turn to interrupt. "Mr. Cameron, for once I want you to listen. My husband was killed yesterday and my daughter was critically injured, and I'm not apologizing to anyone. Your secretary knew I had an emergency and"—She started crying again but composed herself quickly. 'I won't be in to work for a while. I'll be in touch with you next week after Mick's funeral and discuss what I am going to do."

"Beth, I am so sorry," Mr. Cameron said. I didn't know. Is there anything I can do?"

"Please call Laurie for me," she said, and hung up.

She had been rude, but damn it, she had a right to be, and right now she just didn't give a shit. Beth lay down on the couch and cried herself to sleep, while Brandy curled up next to her and licked her tears away.

From the moment of the shooting to the time Larry had come out of the anesthesia, the police department had a good idea who might have done this. Larry's eyewitness account to Captain Wicks put the lid on it.

A warrant for the arrest of all three of the Sanchez brothers went out and they had been arrested at home without incident at 11:45 p.m. on Friday night. They were transported downtown and jailed, but none of them was saying anything. Carl Huebnor, who was the family attorney, gave a brief statement saying all three of the men had solid alibis and were innocent of the charges. Under the direction of Judge Susan Werness, they were ordered to be held without bail until a grand jury could be convened on Monday to consider the charges. All three men were shown on local T.V. being escorted into the courthouse and jail. Manny held up his fingers in a V sign and flashed a big toothy smile. Diego also seemed to be in good spirits. Only George seemed to be subdued.

The morning paper on Saturday came out with a headline that said, **"Three Local Men Arrested in Cop Killing."** There was no mention of Sarah.

When Beth woke up she smelled coffee perking and realized that someone had covered her with a blanket. The lights were on in the kitchen and she walked in still wrapped in the blanket. Her dad and Laurie were at the kitchen table. The clock over the stove said seven p.m.

Beth's dad slid his chair out and went to his daughter and held her in those big arms that had soothed her so many times before. Laurie began crying at the table and got up and joined in the hug. Just then the phone rang, and Beth broke loose to answer it. It was Lester Strom.

"Beth, I hate to bother you at a time like this, but I just wanted to tell you that all of the arrangements have been accomplished. With your permission, the funeral will be held next Tuesday morning at St. Ann's. The wake will be the night before, here at the funeral home. I have talked with Captain Wicks from the police department and he will take care of the clothing, if that is all right with you. You do want Mick to have a full police funeral, don't you?"

For a moment she hesitated. Had she really gone and made arrangements for Mick's funeral? Yesterday was just one big, blurry horror story, but then she remembered being there. How she had done what she did yesterday she couldn't comprehend. Not the way she felt right now. "Yes, I guess so," She said quietly.

"We have procured a grave site at Sunset Memorial, if that is ok? If you want I could take you out there to see it."

"No, that's fine," Beth said. "Thank you for your help." She handed the phone to Laurie who hung it up.

"I need to go to the hospital," she said. "Will you go with me?"

Both Laurie and Beth's dad said they would come.

"Dad, while I get dressed will you call Mick's parents? The number is there in the rolodex." She pointed to the desk in the corner. "I'm not sure what to say to them. We never where very close, them living way out there in California and—." Her voice trailed off. Beth went upstairs and dressed in black slacks and a white sweater with a black turtleneck under it. No jewelry, but she did put on some makeup.

She started sobbing again and Laurie, who had accompanied her into the bedroom and was brushing out her hair, sat on the end of the bed and held her for a few minutes until she calmed down.

When they came back down Beth was holding a pair of pajamas she had taken from Sarah's room and a stuffed rabbit that was one of Sarah's favorites. She slept with it every night.

They walked out into the cold April evening. The street was quiet and deserted and Beth saw that her dad had moved the lumber pile into the back yard. They took Laurie's car and Beth, staring out the window silently, ate an apple on the way, the first thing she had eaten in a day and a half.

The sight of the hospital made her upset again, so she sat in the car for a few minutes until she calmed down, and then they all went in together. Walt and Laurie stayed in the back of Sarah's room while Beth pulled a chair over to the side of the bed just like she had yesterday. Her face was ashen, her hands trembling. She took Sarah's small hand in hers. It felt lifeless, and when there was no response she squeezed it and broke down again.

Laurie moved behind Beth and held her, but she was crying so hard herself that she wasn't much help. Walt, too, had tears running down his face when he saw his little granddaughter lying there like that.

After a few minutes a nurse came in and Beth asked her if she could put the pajamas she had brought on Sarah and fix her hair.

"Certainly," she said. "I'll help you with the tubes."

Sarah looked so much better in her pajamas with little clowns on them and her stuffed rabbit under her arm. She looked very frail, however, and her hands were still clinched into those tiny fists almost as if she were angry. Beth brushed her hair and put some barrettes in the sides to keep it in place. The machines that were keeping Sarah alive whirred and hissed while drawing in air and forcing it into Sarah's lungs. Her tiny chest rose in response and then seemed to deflate like a limp balloon.

While Beth sat and cried at her child's bedside and Laurie sat on the other side crying almost as hard, Walt went out to the nurses at the station, identified himself as Sarah's grandfather, and asked about her condition.

"Let me have you talk with Dr. Hurst," the nurse said. "She just finished with her rounds and might be available." She dialed a phone and said something to the party on the other end. "She will be right down. Why don't you have a seat?"

Dr. Hurst looked tired. It had been a long day and she wanted to get home to her family. Walt introduced himself and they went into a small office behind the nurses' station.

"I wish I could tell you something good," Dr. Hurst said to Walt as she shut the door. "Sarah's injury was not severe enough in itself for her to be this critical, but the loss of blood was great. When she arrived at the hospital she had lost almost two thirds of her blood supply. Her brain was without oxygen for a long time."

She shifted uneasily in her chair stopping to straighten her skirt. It was almost as if she didn't want to talk anymore, but she had to. She tried to keep eye contact with Walt but it was uncomfortable because he was crying and she could see the pain. This was the part of being a doctor that she had never gotten used to.

"Right now," she continued, "Sarah's brain function is minimal. The chances of her regaining any of that are very small, and they decrease with each hour that passes. I'm glad you're here, Walt, because I just don't know how to approach Beth about this."

"Beth is a smart woman," said Walt. He stopped talking long enough to blow his nose and wipe his eyes. "I think she knows the score."

"Let's do this," said Dr. Hurst. "Let's wait until after her husband's funeral. At least a couple of days, anyway, and then I will talk with her. In the meantime, maybe you can help her understand." Dr Hurst stood up and walked over to Walt and took his hands. Hands, she noticed, that were still covered with calluses from long days of tilling the fields.

"Walt, I know this is difficult for you, and that I am asking a lot, but right now you are all she has for family, and she needs you very much. I'm sure Sarah meant a great deal to you, also."

She had referred to Sarah in the past tense and Walt had noticed it right away. His hands were shaking and his broad shoulders drooped. Slowly he nodded his head, and then standing, said to Dr. Hurst, "I just hope she can cope with all of this." He turned and walked out of the room and went across the hall to Sarah's room.

If Beth knew he had come back, or had even been gone, she never acknowledged it. At about nine p.m. she got up and told Walt and Laurie, "I want to go see Larry."

-14-

Larry was sleeping when Beth came into the room. He was still feeling the effects of the anesthesia as he had just had his second spinal surgery in two days. The doctors fused his spine to keep his back rigid, and Larry would never again feel anything below his waist.

He did retain his bowel and bladder function, and that was a good thing. At least, for his pride it was. There was a plant on the credenza from all of the people down at the police station and someone had tied a balloon to the end of his bed. The draperies were closed and it was dark in the room except for a small night light shining above the bed. Unlike Sarah, he was free of tubes and bottles.

Beth sat down beside his bed and took his hand. Larry looked like he had aged ten years in the last two days. He opened his eyes, a little startled, and looked at her. "You're back. Oh! Beth, is that you? My sister just left and I thought she had returned. Oh, God, Bethy, how is Sarah? I'm so sorry—we never should have taken her in the ca—"

Beth put her forefinger to Larry's mouth to stop him from talking." Larry, how bad are you hurt?" She took his hand and held it in hers. Her other hand brushed his hair back.

"Bethy, I'm paralyzed. They shot me in the spinal cord. I'll never walk again, but I will live, and I will live to see those bastards pay for this." Larry tried to raise himself up in the bed but quickly gave up and let himself fall back onto the pillow.

"Did you see them, Larry?"

"Yes, I saw them and I heard them yell at me. It was the Sanchez Brothers. All three of them."

"I heard on the news that they were arrested."

"That's a start, Beth. Let's hope they all rot in prison for the rest of their lives."

"I have to go for now, Larry, but I'll stop to see you tomorrow." She slowly let his hand slide through hers as she rose to leave. Kissing her fingertips she touched his lips, and whispered, "Take care, my friend." She had to leave before he asked about Sarah again.

Walt stayed outside the room with Laurie as Larry could only have one visitor at a time. When Beth came out, Walt asked her to wait a second while he popped in just to say hi. Beth sat down with Laurie in the hall in a small waiting area. Feeling faint, she laid her head on Laurie's shoulder and then everything went round and round and she passed out.

When she came around a nurse was holding a smelling salts capsule under her nose and talking to her. With Laurie on one side and the nurse on the other they walked Beth to the nurse's station. There they gave her a shot of Dramamine and some hot cider laced with sugar to drink. A few minutes later another nurse came back with a chocolate malt that he had gone down to the cafeteria to get for her. They made her stay until she had drunk the whole thing.

When they got home Laurie stayed long enough to make coffee. The three of them sat at the kitchen table for a while, with everyone at a loss for words. After a particularly long silence Beth said, "Dad you need to go to bed, and Laurie needs to go home. I need to be alone."

As soon as she was alone Beth could hold back no longer, and she went in the living room and lay on the couch. She put a pillow to her face to muffle her sobs and cried until she could cry no longer. She cried until her chest ached from heaving and her throat was sore and raw. She cried until there were no more tears, and finally sleep took over.

On Monday morning the grand jury met to consider charges against the three Sanchez brothers. The County Attorney presented Larry's eyewitness testimony identifying them as the shooters. It was all the evidence they had at the time.

The lawyer for the three brothers, Carl Huebnor, gave a long dramatic explanation of his client's innocence. He told Judge Susan Werness that the Sanchez brothers had been wrongfully accused. That the grand jury was being asked to believe that a critically wounded cop, lying in a hail of gunfire was able to identify his assailants was in his words, naïve on their part.

His clients had been home, the attorney said, all day on Friday, and they had witnesses to collaborate their story. There was no other evidence that the police could bring forth at this time to tie them to the shooting. The getaway car and the guns had not been found anywhere.

In fact, as the inquest was being held, police with a warrant were searching the Sanchez residence, much to the dismay of Momma Sanchez. They found nothing.

Susan Werness had been a judge for twelve years and had seen a lot of guilty people released from the courts because of lack of evidence. That was the way of the law of the land, and this particular case was one of those where she just knew in her gut they were guilty. She was frustrated because her hands were tied.

Finally, at twelve noon after the grand jury had refused to indict them, she recessed the court and released the three men from custody. There was nothing else she could do without more evidence.

Outside the courtroom the media circus had just begun, and reporters and photographers lined the stairs and hallways. Manny smiled and slapped the hands of a few friends who had showed up. "Let's go down to Wales," he said. "I want to buy you all a drink."

Diego was also in an upbeat mood, but he didn't talk to anyone, waving off the reporters with a smile and a "no comment." He just hailed a cab and left the scene for home with George.

Huebnor stood on the courthouse steps and gave one last performance. He accused the police of being out to get his clients every time something bad happened, and threatened a lawsuit against the city for false arrest.

Channel Three reporter Trish Lawson and her cameraman were there to catch the entire performance and had it not been a slow news day, it might have gone unreported.

As it was, today it was their lead story on the 1 p.m. news.

Beth slept until 7:30, Monday, waking in a cloud of confusion as to what she needed to do next. She wanted to be with Sarah, but the wake was tonight and she needed to get her hair fixed. Theresa, her hairdresser, didn't open until nine and she wasn't sure she could get in anyway, but she would call right at nine.

Beth laid out several outfits on the bed trying to decide what she should wear tonight. It was the first time she had been back in their bedroom for any extended period of time since the shooting. She reached over and took Mick's pillow and held it to her face. His smell was still there in the linen, and waves of grief came over her and she slid to the floor sobbing into the pillow.

She cried until she could cry no more. She had used all of her tears. Her throat was sore and dry and her whole body ached from sobbing.

The sound of Walt down in the kitchen brought her back to reality and she pulled herself to her feet and walked downstairs. She didn't know what she would wear tonight, and right now she just didn't give a damn.

Walt was at the stove when she walked in and he saw her red eyes, and tear-stained face and went to embrace her.

"Sit down, Bethy. You have to eat something." He set a cup of hot coffee in front of her. Going back to the stove, he came back with a piece of French toast and put that in front of her, also, but she pushed it aside.

"Dad, I need to go to the hair dresser this morning. Would you go with me?"

"Yes, of course," Walt said.

"Then we can go see Sarah afterwards, okay?"

"Sure, sweetheart. Now eat your French toast before it gets cold."

She nibbled on the corner of it but as soon as Walt left the room she went to the sink and shoved it down the disposal. She would vomit if she ate.

Beth showered and fixed her face and then called Theresa, who told her to come right in. Theresa didn't mention the shootings, and Beth wondered if maybe she didn't know.

When they got to the shop the door was still locked, but Theresa was waiting and turned the deadbolt to let them in, then locked the door behind them. It was then that Beth remembered that the shop was closed on Mondays.

Theresa knew. Beth could tell by the sad look on her face. She grabbed Beth and embraced her, saying over and over how sorry she was. At last she sat Beth down in the chair and draped a towel over her shoulders.

"I'm glad you called when you did," Theresa said. "I was just down here cleaning the shop and was going to be leaving soon."

"Thank you for letting me come," was all Beth could say.

It was close to eleven a.m. when Beth and Walt arrived at the hospital. It was starting to feel like Sarah had been here forever.

Beth had prayed this morning that when they got there Sarah would be sitting up in bed and smiling at her, but deep down she knew that was not going to happen. It wasn't that she believed that God couldn't make her well.... He could if he wanted to. She just believed that God's will was being done, and although she didn't know why, he was going to take her daughter from her. Sarah looked worse than she had the last time Beth had been there. She was so pale and her lips and ear lobes had taken on a grayish cast. The bag on the side of the bed that was attached to her bladder was nearly empty, and the nurses were suctioning out her throat on a regular basis now.

Beth took her tiny hands in hers. Today they felt cold, so cold. Much colder than yesterday. She worked her fingers around Sarah's wrist to try and feel her pulse but she couldn't find it anywhere.

She isn't alive. It's just that damn machine that I am sitting here talking and praying to, she thought. Beth cried again, but this time it was more controlled, quieter. Walt sat beside her, crying softly, too.

Beth had brought clean pajamas again for Sarah and she rang the bell and asked the nurse for a pan of warm water, some soap and a towel. She undressed Sarah and washed her tiny body, remembering the times when she was a baby or a toddler, and she used to take her in the tub and play with her for hours.

She dressed her in her clean pajamas, then rolled the others up and stuffed them in her bag. Walt walked over to shut off the television that had been playing since they came in the room. Just as he reached for the dial a news anchor came on with the 1 p.m. news. The war in Iraq and a fire on the near north side were the headlines, but the anchor had mentioned something about accused cop killers. Walt stood, his eyes frozen to the screen.

They broke for a commercial and then the newscaster was back.

"This story is just breaking out of the courthouse, but here is what we know right now." The anchor had led off the story and now his female counterpart took over.

"Judge Susan Werness released the three men who had been arrested in the killing of Police Officer Mick Motrin this morning. The grand Jury was unwilling to press charges at this time without more evidence. This does not mean, however, that they can't be charged later, if more evidence is forthcoming."

The camera switched to a shot of Manny Sanchez on the courthouse steps, beaming from ear to ear and flashing the V for victory sign. In the background he could be heard over the talking of the reporter inviting his friends down to Wales, which was a trendy nightclub on the north side of the Loop that catered mostly to singles. It had its share of prostitutes and drug dealers and the police department kept a close eye on the place.

Diego, smiling and looking victorious, was walking behind Manny with George, who was wearing wrap-around sunglasses. Diego made no attempt to hide his face, but George was half hiding his behind some rolled up papers.

Beth had been half-lying on the bed, holding Sarah's hand and looking straight at the television screen. She appeared unemotional about the news and sat up and told Walt, "We'd better be going. I need to see Larry, and then I have some things to do."

Larry was up and sitting in a wheel chair when Beth and Walt came into the room. Beth's appearance seemed to cheer him and he turned the chair from the window to face both of them.

"Beth, sit close so I can touch you," he said. She pulled a chair right along side of him and reached over, taking his hand in hers.

"My sister just left," he said. "She had to get back to her life, but it sure was good to see her."

"I wish I could have met her," Beth said.

"I may have talked the doctor into letting me out to attend Mick's funeral tomorrow. He said he has never had anybody heal as fast as I have. At least physically. It is going to take a long time to get used to being so handicapped and not being able—" Larry's voice trailed off. After a moment he asked, "Sarah?"

Beth shook her head slowly no. A few tears ran down her face but she quickly dabbed at them with a Kleenex.

"Larry, did you see the news?" she asked, quickly changing the subject. Not waiting for his answer, she dove right into it. "They let them go. The courts released them, saying that there was no evidence to hold them. They don't believe you."

Beth turned her chair around so she was facing Larry straight on. They were both on the verge of crying and Larry's lip was quivering. Beth gave him a moment to compose himself. She took both of his hands, holding them to her chest. Walt, who had remained standing, now sat on the edge of the bed behind Beth, looking concerned.

Their eyes met and locked, and Beth said. "Tell me that what you saw was who you said it was, Larry. Tell me there is not a doubt in your mind, I have to know."

"Bethy, it is an indelible picture that I'll never forget. Manny Sanchez's face looking out of that car window, grinning from ear to ear, with that gun still smoking in his right hand alongside of the car door. His brother Diego still was looking down the sights of the barrel on his weapon while he looked out the back window, on the same side of the car. Then Manny's sneering voice yelling, "That one's for Raul.""

"The third brother?" asked Beth.

"Beth, there was another man in the car but I can only assume it was George. I know all three brothers, but I did not see his face." As an afterthought he said, "It had to be him."

She dropped Larry's hands in his lap and taking his head with one hand on each side of his face, she bent forward and kissed him on the forehead.

"Thank you," she said. "Please sit with me at the funeral."

Walt reached over and squeezed Larry's shoulder. "See you tomorrow," he said, as he and Beth walked out of the room.

Something had changed for Beth with this visit. She had more of a defiant look on her face and she seemed to walk a little taller. For the better part of three days she had been beaten down, but right now some inner strength from somewhere had taken over. At least for the time being, it had.

-15-

At the last minute Beth decided to go with a dark blue pants suit with a light blue turtle neck sweater, and a simple gold chain with a cross and small gold earrings for the wake. Mick had given her the set for their anniversary a year ago. She wanted to cry when she put them on, but that mysterious inner strength kicked in again and she knew there would be time enough for crying later on.

When Beth went back into her bedroom after coming home from the hospital she noticed the room had been straightened and the bed made up with fresh sheets. A basket of tulips was on the nightstand. Laurie must have been here she thought. Walt had been with her and there was nobody else.

Beth had talked with Laurie before she went to the hairdresser's. Muriel had called from the funeral home and left a message on the recorder. They needed pictures of Mick for a collage they wanted to set up for the wake. She just wasn't up to looking at pictures right now, so she asked Laurie if she would do it for her. All of their pictures were in albums in the bedroom closet, and she told Laurie where to find them.

Brandy followed her around the house looking for attention from the moment they had come home. Beth stopped and sat down on the upstairs steps and held the pup. *What a carefree world you live in,* she thought. She set Brandy down before she licked off all of her make up and got dog hair all over her clothes.

Walt had left again, going down to the shopping center to get a haircut. It was about three p.m. right now, and they would have to leave for the funeral home in a half hour. Hesitating for a second on the steps, Beth went back up and opened Sarah's bedroom door.

Walt's suitcase was on the end of the bed, but otherwise the room was just as Sarah had left it. She walked slowly around, touching each furry little animal and looking at the pictures Sarah had drawn in school and stuck on the walls.

She had a little corkboard that Mick had made for her and installed over her desk in the corner. Right in the middle of it was a picture Beth had taken of Sarah and her dad, sitting on the front steps holding Brandy, the day Mick brought her home.

Beth sat down on the edge of the bed, and like this morning in her bedroom, smelled Sarah's pillow, but her scent wasn't there. Laurie had changed the bedding here, also, and all she could smell was freshness and soap. Her fingers traced the edges of the lampshade on the nightstand, a Mickey Mouse lamp that they had bought for her at Disney World.

Stopping at the window, she pulled the frilly white curtains back and looked out into the back yard at the swing set Mick had put up for her so many years ago. One chain was unhooked and the swing seat lay on the ground. It looked broken, empty and lonely, just like her heart, she thought. Sarah's bicycle was parked leaning against the apple tree where she had stood on a lawn chair to smell the blossoms that now lay on the ground wilting.

In the corner of the yard, a sand box that Sarah had played in for hours when she was smaller was now over-grown with weeds, and there was hole a in the middle of it where Brandy had been digging.

A car door slammed. *It must be Dad back from his haircut,* Beth thought. Quickly she got up and walked out and down the stairs to the kitchen.

There were only a few cars in the funeral home parking lot when Beth and Walt arrived. From four until five p.m. was set-aside for the immediate family, and then there would be a reception for all the others until eight p.m.

It had rained last night and the lawns had taken on new look with a dark shade of green that comes only in spring. Small beds of flowers filled with daffodils, tulips and crocuses were scattered along the walk going into the funeral home. In the distance the sound of thunder gave an ominous warning of another watering that was on its way.

Lester Strom was waiting for them and looked regal in his black suit and scarlet tie. His gray hair glistened like freshly cleaned silver, and the look on his face was one of sincere compassion.

"Beth, I hope everything is as you would like it in this difficult time. I want to let you know that I am here tonight until closing, and if there is anything I can change or do for you, please let me know."

"Thank you," said Beth.

She glanced around the spacious lobby at the displays of pictures that had been set up. She would take a better look at them later. Right now she needed to be with Mick.

The double doors into the chapel where Mick was laid out were open, and from the doorway where she was now standing, trying to catch her breath and work up the courage to proceed, Beth could see some of his hair and his forehead above the edge of the casket.

The room was empty except for flowers everywhere and soft music seemed to come from no particular place, just flowing from everywhere. The lights were bright but still soft and the dark red carpet felt as if she were walking on a cushion.

Beth turned to Walt who was standing beside her and holding her hand. "Dad, I need to be alone for a few minutes. You understand, don't you? Please close the doors for a few minutes."

She walked slowly down the aisle, her hand touching the back of each chair she passed as she approached the casket cautiously. Each footstep brought more and more of Mick's body into view. At last Beth stood looking down at the man who was her whole life, her lover, her friend, her very soul-mate and the father of their child who would soon join him, she was sure.

. Her eyes glistened with tears, but they had not spilled over and she was remarkably composed for the time being. They say a person goes from grief to anger to acceptance. This thought ran through her head, but she was not sure where she was in that process, and right now it was not important.

Mick was dressed in his police dress uniform with his hat with the gold band tucked under his arm. The light above him glistened off the gold badge and buttons on his chest. His skin was too heavy with make up and his hair was not right. Beth took her hand and fixed it. Gone also was that impish grin that was just a part of Mick. No one could ever bring that back. Slowly she settled onto her knees on the kneeler. Beth reached into the casket and laid her hand on his.

"Mick, I want you to know, where ever you are right now, darling, that I loved you as no woman has ever loved a man. We were so perfect, Mick, and so good for each other. We were as happy together as a family can possibly be. We had the perfect child, Mick, and she too, is being taken from me. I can only hope she finds you again and you can go on being the great father you were and keep on watching over her.

I don't know how to continue without you. The easiest thing would be for me to join you and Sarah, and then we could all be together once more. Maybe that will happen, darling. I don't know. I am so confused right now. I need to finish some things I have to do. Then I will deal with that."

Beth stood and composed herself. She wiped her eyes, blew her nose and simply willed her chin to stop trembling. She walked from plant to plant looking at the cards and notes, stopping to cry at some and smile at others. There were flowers from neighbors, family, friends, and co-workers, and even people she had not thought about for a long time. A flood of memories came back, and for a brief moment when she looked at Laurie's card and flowers she lost control, sobbing, but once again she bounced back.

At last she walked to the back of the room and opened the doors. She took her dad's hand and they both walked back to the casket, followed by family members she had not seen for a long time.

Throughout the night Beth accepted people's sympathy and best wishes. Laurie came and was her constant companion for the evening. There were so many members of the emergency services in attendance … highway patrolmen, sheriff's deputies, fire fighters and EMS people, and Mick's fellow officers, so many she lost count. At five p.m. two police officers in full dress uniform came and flanked the casket, standing at attention for the duration of the evening.

Almost all of the teachers from Beth's school were there, along with Mr. Cameron, the principal, who apologized again for his phone call. There were a lot of their neighbors there, too, including Mrs. Crowley, who cried so hard that it was Beth who ended up comforting her.

At seven p.m., Father Quinn came from St. Ann's and held a short prayer service. Then, just before leaving, he blessed Mick's body and gave a special blessing to Beth. His words were comforting and Beth would have felt better after he left; except for his last sentence … "I'll see you in the morning."

Captain Wicks was there for most of the night. Shortly after arriving, he took Walt aside and talked with him for a few minutes and then spent a lot of time talking with police officers. Beth noticed this, but thought little of it at the time. He did spend a few minutes with Beth, but seemed very uncomfortable, and did not mention the investigation into Mick's killers.

At last the evening came to a close and the last guest had left. Beth, Laurie and Walt sat in the lobby, all talked out. It had not been that long since Beth's mother had died, and it brought back some sad memories for Walt. He and Beth said goodbye to Laurie and walked slowly to the car.

"A few minutes at the hospital, Dad, and then we can go home," Beth said, and switched the radio in the car from a news report to something lighter as Walt drove. Though her mind was tired and foggy, she suddenly realized that Laura

Branigan was singing, *"How am I supposed to live without you? How am I supposed to carry on? All that I am living for is gone."* She and Mick had listened to that song together so many times, but it never had the meaning then that it did now. Beth reached over and shut it off.

As they pulled into the hospital parking lot, Beth turned to Walt and said, "Why don't you wait in the car, Dad? This will only take a few minutes. I won't stay long."

It was then she saw the cardboard box in the back seat and said, "Where did that come from?"

"Oh, that," said Walt. "That's from Captain Wicks. Some of Mick's things."

Beth did not wait for the elevator but took the stairs up to Sarah's floor. She didn't want to meet other people right now. She walked quickly with her head down until she got to the doors that took her into I.C.U. "Mrs. Motrin, can I help you?" the nurse behind the desk asked.

"I want to leave a message for Dr. Hurst," said Beth. "I need to meet with her sometime and I wonder if she could call me tomorrow after 3 p.m."

"I'm sure she can," said the nurse. "I know she wants to see you, also." Beth turned and walked across the hall to Sarah's room after a short "thanks" to the nurse.

There was a new machine hooked up to Sarah now, but it mattered little to Beth. She knew and believed that what was lying in that bed was only Sarah's body. Sarah had gone to a better place.

Beth bent over and kissed her, but her skin was cold and dry. She didn't even smell like Sarah any more. Beth took her hand and said, "One more day, sweetheart. One more day and mommy will come and end your suffering."

She found herself praying, *"Dear God, please take my little girl into your heaven and care for her there. Please let me live a good enough life that I can be with her again in your heavenly home. Amen"*

The nurse sitting right across the hall never saw her leave. She was there one minute and gone the next. Her stay had been so brief it puzzled her. She walked into the room, adjusted a few things and dimmed the lights for the night.

Walt went straight to bed when they got home. It had been a long day for an old man. Beth sat at the kitchen table with a glass of wine. She was more relaxed now than she had been since all of this started, but was still deeply troubled about what was ahead for her. She wanted tomorrow to be over with and she did not want one more person to tell her how sorry they were, or how much Mick was going to be missed. No one knew that better than her.

The day of the funeral dawned cold and windy. Beth wore a black suit with a dark green blouse and the same necklace and earrings as yesterday. Black hose and flats completed her outfit.

She had experienced a crying session again shortly after she had gone to bed last night that lasted into the small hours of the morning. Beth spent most of the night in her white bathrobe sitting in a chair by the window holding Brandy. It left her exhausted and not thinking straight. She wore very little makeup today; she didn't have the strength to make herself look her best.

Laurie was over early and helped her get organized. What a wonderful friend she had been over the last few days. How could Beth ever repay her? Laurie had made all of the arrangements at the church that the mortician couldn't, even going so far as to arrange a good part of the service, as Beth knew she was in no position to do it.

The funeral was at eleven a.m., but they were to be there around ten thirty to greet guests and say goodbye to Mick with the closing of the casket.

The church was filled with flowers and a small display from last night had been set up in the entryway. Mick lay just inside the doors where people could pass by him on their way in. A rack of candles behind him flickered in the breeze coming through the doors. A flag was laid across the casket and a bouquet of red roses with a ribbon that said 'Father and Husband' was on the closed end of the casket.

Beth and Walt had parked behind the church and come in the back way, walking through the church. Beth stepped through the front doors to the outside and looked down the street at what looked like a never-ending parade of emergency vehicles that had formed behind the hearse and the limousine behind it. Men and women in uniform were everywhere, looking somber and talking quietly among themselves. She walked back into the church and took her place on a chair next to the casket, and Walt stood behind her, being as supportive as he could under the circumstances.

The line of people coming in became a blur for Beth. Some she recognized, but the majority of them were strangers who filed by awkwardly, not knowing how to show their respects. Some of the officers, those close to Mick, cried openly. She had never seen that side of them before; they had always seemed so strong. *But everybody has a breaking point,* she thought.

Father Quinn came down the center aisle of the church with two altar boys who were carrying candles and a crucifix. He welcomed Beth and asked her to stand with him at the casket as he blessed Mick's body with holy water and prayers. Then Beth stepped forward to kiss him for the last time. The lid was closed and the casket was wheeled out into the center aisle with Beth, Father Quinn, Laurie and Walt behind it.

Beth heard a murmur behind her and, turning, saw Larry being wheeled into the church in a wheelchair. A wide strap held him against the back of the chair and a young male nurse was pushing him. She left the small group and went to him and couldn't hold the tears back any longer as she held his head in her hands and kissed him.

"Please bring him up here," she said to the nurse and pointed right behind the casket. With a signal from Father Quinn to the organist, the music began and the overflow crowd stood in silent respect as the procession made its way to the front of the church. Beth walked slowly behind the casket, one hand being held by her dad and the other holding the back of Larry's wheelchair. His nurse, feeling out of place, walked with his head bowed as he pushed him. The organ music stopped and somewhere in the back of the church the bag pipers began playing "Amazing Grace." The church was a sea of blue and black uniforms all standing in rigid respect. Some even saluted the casket as it passed. Father Quinn waited patiently at the steps to the altar, his hands crossed over his texts.

Beth sat unemotionally through the Mass part of the service with her head on her dad's shoulder and holding a rose in her hands. Her handkerchief was inter-twined around her fingers. She wept quietly from time to time, but for the most part was composed, listening to Father Quinn's eulogy. She had taken a sedative this morning and it made it hard for her to concentrate. Most of the time she had a far-away look that suggested she had other things on her mind.

At last Father Quinn closed his notes and walked down the aisle and handed the microphone to Larry who was sitting in the aisle next to Beth. His chair was turned around so that he faced the crowd and Father Quinn retreated back to the altar area where he sat down on the steps to listen.

Larry seemed to take a moment to collect his thoughts but then raised the microphone to his mouth and began to speak softly. The large crowd hushed and those in the back were carefully stretching their necks to see who was talking.

"For those of you who don't know me, my name is Detective Larry Sorenson. Mick Motrin was my partner, my dearest friend and my mentor. He was the brother I never had, and no one has ever impacted my life more than he did. Beth, Mick and Sarah were my extended family. We did so much together because we truly loved each other.

"I come here today a shattered man both in body and spirit. I come to say goodbye to Mick and to tell Beth how terribly sorry I am."

For a brief moment Larry dropped the microphone to his lap and wiped his face with his sleeve. There was a look of anguish on his face and his hands were shaking slightly. Beth reached out from where she was sitting next to him and squeezed his arm, smiling softly through her tears.

"There were always times in the past when I wondered where life would take Mick and me," Larry went on. "This is a dangerous business, but never in my wildest dreams could I have thought that things would end like this. So often in a eulogy you try to tell those who are here what this person was really like. For me to do that would take much more time than we have. So I will be brief. Mick Motrin was a cop's, cop. He was the poster child for all policemen. He could be as compassionate as the priest sitting behind me, or he could be the voice of authority when he had to be. I never felt safer than when I was under his command."

For a brief moment Larry looked right at Captain Wicks who was seated just a few pews back on the end. Wicks shifted nervously in his seat and looked down at the floor, averting his gaze.

"Mick loved his family with all his heart and spent hours talking about them. They had just returned from a long overdue vacation to Florida, and he was already planning the next one. He talked about the opening of fishing and building a new deck on his house next week. He talked about how lucky he was to have Beth, and Sarah, his beautiful daughter. Mick was optimistic about what the future held for all of them. Yes, he was very happy with his life. The world will be a better place to live in because of Mick Motrin, and I am a better man for having known him. If he were here today, he would be the first one to put a positive spin on all of this, if there is such a thing. We all need to take his example."

"For those of you who didn't know it, Mick and Beth's daughter, Sarah was critically wounded in this cowardly shooting, also. I ask all of you to pray for her recovery. I also ask you to pray for Beth, Mick's wife, for the strength to carry on, and I ask you to pray for justice."

Larry hesitated as if he had more to say, but then handed the microphone to the nurse, who shut it off and gave it to the priest who had come down for it.

At the conclusion of the service, six police officers clad in dress uniforms with their badges covered with black transparent cloth came forward to escort the casket to the hearse. All the other officers in the crowd gave a hand salute as the procession passed by them down the center aisle. Beth and Larry, side by side, came next, with Walt and Laurie behind them.

The procession, which seemed to stretch forever, followed the hearse and limousine through the city streets. At every intersection squad cars blocked the traffic, and the officers assigned to them stood beside their cars at attention. At last they were on the outskirts of town and slowly winding through the large stone arch that marked the cemetery gates. They passed hundreds of monuments and grave markers until they stopped high on a hill that overlooked the entire cemetery.

Squad cars, too numerous to count with their emergency light's flashing, slowly came to a halt. The same six officers who had carried Mick's body from the church came forward again, and as bag pipes played, carried him up a slight rise to his final resting place.

Father Quinn gave his final blessings and prayers. Beth stepped forward and placed a single white rose on Mick's casket. Then she watched as it was slowly lowered into the ground. They were not just burying Mick Motrin, she thought. They were burying all of her dreams and aspirations along with him. "We will be together soon, sweetheart," she said softly to herself, as somewhere behind the hill and out of sight, a bugler played taps slowly and mournfully.

Then it was back to the church for a reception and lunch for the family. Mick's parents, who were old and frail and who lived far away, had not been able to come, but it was good to see some of the aunts and uncles and so many old friends. By two-thirty it was all over and Larry, who had not been allowed to go to the cemetery and had waited at the church, had been taken back to the hospital.

Beth knew that somehow she had to gather the strength to finish what had to be done. She would meet with Dr. Hurst tonight about Sarah. A message was waiting for her on the machine when she got home saying that the meeting was set for 5 p.m.

-16-

Beth went to the hospital by herself. She told her dad she had something to do, and that it was going to be a very private moment. As much as she loved Sarah's grandfather, she needed to do this alone.

She changed Sarah once more into a pair of white cotton pajamas with little blue angels on them and brushed out the little girl's hair as best she could. Her naturally curly hair seemed limp and lifeless, and there was liitle she could do with it. Sarah's complexion was almost as white as the pajamas that she put on her. Her lips and ears were turning bluish-gray and there was a blue-grayish tint to other parts of her body too, especially her stomach and back.

Not long after she finished, Dr. Hurst came in, and the two women sat side by side next to the bed. They didn't need to talk, they both knew what they had to do. They sat silent for a few minutes looking at Sarah. Dr. Hurst had some papers and charts but she made no attempt to share them. The door was closed and the draperies that went around the bed were closed.

Dr. Hurst spoke so softly that Beth could hardly hear her over the noise of the respirator. "Beth, Sarah hasn't actually been with us since the moment she was brought here to the hospital. Sometimes we do things to give us time to explore all of our options. Maybe we hope against hope. Pray for the impossible. I wish there had been more we could have done for her, she is such a beautiful little girl. I don't think that I'm telling you anything you don't already know," she went on. "Maybe you are just making my job easier by reacting the way you are. I don't know. I have two daughters myself, and I don't know what I would do if I were in your place." Beth reached over and took Dr. Hurst's hands in hers. Both women were crying softly.

"Let's not talk anymore," Beth said. "I want to hold her while you shut the machine off."

Dr. Hurst stood and removed all of the tubes from Sarah's body except the respirator tube that was in her mouth. Beth sat on the edge of the bed holding Sarah in her arms. She stroked her hair and kissed her one last time. She was sobbing quietly, her tears falling on Sarah's face. She looked at Dr. Hurst and nodded.

Dr. Hurst reached up and shut off the machine, and for a moment it was very quiet. Beth watched Sarah's chest for the miracle that did not come. Dr. Hurst went over and looked out the window at the traffic going by on the street below. Two young girls about Sarah's age were walking along the top of a retaining wall, their arms held out to maintain their balance. They were laughing and giggling, so full of life, not a care in the world. No one had ever prepared her for times like this. It was the part of being a doctor that she would never get used to. When she turned to look back at the bed, she saw that Beth had laid Sarah back on the pillows and was lying beside her. She had removed the tube from her mouth. Beth's eyes were closed but her lips were moving in silent prayer. Dr. Hurst left and told the nurses at the station across the hall that Sarah had died, but that her mother was still with her. They would know what to do. She told them to note the time.

Beth stayed for about half an hour, then she got up and gathered all of Sarah's clothes and the stuffed animals she had brought, and put them in her bag. In the bathroom, Beth wiped her face and blew her nose. She came back out and gazed at the still form of her child once more, then slowly turned and left the room. She walked slowly down the hall and through the swinging doors for the last time, then went down the elevator and out to the car.

It was dusk, and the last threads of daylight were disappearing over the rooftops as she drove into the fading sunset toward home. As sad as she was, and although she felt empty, frightened and alone, she also felt some sense of relief that it was over.

On Thursday morning, Sarah was laid to rest next to Mick in a very private ceremony. Father Quinn presided and only Beth, Walt, Laurie and a few relatives were there. Larry was brought from the hospital once more. He was sad and withdrawn, and didn't talk to anyone but Beth.

Sarah's small white casket was covered with a spray of spring flowers and an array of stuffed animals. There were no pallbearers; the casket was in place when they arrived, and the hearse was parked down the road. A small altar had been set up and Father Quinn had the funeral service beside the grave. He had been reluctant to do the funeral this way, but Beth begged him, saying she couldn't take another church funeral. In the end, out of pity, he gave in.

The noise of heavy equipment from a nearby construction sight made it hard to hear him but he spoke louder when he had to. About thirty steel folding chairs had been set up next to the grave site and they had sunk into the soft ground so that they sat leaning every which way.

Beth tried hard to keep her mind on what Father Quinn was saying, but she was so distraught that it was hard to concentrate. The fresh soil on top of Mick's grave was a stark reminder that he was there with them. She could only hope and pray that father and daughter were together again.

The ceremony did not take long. As much as Sarah deserved more of a funeral, Beth knew that she couldn't go through that again. There was a reception at the church put on by some of the teachers from the school, but it was small and lasted only about an hour. Pictures that Sarah's classmates had made were taped up on the walls along with messages to Sarah and Beth. She walked from picture to picture, and at one point was so overcome by emotion she had to sit down for a while, her head buried in her lap sobbing uncontrollably. "Why, God? Why her?" she said out loud. It was so unfair. Mick was a cop and he accepted the risks that went with the job. But Sarah? What possible reason could there have been to kill her?

The box that Captain Wicks had put in the back seat of her car was still there when they got home that day, and Beth took it upstairs and set it on a chair in the bedroom. She wasn't in any mood to go through it right now.

Walt had taken quite a shine to Brandy, and he had taken her for a walk, while Beth sat down at the kitchen table to write a letter to Principal Cameron, asking for a leave of absence for the rest of the school year. So much had happened in such a short time that the enormity of all of it still hadn't sunk in. Her grief was still immeasurable and she had put so much on hold. Now it was a time to tend to business. She had slept fitfully and eaten little since last Friday when the whole thing started. Laurie and Walt had helped so much, and she owed them both such a debt of gratitude. As for herself, it was going to be one day at a time for a while. Maybe even one minute at a time.

Having lost her train of thought for a while, Beth now shook her head to clear it and started writing again:

Dear Principal Cameron,

This is a formal request for a personal leave of absence for the rest of the school year. I am sure with the recent events that have happened in my life I would not be an effective teacher if I were to try and continue. Please let me know as soon as possible if this is acceptable. Since I will not be home for a few days, please contact me on my cell phone at the number you have on my record card.

Sincerely, Beth Motrin

Beth stuffed the note in an envelope and addressed it. She would mail it in the morning on their way out of town. She was going to her dad's place to try and work things out, thinking a new environment might help. She had seriously considered taking her own life several times in the last few days. Only the responsibility of Mick and Sarah's funerals had kept her mind off it, and now that was taken care of. What did she have to live for now? So she could walk around each day, reminded at every turn, of what she no longer had? They had lived as a family, and maybe that's the way it should end. It was futile to think that she could ever get over this.

Brandy ran into the kitchen and put her front feet up on Beth's lap and started licking her face. Walt stood in the doorway smiling.

"Wow, that was quite a work out," he said rubbing the backs of his legs.

"What time do you want to get going in the morning, Dad?"

"No hurry, Beth," he said.

"I need to stop and see Larry and Laurie before we go. I only have myself to pack for and it won't take me long, so we can leave early." As she said this, she broke down and started crying.

Walt came over and hugged her. "We'll get through it, baby. We'll get through it together."

The box that Captain Wicks had left in the back seat of the car at the wake was still upstairs on the chair where she had put it. She had seen it several times but didn't want to bother with it then. *Now*, she thought, *I better deal with it now, before I go to Dad's.*

It seemed to be too heavy for just the pictures and papers that she could see on the top. Beth picked it up off the chair and set it on the end of the bed. She sat down beside it and started to take things out one item at a time.

A framed picture of herself, Mick, and Sarah, taken on the front steps was right on top. She had seen it on Mick's desk many times. Sarah was squinting with the sun in her eyes and Beth was trying to keep from laughing because Mick had his hand on her butt behind their backs. Even now it made her smile through her tears.

Trying hard to not cry, she set it aside and went through the rest of the pictures and papers until she came to something heavy wrapped in a towel at the very bottom of the box. It was Mick's service revolver from work. A 9 mm Smith and Wesson automatic. Beside it lay a full clip of shells.

The gun was heavy and cold. This was the gun that had shot Raul Sanchez. The gun Mick depended on to protect him. The gun that had never made it out of his holster the day he was shot.

She had shot this gun at the farm once and it had scared her so much that she had dropped it when it went off. Mick had laughed and teased her all the way home. Beth picked up the clip and put it in the handle. It snapped into place almost as if the gun had sucked it in. She knew she only had to pull the slide back, release the safety and it would be ready to fire.

This gun represented all that was evil in this world to her right now. A police officer would see it as his friend. 'His comforter' he had called it. In Beth's mind it was the reason she was now a widow, and a childless widow, at that.

Beth put the gun back in the cloth and wrapped it back in the towel. She would put it on the top shelf in the closet with Mick's other pistol until she decided what she was going to do with it.

Getting the bedroom chair and putting it in front of the closet, Beth climbed up and felt around under the blanket where Mick had put his other gun up high so Sarah couldn't get at it. It was in a holster and in a metal box. She had seen it many times. It was a .357 caliber Colt Python with ivory grips.... Mick's first gun when he joined the force. She could feel the box, but it was pushed too far back on the shelf to get a grip on it.

Beth got down, and moving the chair closer, took the box off the shelf and went over to the bed with it. There was a latch on the front but it wasn't locked. The pistol was wrapped in an oily rag inside the box and she could smell the gun solvent that had been used to clean it. It had a four-inch barrel and the cylinder held six bullets. Beth could see five of them looking at it from the barrel end.

The police department had made all of their officers carry automatics and Mick had been forced to shelve it, although he said he would never get rid of it. Beth liked this gun. It had never hurt anyone, and it was pretty with its white handles.

It would be so easy to just pick this up and put it to her chest and pull the trigger. Then she wouldn't have to deal with this pain and suffering any longer. For a moment she wished Walt wasn't here right now. He was the only reason she couldn't go through with it. But things could change. There would be a time and a place.

Beth put the .9mm automatic in the box in the Python's place and put it back up on the shelf. She was going to keep the revolver with her for a while.

Putting a large suitcase on the end of the bed she started to pack things to take to her dad's. The revolver went into a zippered pocket on the side.

Beth called Laurie and asked her if she would keep an eye on the house for a few days. "I really don't know how I will ever thank you, Laurie, for all you've done for me. I'm not coming back to school anymore this year. I just need to go somewhere and let it all sink in."

Laurie was in agreement with her. "Heck, there is only a month left in the year, Beth. "Don't worry about the place. Don't worry about anything. Just get healed up and know that there are a lot of people here that love you and need you in their lives."

"I love you so much," Beth said, and hung up the phone.

She had wanted to go see Larry, but time had just gotten away from her so she called him and told him her plans.

"I'm being moved out of here the day after tomorrow," Beth, he said. "They're taking me to a rehabilitation center to learn how to live without the use of the lower half of my body. You need to take time to sort out your life. I hope when you're finished there will be room for Larry in there someplace."

"Until I die, Larry," she said. "Until I die."

Captain Wicks was furious about the lack of progress in the case. Every lead that seemed like it might go somewhere turned out to be a dead end. Snitches that the department had relied on for years for information suddenly knew nothing.

There had been a security camera outside of the drug store, but it gave them only a grainy photo of the lower half of the sedan. It gave them a good photo of the police car, however…. what had gone on inside of it and the hail of lead they had been subjected to.

The only eyewitness that had come forward was an old lady who was coming out of the flower shop next door to the drug store. She had seen the older blue car which she said had three men inside, or was it four? She wasn't sure. The shooting had scared her so much that she turned and ran back into the flower shop and hid behind a counter. By the time she looked out again the car was speeding away down the street.

The whole thing had happened fast and without warning. On the security camera film, Mick's head had been jerked violently to the side from the impact of the bullet that hit him. Blood and gore splattered the window opposite him. His whole body slumped forward against the dash just a few frames after the impact of the slug hitting him. There was no picture of Sarah, as she was shielded from the camera by Mick's body until he fell forward, and she was down, out of sight after that. Larry lay back in the seat writhing in pain. The parking lot had been littered with spent shell casings, but without the guns to match them against they were useless.

The search of the Sanchez residence had turned up nothing of importance. There were a few hunting guns and knives that could be found in almost any house in town, but there were no pistols or AK 47's, and nothing that could be called evidence. The break in the case would have to come from someone who knew or had seen something. Without that they were dead in the water.

George Sanchez sat with his mother on the patio outside of their home nursing a beer and watching the cars go by on the street out front. They had been talking for some time, as George had told her he was leaving. His mother was lecturing George on loyalty and how he owed it to her and the family.

"Your father worked very hard to make this business what it is, and he expected you to take care of it, not turn tail and run when the going got tough. Your brother Raul is looking down on you right now, and he is pissed at your selfish attitude. I, for one, will not let you leave, George. If you leave this business, you leave this family. You leave me, and you leave your brothers also. You have no right to do that."

George was tired of arguing with his mother. He was tired of drugs and crime and killings. He wanted to be a good father and husband. He wanted to come home to his wife and daughter each night proud of what he had accomplished that day, not sneaking around, afraid of what was waiting for him around the next corner.

"Momma, I've made up my mind. I am taking my family and we are moving to Chicago," he said wearily. "I have a job waiting for me with a friend, and I'm going to make an honest living for a change. What's done is done and I'll never speak of it again. But I'll never do it again, either."

Momma Sanchez walked over to George and glared at him. Her hands were shaking in anger. Suddenly she cleared her throat and spit in his face. "Go, you bastard, and never darken my doorstep again." She went back into the house, slamming the door so hard that the glass shattered.

-17-

The trip back out to the home place seemed to be over before it started. Walt drove and Beth sat in the passenger seat with her faced pressed to the side window. She was quiet, and her dad could tell that she wanted to be alone with her thoughts, so he said very little. Beth was not feeling good this morning and had thrown up when she got up. No sleep, severely depressed, and nothing but junk food for six days had taken its toll on her.

It was hard to think about anything for any length of time. Her attention span was measured in seconds not minutes. She was wallowing in self-pity and had never felt this low in her whole life, or had even thought someone could reach this level of hopelessness. On her lap was a shoebox full of cards and letters that she hadn't opened yet. "Maybe I can go through these on the way out to the farm," Beth said to Walt before they left, but when they arrived she hadn't even taken the cover off the box.

Walt stopped at the mailbox to pick up his week's worth of mail. The drive up to the house was almost half a mile long. The little house Walt had made for his daughters to wait for the school bus in on those cold mornings still sat on the corner of the driveway. The paint was gone and a windstorm had removed most of the shingles. Beth remembered the cold winter mornings when her and her sister would huddle in there and giggle after Dad had given them a ride down there in a warm car. Life was so carefree back then. Dad was always so protective of his girls, and that included Mom.

About half way up the driveway was Mom's vegetable garden. Beds of perennial flowers surrounded it, and right now tulips, irises, and peonies were trying hard to peek above the weeds that had over taken the gardens. The vegetable gar-den was in the middle, and Beth could still picture her mom down on her knees with her big straw hat on, pulling weeds. It had surrendered to those weeds now and they choked out everything else after two years of being idle. Just like the cancer had taken over her body and choked out her life.

Beth had been so close to her mom. They had been more like two sisters than mother and daughter. Those long walks they would take came to mind and how Mom would tell her how proud she was of her.

She remembered when she was twelve years old and had fallen out of a tree she had been climbing. She had fallen right on her butt, and when she got up there was blood in her underpants and she had run all the away home crying, afraid that she was going to die from internal injuries.

She called them 'eternal injuries' and Mom laughed and then sat her down and talked to her about what was happening to her body. She took her little girl into the bathroom and showed her a sanitary napkin and how to wear it when those times came each month. Then, her eyes filling with tears, she had said, "My little girl is growing up."

Brandy was so happy to get out of the carrier and run, she was like a calf out of the barn in the springtime. Beth thought she would ask Dad to keep the pup here on the farm where she could run and explore. The pup had been Sarah's, and she didn't need the memories. Rascal, Walt's old black Lab, was still over at the neighbors. They had watched him while Walt was gone. He couldn't wait to introduce him to Brandy.

The house smelled stale after being closed up for the week, and Walt opened a few windows while Beth started a pot of coffee and some hot dogs for lunch. After lunch she would get started on the cards.

That evening Beth and her dad walked down the lane and they talked about what lay ahead for both of them. He told Beth she was welcome to stay as long as it took for things to get better, but Beth knew that that was never going to hap-pen. Not the way she felt now.

It was nearly dark when they got back from their walk. "Want to play some rummy," Walt asked?

"I think I'll just go to bed, Dad, but thanks anyway." Beth could see by the look on his face that he didn't really want to play. He was doing all he could to keep her busy.

There were two bedrooms upstairs in the old farmhouse, one on each end with the staircase and a small landing in the middle. When Beth was little, her older sister Nancy and she had shared one bedroom while the other room was a guest room. As they got older sibling rivalry took over, and Mom had separated them, giving them each their own room.

Nancy was 5 years older than Beth, so they never were really close. When Nancy graduated from high school she told her folks she would never live in the country again and was moving to the city to seek her fame and fortune. She came home for her mother's funeral, but Beth hadn't seen or heard from her since. Walt never talked about her, and Beth suddenly realized that she hadn't made any attempt to tell her about Sarah and Mick. *Maybe it was best*, she thought. *She never wanted to share my good times, why bother her with my grief.*

Her bedroom was just the way she had left it 15 years ago. Her high school yearbook was still on the bureau top and the dresser drawers still held a lot of the clothes she had worn back then. There was a single bed, and the last time she had slept in it was the night before her and Mick's wedding.

She sat on the edge of the bed and looked out the window, remembering the nights she laid there propped up on her pillow, watching the tractor lights go back and forth in the fields as Dad cultivated corn into the wee hours of the morning. She opened the window a crack to chase away the mustiness, and just like way back then, she could hear the frogs and crickets giving their evening concert. Somewhere out of sight a crow gave a solitary 'caw, caw,' and somewhere farther away a volley of 'caws' came back.

Lying down on the bed, Beth pulled the comforter at the end over her. She was too old to start over. "W*hy, God, when things were so perfect did this have to happen to me? Why did you give Mick and Sarah to me in the fist place if you just wanted them back?"* She pulled the pillow over her face to muffle her sobs.

There are several stages of grief that people go through. Beth was somewhere between the first and second stages … somewhere between profound grief and severe depression. Anger and acceptance were yet to come someday, God willing.

She cried herself into a fitful sleep, tossing and turning most of the night. When she awoke because she had to go to the bathroom, it was three-thirty in the morning. She had to go downstairs to use the bathroom, and on the way back up she brought her suitcase, which had been left at the foot of the stairs. She set it on a chair in the corner.

The only light in the room came from the full moon that was shining through the window. It had become chilly outside, and Beth went over and closed the window.

Sitting down on the end of the bed she began going through her suitcase, looking for her toiletries. In there someplace were some throat lozenges, and her throat was raw from crying. Her crying was now tearless. Like someone who vomits until there is nothing left to vomit, she had cried until her tear ducts had simply run dry.

Her knee pushed against the bulge in the zippered side pocket of the suitcase and then she remembered the gun. Slowly unzipping the pocket, Beth reached in and took out the shiny steel revolver. For a moment she sat with it in her lap, her fingertips tracing the outline of the pistol almost as if she was blind and was trying to make out what she had lying there in her lap.

Finally she picked the weapon up in her right hand and lay down on the bed. Her pillow was wet and it made her uncomfortable. She angrily flipped it over, impatient with these interruptions to her train of thought.

Beth was lying on her back, the cold steel gun in her right hand resting on her chest. The barrel pointed toward her feet. Looking out of the lower half of her eyes she stared at the weapon. It would be so easy to just turn it around and point it at her chin. One squeeze of the trigger and she would either be with Mick and Sarah or she would just be dead. Either way, the hurt would be gone.

She remembered that when she was a young girl the priest had told them in religion classes that it was a mortal sin to kill yourself. That it was killing just as much as if you killed anyone else. That God could not allow you into heaven if you died that way. But things had changed, and those rules must have changed, also. What the hell … it used to be a sin to eat meat on Friday and use birth control, but they didn't say much about that anymore. God was a compassionate God, was he not, and he would understand that she had been driven to doing this. A week ago it was the farthest thing from her mind, but now she thought it was fast becoming her only out.

A toilet flushed downstairs. Dad must be up. Poor Dad … he had been through so much, too. He tried to be a pillar of strength for her, but he had faltered several times. He had loved Mick and Sarah, too, and he loved Beth, and what was blowing her brains all over her bedroom going to do to him?

Right now Dad was the only thing between her and eternal relief and it pissed her off that she had to live to make him happy. *What a selfish person I am*, thought Beth. But then, maybe I'm not the person who should die. Maybe the bastards who did this to me are the persons that need to die.

Beth pushed the gun off her chest and it slid down beside her. Maybe it would go off accidentally and that would be all right. Accidents couldn't be held against her, *right God?* Rolling onto her side, she cradled the gun once more in her hands but this time she pointed it across the room.

She fell back asleep for a while, and when she woke up the gun was lying down by her legs. Sitting up, Beth picked the pistol up and then walked over to the dresser. The top drawer was full of her old clothes and school mementoes. A picture of Kyle Simmons was lying on its side against the end of the drawer. Kyle had been her first love. They started going together when they were in the 10th grade, and he had taken her to the junior prom. She had never let him make love to her, but they had petted and touched each other. How well she remembered his clumsy, fumbling touches. He was a big farm boy with well-developed muscles from hard work and nothing was gentle with him. Kyle had dark blond hair that he wore in a crew cut, and Beth had worn his class ring around her neck on a chain because it was so big that it fell off her thumb.

He was also full of himself, and that was why, one night in their senior year, she had given him back his ring and told him she didn't want to see him anymore. It was the talk of the school for a week and her mom had told her to reconsider because Kyle came from a good family. He was Catholic like her, and they had so much going for them.

But Beth didn't want to be a farmer's wife. Right or wrong, she didn't love Kyle. She took the picture out of the frame and crumpled it up and threw it in the wastebasket beside the dresser, but not before the thought passed through her mind that had she married him he might still be alive.

The next drawer down, the deep one, had only two round boxes in it that she'd never seen before. They looked like hatboxes, but when she opened one she found a wig inside. A black wig. She had never had a black wig or any wig, for that matter. Then she remembered that it was her mother's, of course … the wig she had worn when she was going through chemotherapy and all of her hair had fallen out. The other box was empty. *I wonder where this wig went.* Beth thought. The she remembered *"It was on her head, silly, when they buried her."*

She remembered now how her mother had looked in that casket with that wig on. She hadn't looked at all like herself. Her skin had been stretched tight over her skeleton-like body. Her eyes were sunken in her head. Her hands and arms were full of bruises from all of the needles that had poured an endless supply of painkillers and drugs into her. Beth had seen the scars on her chest after her breast had been removed, and it looked like someone had shot her with a shotgun and then sewed it up. She looked back at the gun that was still on the bed. She would leave the gun here for the time being. She needed to think this out some more and give it time. There had to be a way. She lifted the wig and slid the gun underneath it. Putting the cover back on the box, she slid the drawer shut.

When dawn finally spilled the sun's warm rays through the bedroom window, Beth was feeling better. She took clean clothes and her toiletries and went downstairs to the shower. Her dad was up and gone, but there was a note on the table saying he had gone to town for some things. The coffee was on and there was a cinnamon roll in the breadbox.

The note made her smile and she poured a half a cup of coffee and took it into the bathroom with her. The shower and clean clothes did wonders for her. Afterwards, with her hair still wrapped in a towel, she went out and sat on the back steps with her coffee and the cinnamon roll, sharing it with Brandy and Rascal. Both dogs were wet from the early morning dew and Beth yelled at them to not get her dirty and wet.

A gray goose with six little goslings following her, approached and stuck out its neck for a sample, but the dogs chased her away with a volley of barking. Mother goose retaliated by going after Brandy with her neck outstretched, hissing and screeching, and the pup hid under the porch, much to Beth's delight. It was the first time she had laughed in a week.

Dad came home shortly afterwards, the truck seat full of groceries. He seemed to be more upbeat today too. Beth helped him carry in the groceries and put them away.

Needing to get back to the cards and letters, Beth poured them out on the tabletop in the kitchen. There was a letter from Darla in Florida expressing her shock and sympathy.

Dear Beth,

I learned of your tragedy this morning from my mother, who still lives in your city and saw it on the news. When you guys were here at our house, Mick seemed to me to be the best, and I am so sorry for your loss. I, too, have lost my husband because I left him, but now is not the time to get into that. I will write you more later, and God bless you and Sarah.

Darla.

Beth set the letter down. Darla didn't know about Sarah. How many other people did not know that Sarah was killed, also? She pushed the letter to the side. *I need to write her,* she thought.

The next day was Sunday, and Beth went to Mass with her dad in the morning. The priest was the same old priest who had been the pastor of the church for forty-some years and had married her and Mick over thirteen years ago. Beth remembered him as a younger man full of spirit and vitality. Now he looked tired and frail.

His homily this Sunday was on the beatitudes, and he talked a little about each of them and how we should use them in our lives to build our character. "Blessed are those who mourn, for they shall be comforted". Beth swore he was looking right at her when he said it, and she shifted nervously in the pew.

"Blessed are the peacemakers, he continued for they shall be called children of God." She raised her face to look at him. It was time to think again of Mick and Larry. But when he continued on saying, "Blessed are they who hunger and thirst for justice, for they shall be satisfied," the words "That remains to be seen" were on the end of her tongue.

After Mass, Beth stopped to say hi to some old friends, but was uncomfortable so she went to the truck to wait for Dad. She made up her mind to go home tomorrow. She would finish her cards and thank you notes there. There were bills to be paid and plans to be made. The words, 'those who thirst for justice' kept flashing across her mind.

They had a big Sunday dinner with roast chicken and biscuits like her mom used to make. Afterwards, over coffee Beth told her dad that she would be leaving tomorrow.

"I'll come back and spend some more time with you in a few weeks, Dad. Right now there are some things I need to get done. And you have things to do besides comfort me, as much as I love you for that.

Walt reached over and patted her hand. "I love you too, Bethy, and you're about all I have left in this world. But you do what you have to do."

That afternoon while Walt napped, Beth, Brandy and Rascal went for a long walk down to the river where she had played as a young girl. The water was high from the spring rains, and sitting on the bank she could hear it gurgling and rushing on its way downstream. The dogs were in a lazy mood, and they all sat on the riverbank in the sunshine like three peas in a pod, the dogs were dozing and Beth was daydreaming. She was thinking of Mick and the time they had come here and he had talked her into going skinny-dipping, but she had been shy and left her bra and panties on. When they come into shallow water to come out, she saw that the wet panties were sexier than if she had been naked. They had made love right here on this river bank on the grass, and Mick had made her feel like she was the most beautiful woman in the world. He said that she was more beautiful than Cleopatra on the banks of the Nile, even more beautiful than Deborah Kerr on the beach in *From Here to Eternity*. After they were finished they had lain and held each other for a long time, wrapped up in a blanket Mick had magically produced from his backpack which was supposedly filled with fishing gear. He was always full of surprises. Beth was crying again and the dogs sensed her sorrow and snuggled up to her, licking her face. Her tears stopped and she hugged them and they headed home.

The next morning she thanked her dad for all that he had done. She would take his car back. It was a vehicle he seldom used, and Beth said that maybe Laurie and she could get it back to him.

"No hurry," Walt said.

"I'll be back to pick up Brandy and see you in a few weeks, Daddy. I love you so much." They hugged once more and then Beth got in the car, put it in gear and started down the long driveway.

In the back seat were her suitcase and the wig box. In her mind was the beginning of a crazy plan.

-18-

The first thing Beth had to accomplish this week would be sending thank you cards and acknowledgments to all the people who had expressed their sympathy in so many ways. The outpouring had been enormous, including people she had never heard of. The box of cards she had taken to her dad's was only the tip of the iceberg. The mail Laurie had brought inside while she was gone and piled in the middle of the kitchen table contained many more.

The red light on her message machine was blinking and there were twenty-three messages. Most of them were sympathy messages from friends and relatives, but a message from Captain Dan Wicks at the police station sounded serious enough to get her attention, and Larry had also asked her to call as soon as she was home.

Beth opened some windows to air the house out, deciding that she had to get on with what life she had left. She made plans to go grocery shopping and started a load of laundry.

"Hi, Laurie," Beth was standing in the kitchen twirling the phone cord around her fingers.

"Beth ... you're home. I would have thought you might have stayed longer."

"No. That wasn't a good place to go and try to forget. There are as many memories there as there are here. Dad, bless his heart, was trying very hard to make things easier for me, but I think having him around was only making things worse.

What's new at school?"

Laurie was astonished at Beth's rapid recovery, and although happy for her friend, she thought something was not passing the smell test here. They made plans to get together in a day or so to talk.

"Laurie," Beth seemed to have hit a serious note, "I know I've thanked you, but I just want you to know I would never have gotten through all of this without you. You are a dear, precious friend."

All Laurie could think to say was, "I love you, Beth."

Larry had asked her to call him at a phone number she had not seen before, and when Beth called, he answered as if the phone was already in his hand.

Recognizing her voice immediately, Larry asked, "Beth, when did you get back?"

"Just today," she answered.

"Hey, you've got to come and see me. I'm at a new place that's just fantastic. They're teaching me how to live without the things I lost, and I need you to help me get through this." His voice was cracking.

He had started out so chipper but had become serious in a hurry. *He needs me to help him get through this. Who's going to help me get through this?* Beth shook her head to clear her negative thoughts.

"Give me your address, Larry. Maybe I can come in a day or so, but not tonight. I've got too much to do."

After hanging up with Larry, she dialed Dan Wicks' phone number but got his voice mail. "Dan, Beth Motrin. I just wanted you to know that I'm back and should be in most of the day. You can call me at home."

She went upstairs to the bedroom and opened the closet. Half of the clothes in there were Mick's, and right now this house was a Mick Motrin museum. She was not going to be able to go on while being reminded at every turn that he was gone. She took clothes by the armfuls out of the closet and carried them into Sarah's room and piled them on the bed. Next she cleaned off Mick's nightstand and emptied the drawers in his dresser. This was hard to do and she was getting emotional again. But there was no time right now to sit and cry. "I will make this right, Mick," she said aloud, "You just have to be patient with me. For now, all of your stuff is a distraction."

The phone ringing jogged her back to reality and Beth picked the receiver up at Mick's nightstand, and sat on the edge of the bed.

"Beth, Dan Wicks. I know this isn't giving you a lot of time to let things settle down, but I need you to come in and go over some things with me. There are insurance policies that pay for officers lost in the line of duty. There is some question about Mick's status at the time he was killed, but we're doing all we can to have this processed as an on-duty incident. I don't want to go over all of this on the phone. I could come to your place, if it's more convenient."

"Yes, that would be fine," Beth replied, and then catching what she had just said, she corrected herself. "I mean, I can come in to see you. When and where?"

"Tomorrow?" Wicks answered. "Say ten a.m. at my office."

"I'll be there, Dan," she said softly, and hung up the phone.

After a striping the room of all Mick's things, she moved the bed to a different wall and made it up with new comforter she had gotten for Christmas but never used. Beth closed the door to Sarah's room. Maybe some day she would be able to do something with that room. The trips she made in with Mick's things were hard enough.

There were a lot of people in the grocery store for a Monday afternoon. She found herself picking up things that she didn't really like but that Mick did, and then putting them back. Sarah's favorite cereal stuck out like a sore thumb from the shelf when she passed it and she had to stop and catch her breath. For how many years had a box of Fruit Loops been an automatic purchase?

This was a different store, out of the way, because she didn't want to see anybody she knew. Everybody meant well, but it would be so much better if the attention was dropped for now.

After shopping, she went back home to find more cards in the mail and her paycheck from the school, along with a letter that said her leave of absence had been approved by the school board. *Maybe she should have gone back,* she thought. *It would have gotten her mind off things, but she had something to do now, and it didn't include teaching. Maybe it was going to be difficult and maybe not, but it was a whole new role for a fourth grade school teacher, that was for sure.*

Beth worked late into the night on thank you cards and thought maybe she was going to come off as not sounding very sincere in some of them, but there were just so many ways to say it, and she had worn them all out.

At ten o'clock she flipped on the television to catch night time news. It had been a few days now, and there was nothing on the news about her husband's killers. She watched the weather, then shut off the television and headed to bed, unbuttoning her blouse as she walked up the stairs.

There were clean sheets on the bed and she needed to be clean too, so she shed the rest of her clothes and headed for the shower. She needed to clean the bathroom out, too, she decided. Mick's shaving cream and razor went into the wastebasket, along with some hair dressing and deodorant.

The shower felt soothing and she soaped up her sponge and scrubbed her legs and back, feeling some of the day's tension leaving her with the soapy water.

Soaping up the sponge once more she carefully washed her neck and chest. The soap always smelled so clean it almost cleared her head.

For some reason, her right breast seemed tender. She felt the breast and something was different. Maybe she had bumped herself or leaned wrong on it. She raised her arm in the air feeling for lumps, but nothing was suspicious ... or was that a lump? No, that was there before, wasn't it? Her other breast, also, was tender, but nothing like this one. She looked at it and the nipple seemed darker than normal. It was darker than the other nipple.

For a moment she shut off the water and tried to compose herself. *This was foolish*, she thought. *She was getting paranoid now and imagining all kinds of problems, but was this the way her mother had felt when she first noticed a lump?* Beth had never really talked with her about it. What were her other symptoms? She was much younger than her mother was when she got sick, but this was a genetic problem in women. She had read that in a magazine sometime back, and she knew women younger than her who had had problems with cancer.

Upset now, she got out of the shower and dried herself off. She grabbed her robe and went in and sat down on the bed, brushing her hair out. Then laying down her brush, she undid her robe and examined her right breast again. Something is wrong, she decided, and that's all there is to it.

She sat on the bed thinking. Wouldn't this just top it all off.... she loses her husband and daughter, and now she has inherited the same deadly disease that took her mother's life two years ago. "Well, you know what?" she said out loud. "I don't give a shit. I don't care if I have a cancer that grows so big it will look like I have three tits. Give me cancer if you want to. I have nothing to live for, anyway."

She wiped a tear away. Hell, it wasn't worth crying about. Maybe it was God's way of helping her out. She couldn't take her own life when she had wanted to. She had tried and failed. But he could do the job for her, couldn't he? But you know what? She was not going to die tonight or tomorrow, or even a month from now. This was still not going to spoil her plans and now she truly had nothing to lose.

When Beth woke up she was lying on the end of the bed wrapped in her robe. The digital clock said 3:45. She got up and went downstairs to the office, where she got out the medical dictionary.

"I wish we weren't having this conversation, Beth. I didn't get a chance to talk to you at Mick's funeral, and I also didn't get a chance to express how bad I felt about your daughter." Dan Wicks was sitting on the corner of his desk, while

Beth looked up at him, nervously playing with the string ties hanging from the bottom of her jacket. She hadn't dressed up, and wore blue jeans, a sweatshirt and white tennis shoes. She had put her long hair in a ponytail and looked much younger than he had remembered her.

Beth didn't respond to his comments but watched him with a gaze that said 'I heard you, now get on with whatever else you brought me here for.' She had never liked Dan Wicks because he was a man who abused his authority. As Mick had said, he was the boss and he never wanted you to forget it.

She had left the office door open when she came in and he left his perch to close it, looking both ways down the short corridor before he did. When he came back he didn't return to the desk corner, but sat down in the chair next to Beth. Maybe, she thought, for a while he was going to come down to her level.

"Beth," he said, "there are two insurance policies that covered Mick as a police officer. One is from the State of Minnesota, and the other is a federal policy. Together they amount to about two hundred and fifty thousand dollars. To be eligible for these you have to be killed in the line of duty. This department believes that Mick and Larry were still on duty when this happened. The Feds are questioning this, but we'll go to bat for you. The thing you need to do is apply for the benefits. I've put all of the paper work together for you and I need you to take it home and fill it out. Attach the documents they need, like a death certificate, marriage license, etcetera, and get it back to me." He reached over to his desktop and picked up a manila folder and handed it to her.

Beth did not open the folder but laid it in her lap. "Dan, I wanted to ask you how the investigation is going and when these men who killed my family are going to be arrested." Her tone was almost sarcastic and he could feel the underlying anger.

"Beth, it's just matter of time before we move on them. We tried for an early arrest and the courts shot us down, saying we didn't have enough evidence. These men are smart and they're good at covering their tracks. They also have money and good attorneys. And you have to remember that when we arrest them; we only get one shot at taking them to trial."

"Tell me about the Sanchez family," Beth replied.

Wicks shrugged his shoulders. "Not much to tell, Beth. They have lived in this city for many years. The father started a tobacco wholesaling business many years ago. To start with, it was a legitimate business, but as the years went by, and especially after his death, they started selling drugs. They were smart and never got caught on the streets with it. They were just the wholesalers, not the pushers. Can I get you some coffee?" He started to stand up.

"No, no thanks. I just had breakfast before I came." She gave him a smile and turned in her chair so she could see him better. "There were four boys in the family?" She asked.

"Yes, there were four boys. Actually they're men now. One of them was killed in that shoot-out with Mick." He wanted to drop that subject as soon as he could. "We believe that Mick's killing was in retaliation for what happened there." Wicks had turned his chair now so they were both sitting parallel to his desk.

"The oldest of the three is George, and he kind of runs the show, now. We rarely see him or Diego, the next in age. Diego is believed to be the enforcer in the family. He's a loner, that's for sure. Manny, the youngest, is the one we know the best and he has a rap sheet a mile long. He likes to party, and hangs out a lot downtown."

Beth wanted to keep the conversation going, but Wicks realizing that he had already said too much, stood up.

"Look, I promise you that you'll be the first to know when we have what we need to charge these guys," he told her as he took both of her hands in his, helping her up. "No one wants them behind bars more than we do, Beth. Please believe that."

Beth realized the conversation was over and was uncomfortable being here any longer, especially holding hands with Wicks. "I'll get these back to you soon," she said.

"Thanks." He dropped her hands and put his in his pockets.

It was a beautiful day and the sun made her squint as she walked out the front door of the police station and across the street to her car. She was glad the meeting was over and hadn't got any more personal than it had. She needed to go to the library to look at some old newspapers, so she drove downtown. Parking in a ramp, she crossed the street to the library. The place was almost empty and the only librarian on duty looked up as she approached the counter.

"Do you have back copies of the Tribune?" Beth asked

"We do, but they're on microfilm. Will that work for you?" She seemed a little irritated that Beth wanted something from her. She had been eating her lunch and it looked as if that was something she did a lot of.

"Yes, that will be fine."

"Well, the machines are right around the corner. If you give me the dates I will bring you the appropriate film."

Beth thought for a second before answering. "I would like to see them for everyday for the last ten days, including today."

The woman disappeared into the back room. Her perfume, which Beth thought she must have bathed in, hung heavily in the air, and Beth stepped back a little before her breath gave out.

The woman returned and handed Beth the films saying, "The instructions are right on the screens, but if you need help come and get me."

The first film was for the day Mick was shot, but it was too late to make the papers that day so she never looked at it. The next day, Saturday, it made the headlines, and Beth bit her lips as she saw Mick and Larry's pictures. They mentioned Sarah, but there was no picture, and it was almost as if her injuries were minor. There was no mention of the Sanchez brothers; it just said the police investigation was widespread.

Sunday's edition had the first mention of the Sanchez Brothers being arrested and brought in. Pictures of all three of them were on the front page, along with the story of their arrest.

There was just a short article on Monday about the grand jury meeting on the case, but Tuesday's edition had a lot of coverage of the Sanchez brothers' release, due to lack of evidence. There was also a direct quote from Manny to the Tribune reporter that they were innocent, and that he would be at Wales that night celebrating if anyone wanted to talk with a free man.

The rest of the papers carried nothing important. Beth took the Sunday clip to the counter and asked if she could get a copy of the front page.

"You can, but there will be a $1.00 charge," the woman said.

Beth reached into her purse and took out a dollar bill and shoved it across the counter.

"I will be just a minute," the lady said, stuffing the bill in a drawer.

After leaving the library, Beth drove over the Third Street Bridge and looked for Wales Night Club. It was there, on the corner of Third and Second Streets in what was a seedy part of town. She locked the car doors, driving slowly by, and then speeded up and headed home.

-19-

Larry didn't know when Beth was coming, so he seemed surprised when she walked in. The place where he had been transferred to was a rehabilitation center for people who had been injured or sick, but no longer needed constant medical care. It was a one story red brick building that looked to be fairly new in a quiet neighborhood, not far from the hospital where he had been treated. The front was covered with so many vines that it appeared to be almost camouflaged. There was a small parking lot in the front that held a few cars, and a one-lane road went around to the back for extra parking.

The only other car in front right now was an old panel truck with something leaking out of the engine area. Beth parked as far a way as possible.

Inside, a young Asian man in a gray sweater and slacks was sitting at a computer typing when Beth walked up to the reception desk.

"I'm looking for Larry Sorenson," she said. "I think he was just admitted here today."

He typed something on his keyboard, and then turning to face Beth said, "Larry's in room 106. That's around the corner to the right and about half way down. Shall I call him and tell him you are here?"

"No, let me surprise him," Beth answered.

Larry was dressed and lying on top of his bed looking out the window when Beth walked in. She walked to the end of the bed and squeezed his foot before she realized the futility of what she had done, but Larry had seen her, anyway.

"Beth, I'm so glad to see you." He reached up and grabbed the handle on the support that hung over his bed and pulled himself to a sitting position. Then grabbing his legs, he pushed and pulled himself around, until his legs hung over the bed. Maneuvering his wheel chair into position beside the bed, he slid down into it and looked up at Beth.

"Pretty good for one day's lesson," he said.

"I am impressed," Beth answered and applauded.

He let her push him down to a large assembly area where a few people were watching television and playing cards.

"They say a week or two here and I'll be ready to go home. I've been thinking about it and I might have to move someplace else because the building I live in is not handicapped assessable." He took a pack of gum from his shirt pocket and offered Beth a stick. "Need to quit the cigarettes," he said.

"No thanks," she said. "You should have quit long ago."

Larry didn't answer her.

"Is there anything you need from home?" she asked.

"Not really. All I really need to do now is get my head screwed on right. I'm wallowing in self pity, Beth."

Just what I need, she thought. *I just lost my whole family and now I've got a gay friend who's full of self-pity. That ought to go a long way toward cheering me up.*

She reached over and touched his face. A solitary tear slid down Larry's cheek but he quickly brushed it away.

"Larry, were you very sure that is was the Sanchez brothers who did this to you?"

The question caught him off guard. "Why do you ask that?"

"I—I just want to be sure about what happened. I just want to be sure about the people who robbed me of all I ever had in life, Larry. You were the only witness, and it seems like your word wasn't good enough for the judge or they would be locked up by now."

Larry sat quietly for the moment. He was chewing on the cuticle of his right thumb and looking off into space. Suddenly he turned to face Beth, repositioning his wheel chair so fast that it banged against the wall.

"Beth, there is nothing I am more sure of than that. Their faces are burned into my memory as if they were branded there by a red hot iron." He looked insulted and stared at her defiantly.

But Beth had other questions and she was not going to stop asking now. "Who was driving the car, Larry?"

"Manny was driving and Diego was in the back seat on the same side. They both had AK .47's sticking out the window. You don't forget that easily when you see one of them pointed at you and spitting lead."

"Where was George?"

"You seem to know a lot about these people, Beth."

"Mick talked to me about them before—" She hesitated as if the mention of his name had made her lose track of her train of thought and then recovered. "Before this happened."

"Don't get involved, Bethy." Larry pulled his chair closer to hers. "These people are ruthless killers, and they wouldn't hesitate to kill you, too. I'm advising you to leave it to the police."

Beth stared at him for a second, biting her lower lip and wanting to say, I did leave it to the police and you see what has happened, but she thought better of it and remained quiet.

She changed the subject. She had pushed it far enough. "Larry, I want you to think about coming and staying with me for awhile. At least until things settle down and you get better. We.... I.... have the downstairs office that actually is a bedroom. I could fix it up for you."

"Thank you," he said. "I'll think about that. It's nice of you to offer."

"I have to be going, but I think I can come again on Wednesday. Is that okay?"

Larry slapped his shirt pocket. "Shit, Bethy, let me check my appointment book," he teased. "Oh damn, now where did I misplace that? Well, hell, let's plan on it."

"You screwball," she laughed and ruffled his hair before she bent and kissed him on the forehead. "See you then, and call if you need anything."

"Beth...." Larry began.

She hesitated by the door. "Yes?" she said.

"I don't know who the third person in that car was, but I am sure of the other two."

She smiled but didn't answer him except to wave goodbye.

Beth didn't go right home but stopped at a coffee shop and ordered a latté and read the paper. There was nothing in there about her problems. She needed to schedule a hair appointment tomorrow and get her hair cut short so it would fit under the wig. She felt the ends of her long red hair, her long full red hair. How long had it taken to grow it this length? Oh well, it would grow again if she was still alive, or chemo didn't take it.

Her sore breast wasn't getting any better but it no longer bothered her. The more she fretted about it the worse it got, so it was best forgotten.

I need to go shopping, she thought. *I really have nothing to wear that would look right in the downtown nightclub scene. If I am going down there, I need to look the part.* She finished the last of her latté and headed home.

Tuesday was spent finishing up the last of her cards and letters. She paid some bills and made an appointment with Theresa for the next morning to get her hair cut. Then she stopped by the school and cleaned her desk out for the year. It was lunch hour so the room was empty, but there was someone's sweater draped over the back of the chair that wasn't hers. For a moment she looked around the room at all of the art projects she had taped to the walls. Each desk brought a memory of a smiling liitle face. What was making her turn her back on all of this? She was getting sad again and if she didn't leave she was going to cry. She didn't bother to see anyone, not even Laurie. Beth put the keys to her classroom in an envelope and dropped them at the principal's office.

She had arrived for her hair appointment right on time so the chair was empty when she walked in, and Theresa was waiting for her with a smile. Theresa was happy to see that Beth seemed to have recovered somewhat emotionally from the last time she had fixed her hair.

"Need a trim and a little styling, do you?" she asked.

"Cut it short," Beth said.

"Are you sure you want to do that?"

"Yes, summer's coming and I'm tired of taking care of it."

Theresa cut off several inches and then spun her around to look in the mirror. "Short enough?"

"I want it much shorter," Beth answered.

Beth was quieter than usual. *I guess I'm just used to her being so bubbly and silly,* Theresa thought. She herself didn't quite know what to say, and didn't want to say the wrong thing, so kept the conversation light. Beth wasn't her old self, that was for sure.

When Beth walked out of the shop, her hair was no more than a few inches long. She sat in the car and looked in the rear view mirror. She wasn't sure if she liked it or not, but then, she thought, it wasn't about liking or not liking, was it?

Larry wasn't in his room when Beth got there on Wednesday evening. She had a couple of magazines she had picked up for him in her hand as she walked across the room and looked out the window. Outside was of a small courtyard and Larry was sitting there in the early evening sunshine next to a small fountain, daydreaming.

She tossed the magazines on the bed and knocked on the window loud enough that Larry heard her and looked up, smiling. He pointed to the door and waved his arm in an arc to indicate that she should come outside.

"Hi, buddy," she said. "What did we learn today?"

"I learned to get on the toilet stool," Larry said with a smile. "Here I am, almost forty years old and I have to learn how to go potty and wipe my butt all over again," he said with a frown.

"Just be happy you have a butt to wipe," said Beth "You could have had it shot off." She was sorry that she had said that, and changed the subject as soon as she could think of another direction to go. "Look, Larry," she started to say, but he interrupted her.

"What in the hell happened to your hair, woman?"

"I had it cut. Don't you like it?"

"You look like a biker gal. But a very pretty biker gal, I might add. You're not going to get a tattoo are you?"

"If you hadn't added that part about being pretty I was going to sock you a good one," Beth said with a grin. "Yeah, I might get a big snake tattooed all the way from my wrist to my shoulder."

"Sure, beat up a cripple," he said, ignoring her comments about the tattoo.

"What I was going to say before you so rudely interpreted me, was that I need an answer from you as to whether you're going to come and stay with me."

"I'd like that, Beth, but only if I wouldn't be a bother. I don't want to be a charity case, and God knows you have enough on your mind."

"I don't do charity cases, Larry. I just thought maybe I could help you get back on track. And yes I do have a lot on my mind, but I need purpose in my life more than anything right now. I need someone to talk with and be with, a hand to hold and a shoulder to cry on."

That statement almost had Larry crying until Beth said. "I also need someone who won't try and get in my pants."

Larry slapped the arm of his wheelchair in laughter.

They spent the rest of the evening making plans to get Larry's things moved into Beth's garage for the time being. Larry had some friends from the police department who would come and help her rearrange the house. They would have to hire a contractor to do some work on the downstairs bathroom so Larry could use it, and he said the he would arrange for that.

Beth left on an upper. She was glad he was coming even though she was a little afraid of the challenges it might present.

On Thursday morning Beth went shopping in a shopping center that bordered the University. It catered mostly to young people, and it was the only place she could think of that she might be able to find the kind of clothes she needed to complete her disguise. She needed to look the part, and right now she wasn't quite sure what that part was supposed to look like. Beth walked around the area outside for a while and looked at what the young people were wearing. Was this the kind of crowd Manny would hang with?

It was a hot day in May and a lot of the students were lying outside studying on the lawns and just trying to catch some sun. There was young love in the air, and some couples were expressing their affections for each other, almost to the point of being embarrassing. Beth tried to appear as if she hadn't noticed, but the whole scene brought back a lot of memories of her days in college and she remembered doing many of the same things. It brought back memories of her and Mick's courtship too, and those made her sit down and reflect a little, but it also was going to made her cry and she didn't want to do that. Not here anyway.

Her mission was making her nervous and she was having second thoughts about the whole idea. Then she would think of Sarah, and her resolve would stiffen again. Mick was a cop and there were inherent risks in that job that someday you might be hurt or killed. That just came with the territory, as sad as it might be. But Sarah … they were *not* going to get away with what they did to her baby. Her daughter's image came flooding back to her and she ran to her car and collapsed sobbing. She beat the steering wheel and pulled on her short hair. A passer-by stopped and tapped on the window, mouthing the words, "Are you okay?" Beth nodded her head and, starting the car, drove down to the shopping center and parked.

She bought a short black mini skirt and a white blouse with a scoop neck and also a second blouse with spaghetti straps which was an off white. A pair of fish net tights and a push up bra that hurt her swollen breast and she couldn't wait to get out of, finished it off for clothing, for today anyway.

The clerk who waited on her was cheerful and talked about the nice weather, but Beth responded only with a slight smile and offered her credit card.

She went to a second store and bought some costume jewelry, a pair of large hoop earrings and a trio of bracelets that jangled on her wrist. She had her nose pierced in another shop and a small gold stud put in it. It made her eyes water and her face sting but looking in the mirrors in the car she decided she kind of liked it, and giggled.

The last thing she bought was a small shoulder bag to hold everything she would need. She didn't have a lot of things to carry, but one of them was heavy, too heavy to fit in her regular purse.

Leaving the family had been traumatic for George, but his wife Maria was overjoyed at the prospect of having a life of their own. She had hated Momma Sanchez from the first day that she met her. It had been the source of many arguments between her and George. Their daughter Anna was small now, but she was getting more impressionable every day, and this place was not the kind of place Maria wanted her to grow up in.

She had no love for George's brothers, either, believing Diego to be the epitome of evil and Manny a spoiled rotten brat who was in trouble every time he turned around. Not that it bothered her that he was in trouble ... she wished they would lock him up for good, because it was George who had to get him out of all his petty scrapes. Raul had been the only one she liked, and he was dead.

George left for Chicago on Wednesday, telling Maria he would be back on Friday night with a new life for his family.

Maria was dark-skinned with eyes that bordered on being black. They looked like they were floating in little pools of olive oil. Her hair shined and she wore it long down around her shoulders and it bounced as she walked. She was small, with a tiny waist and a small firm bosom. The only thing anyone could find wrong with Maria's looks was the persistent frown on her face which indicated that she wasn't happy.

On Thursday morning George called to tell Maria that he had met with his dad's brother who was still in the tobacco business. His uncle had heard a lot of stories about the drug dealing, and was reluctant to meet with George at first. He had never forgiven his sister-in-law and nephews for what they had done to his dead brother's business, so when George told him as sincerely as he could why he wanted out of the family business, he gave George a position in the company on the spot. After all, he was his nephew, and family was family.

Maria was so happy she was giddy. A home of their own in Chicago, making an honest living! The frown she had worn for so many years was gone. She picked up Anna and floated around the apartment with her as if they were ballroom dancers.

"Don't say anything to my mother," George had said. "I'll handle it when I get home."

Momma had told Diego about George leaving the family business, and it was fine with him. George was a pain in the ass, anyway, and it would be one less person to split the money with. Now if only Manny would go away, he would have it made. Then it would be just him and Momma.

Momma knew that Diego was not the person to run the business, but for now she was playing her cards close to her chest. She didn't really think George would leave, anyway. They were closer than that. It was his brat wife she didn't trust.

-20-

All day Friday Beth puttered around the house, picking things up that were Mick's and Sarah's and putting them away. It was just too painful to deal with right now and 'out of sight out of mind' was the rule of the day. She had shut the door on Sarah's room and she wouldn't go back in there for anything, except to put more of Sarah's and Mick's things in there. The only light in that room was that which was filtered through the closed shades.

The only exception to her cleansing had been their wedding picture. It still sat on her dresser in the bedroom where it had been since the day they were married. She had lain in bed this morning and looked at it for the longest time. She could do that now without breaking down all the time, so maybe she was healing, or maybe she was just preoccupied with the business at hand. She wasn't sure, but it beat crying all of the time.

She remembered their wedding day so vividly. It would always be the happiest day of her life. It had been a huge church wedding that practically everybody in town had come to. Her mom wanted her to have the wedding she had never had. After the reception, her dad had driven them to the airport in the early evening. They had flown to Bermuda for their honeymoon, and for six days their life had been a fairy tale, filled with swimming and snorkeling in the crystal blue waters and sailing around the island they were staying on in a rented sailboat ... she hadn't cared where she went as long as she was with Mick. Beth had wanted it to never end.

Mick had taken her out to supper each night to a different club and they ate and drank so much they felt ready to burst. They danced each night until the last song was finished and their feet ached. They were two hearts beating as one, with incredible energy drawn from each other.

The thing she would remember the most was their wedding night. They had made love late that first night in their seaside cottage bedroom. The French doors onto the deck were left open to catch the ocean breezes, so they could hear the waves lapping on the shore. The moonlight was shining so brightly in their room that night that they could see each and every pore of their eager bodies. They had been insatiable, unable to get enough of each other. They had explored each other's bodies for the first time feeling free and uninhibited. After all, they now belonged to each other not only on paper but also in the eyes of God. When they were completely spent, they had slept with their bodies pressed together, neither of them wanting to be the one to turn away. They were as one. They would always be as one.

Just thinking about it in bed this morning had brought a whole range of feelings to Beth. First remorse and grief, in knowing it would never happen again. They had been savagely ripped apart and were no longer as one. Next came a feeling of anger at Mick for not caring enough about his family to do something safer for his life's work. The good feelings came rushing back, again, however, as if they would not be denied, and along with these feelings, her physical longing for him, and the realization that you never know how much you could miss someone until you don't have them to hold on to, anymore.

Finally she had retreated to the shower and tried to wash away her troubles and her tears. She sat on the shower floor with her knees drawn up and her head resting on top of them. The shower nozzle was pulsating on the back of her neck and her tears mixed with the stream that swirled and ran down the drain. She felt like her whole life was going down the drain with the water.

Beth sat on the end of the bed with only a towel wrapped around her. She was all cried out and angry again. Her breasts were not getting any better and now they both were sore. She felt for the lump she thought she had found, but it seemed to be gone. Maybe it was just something minor like an infection. But if she had cancer like her mother had, that was all right, too. Life was not that precious anymore. Not to her, anyway. Just for the heck of it she would call and make an appointment with her doctor though, but if it was cancer there would be none of what her mother went through. No chemo, no surgery.

The phone ringing across the bedroom stopped her daydreaming and she picked it up on the fourth ring. It was Laurie.

"Hi, Beth. Hey, listen … I have a pair of tickets to a musical downtown tomorrow night and I know this is short notice …"

"Laurie, I can't," she lied. She couldn't think of any excuse to make up so quickly, so she made none. "Just, just ... sorry, but I can't." Beth could hear the children chattering in the background and knew Laurie was calling from her classroom.

Then quickly she said, "Let's make plans to get together next week. I just have so many things to get caught up on around here right now. Okay, Laurie?"

She could sense the disappointment in Laurie's voice when she said. "Okay." A sudden commotion in the background caused Laurie to say, "I better go. Call me when you can."

"I will." Beth sat and stared at the phone in her hand. What a mess her life was right now. Two weeks ago those would have been her students chattering in the background. She loved to teach and she loved her students. Then this hate-filled act had changed everything. Now all she had were a couple of cold tombstones in a cemetery. A bedroom full of things she couldn't bear to look at, and an increasingly twisted mind. Two weeks ago she was a respected teacher, and now she was reduced to a scheming, vindictive, potential assassin sitting around bawling and lying to her best friend.

She looked up from the end of the bed where she was sitting with the soggy bath towel still wrapped around her. The mirror on her dresser reflected the top half of her body. It didn't even look like her. That pin in her nose and her beautiful long hair gone. Her short hair was still wet and plastered to her head. *Maybe it's time for it all to stop,* she thought. Was killing someone else going to bring her husband and daughter back? Maybe she had the right idea that night in her dad's house. Kill herself and stop all of the pain. It would all be so easy if she could be sure she would go where Mick and Sarah were. Then reality bit back, and with it came the thought that it was murder to kill yourself, and God didn't look kindly on that.

What about killing Manny ... wouldn't that be murder? But didn't that same God say 'an eye for an eye'? She had heard that someplace. She stood up and dropped the towel and looked at herself in the mirror. "You know, I still look pretty good," she said to herself. Her stomach was still flat and her breasts were nice. She turned around, presenting her backside to the mirror. Mick always said she had a nice body. *I have to stop this crap about killing myself,* she thought. *Yes, killing this man isn't going to bring my daughter and husband back, but it might make me sleep easier knowing that this scum won't ever hurt anyone ever again."*

Beth looked in the mirror once more, and this time her sad look was gone and there was a small grin on her face. *I'm mad. I am damn good and mad* she thought. She thought shrugging her shoulders'. *But if that's what it takes, so be it.*

She slipped on some underclothes and her sweats. *Time to get some housework done.*

Dan Wicks was tired. It was Friday and the city had been relatively crime-free for a couple of days, but he was tired just the same, and looked forward to a relaxing weekend. The investigation into Mick's and Sarah's killings was still at a standstill, but he was confident that something would break before too long. They had to be careful because the Sanchez brothers had one of the best attorneys in town. Charging them with anything right now and not having a firm case could jeopardize the whole thing down the road.

He had good news for Beth Motrin though. The feds had dropped their opposition to the insurance payout and she would now get almost a quarter of a million dollars, tax-free. Maybe Monday he would call her with the good news.

It was nearly noon and time to call it a week. Maybe he would take the little lady out for supper tonight. Dan was married but didn't have any children. He grabbed his hat and jacket from the coat tree as he went out the door.

One of these days I need to talk with Larry, he thought. Dan was making some progress on getting him a job as a dispatcher when he recovered. *Maybe things will work out yet,* he thought.

"See you Monday," he said to the department receptionist on his way out. She smiled but didn't answer.

Beth busied herself with washing clothes and general cleaning for the rest of the day. She also called her OB-GYN and made an appointment to get a check-up and a mammogram. She couldn't get in until the first week in June, but that was all right. Then she called Laurie back right after school let out, and they made a date to get together Tuesday evening for supper and a movie. "And wait till you see what I did to my hair," she said.

Beth laid out the clothes she would be wearing tonight on the bed. It had been a hot day, so she was going with the short skirt and the spaghetti strap blouse. She changed into the push-up bra. It hurt her breasts and seemed smaller than it was the other day when she bought it, but oh well, she thought, no pain no gain.

She dug through her panties to find some black ones. There was no way she was going to wear a skirt this short without being covered better than she would be with just those stockings.

It was hard to find where the skirt was supposed to ride. Any higher and her crotch would show, and any lower and her blouse would not be long enough to cover and her panties would be coming out the top. The hoop earrings gave her a little hint of being a gypsy so she added a dangling bracelet that she had. Now some eye make-up and just enough perfume to cover up any nervous odor that might come along. Now her black flats, and one more thing … the pistol. Beth was trembling when she took the hatbox out of the closet and placed it on the bed. She had tried the wig on at her dad's and it was too tight, but she had had all of that hair back then. Now it fit perfectly.

She tried to think of the name of that woman on 'The Munsters'. *Was it Elvira or Sabrina, something like that* … because she was a dead ringer for her in this black wig

With eyeliner she darkened her red eyebrows to match the wig. It looked good. *As long as I keep my panties on no one will ever know.* She giggled at the thought.

She wrapped the pistol in a handkerchief and put it in the bag with her wallet and some make up. She only had forty dollars in cash. Maybe she should stop at the A.T.M. on the way. She preened in front of the mirror for a moment, kind of proud of her new appearance. Then getting a little panicky she thought, *I better get out of here before someone who knows me comes to the door.*

It was about 7 p.m. when Beth got downtown, and she decided to park in a ramp six blocks away and walk down to Wales. The walk from the parking ramp to Wales was an adventure in itself. Several men noticed her and whistled or gave her a catcall. *Maybe parking this far away wasn't such a good idea,* she thought. *Oh well, it would be dark when she went home, if she survived this crazy plan.*

Her hands were sweating and she kept trying to keep her skirt down. She had never worn anything like this before. The net hose made her thighs itch and this push-up bra made her breasts beg for relief. *I am not sure how long I can stand this,* she thought.

The bag on her shoulder was heavy with the gun in it and bounced against her side. If there were metal detectors at the club, she was turning around and going home. It would have to be Plan B after that.

Wales was not friendly for the handicapped, with a flight of about a dozen cement steps going up to the front doors where a bouncer stood twiddling his thumbs behind his back and watching her crotch as she tried to get up the steps without showing too much.

A large neon sign of a blue whale hummed overhead and a sign on the door warned about guns and knives being banned on the premises, but she saw no metal detector. Inside the club there was a long bar along one side of the room with about thirty stools and a couple of waiter stations, and on the wall behind it was a long mirror. Two bartenders dressed in white ruffled shirts and blue bow ties were behind the bar. Booths lined the opposite wall of the room, and there were several small round tables in the middle of the floor, some with four chairs and some with two. There was a small dance floor in the back, and in front of a half round stage a couple of musicians were warming up on a keyboard and a guitar.

Beth took a small round table close to the door. *Mick, Sarah, I hope to hell you know what I am going through for you. Dear God, give me strength,* she thought. The place was almost empty, but it was early. Beth could not wait to sit down and get her legs crossed. She looked down at her chest. Even with the bra her cleavage was not going to win any awards.

Beth had put a zip lock bag, in her bag with a sponge in it. She had no intention of drinking much, although she knew she would have to play the part. The waitress came to take her order. "Can I have a gin and tonic?" she asked. "When does the place start rocking?"

The waitress wrote down the order and shrugged her shoulders at Beth's question, but then said, "Oh, they'll all be drifting in soon enough." She was a pretty black lady with the nicest complexion Beth had ever seen. Her skin looked as soft as velvet. All of the waitresses were dressed in black slacks and frilly white blouses with black string ties. The place was certainly making an attempt to look classy, if nothing else.

By eight the place was filling up. A small heavy metal band was playing much too loudly. The crowd was mostly young Blacks or Hispanics. A few white women were seated at a couple of tables, but Beth was the only one by herself. She felt out of place and was having doubts about whether she should be here or not. She had nursed her first drink long enough and ordered a second. She would have to dump part of this one, as she could already feel the effects of the first one. I *need to keep a clear head,* she thought.

Some of the patrons were smoking pot, passing their cigarettes around under the booths and table tops, and you could smell the sweet smoke drifting throughout the room. No one who worked here seemed to mind, and at one point Beth saw a young waitress take a drag off a cigarette that was being passed around. There must have been at least fifty to sixty people in the place by this time, but no one who looked like Manny Sanchez.

The longer she stayed the more out of place she felt, and by nine Beth figured if she didn't see him by ten, she was out of there. At about nine-thirty she couldn't hold it any longer, and she had to go to the restroom. That meant walking across the dance floor to the back of the building where the bathrooms were located It seemed as if every eye in the place was watching her, but it was either this or wet her pants.

There was no one else in the bathroom, thank God, and Beth went into the first stall she came to. When she was done, she took the sponge out of the plastic bag in her shoulder bag and, holding it down between her legs, wrung it out slowly in the toilet.

She stopped and looked in the mirror as she washed her hands. *Three weeks ago I was dressed in a nice pants suit in front of a classroom full of small children. Life was so good, and now look what's happened to me. Maybe it would be best to stop all of this nonsense. Walk out of here right now and go home and deal with my problems.*

Two obviously intoxicated women came in, laughing and groping each other. They stood in front of one of the stalls and kissed each other passionately. Beth fled out into the narrow corridor that took her back into the bar. She walked down the side of the dance floor nearest the booths. A young Hispanic man was doing an animated dance on the floor, thrusting his pelvis at the woman he was dancing with, and he and Beth collided as he gyrated backwards.

Beth had been looking at the floor but the force of the collision knocked her into a booth and someone grabbed her butt to keep her from falling. The hand-lingered a bit too long and she tuned around to say something, but then looking at the man who had run into her, she realized it was him. It was Manny. She had studied the picture from the paper long enough to know it had to be him.

She said nothing to the man who had groped her, but pulled herself back up and fled across the floor to where she had been sitting, only to find that her table had been taken by someone else. She needed to calm down as her face was flushed and she was breathing rapidly. Going to the bar, she found an empty stool and crawled up on it. The bartender was waiting for her. She ordered another gin and tonic.

Beth sat side-ways on the bar stool, watching Manny as he tried to feel up the young woman he was on the dance floor with. The girl co-operated just enough to keep him there, but he was becoming more aggressive by the minute and had both of his hands on her breasts.

The bouncer at the end of the bar had taken notice and started out on the dance floor just as the music ended and Manny headed toward the bar, the young woman he had been dancing with following a few feet behind. The bouncer intercepted him a few feet from Beth. She swung around quickly to avoid seeing Manny.

"I'm not telling you again, Manny," the bouncer said. "Every time you come in here you make a spectacle of yourself, and this is not your private playground. No more lewd behavior, and no more dope peddling."

"Hey, what do you mean dope peddling? I got no dope on me, man." Manny was getting defensive.

"I know what I just saw, Manny, so cut the crap. You want me to call the cops and let them handle it? You're on their shit list anyway, from what I've heard."

Manny saw he was in a no-win situation and clammed up. "Come on, baby, I'll buy you a drink." He grabbed the young woman's hand and they walked over to an open space at the bar, still within earshot of Beth, with the band silenced for the moment.

"Threaten me with the cops," Manny fumed to his friend. "I know how to handle the cops. I know a couple of cops that won't be coming after me." With this comment he laughed and she giggled.

Beth could not believe her ears. She was beyond irate. She was livid and wanted to reach in her bag right then and there and take Manny out. It was time to get out of Wales for tonight, she decided, but she would be back. Beth needed to think how she was going to get alone with Manny and right now she had no good ideas. She stopped to talk to the bouncer on the way out.

"Who is that obnoxious man?" she asked.

"What obnoxious man? We get a lot of obnoxious men in here, lady."

"The one you just chewed out," Beth, answered.

"Oh him. That's Manny Sanchez. He's bad news. I'd stay away from him if I were you. He's in here every weekend, regular as a clock. Him and all his drugged-up friends. This is like his second home, although we wish he would find another one."

The bouncer's tone turned friendly. "I haven't seen you before. Are you new around here?"

"Yes. I—I just moved in down the way a few weeks back." Beth realized she was stammering as she tried to make up a story. "Nice place … I liked the music. Maybe I'll come back tomorrow night if I have nothing else to do."

Just then a shoving match broke out in the bar area and the bouncer said, "See you later," and headed inside.

It was dark on the streets, and there seemed to be homeless or drugged-up people everywhere. Beth was glad she had flats on and she ran the rest of the way to where her car was parked, short skirt or not. She threw herself into the car and squealed out of the ramp, stopping only to pay the ticket. As soon as she was out on the road she pulled off the wig. Her own hair was wet with sweat from the hot hairpiece. She realized she was speeding and slowed down. *Don't want to get stopped with a gun in the car,* she thought.

It was not until she was home and in the house that she finally relaxed. There was a message from Larry to call him, but other than that the machine was empty. Instead of calling, she went upstairs, showered and crawled into bed wrapped snugly in her white robe.

-21-

George came home on Friday morning from his trip to Chicago. Maria was giddy with excitement and had been packing their things from the moment he'd called and told her about the job.

"How are you going to tell your mother?" she asked. They were sitting in a small café having lunch and Maria was trying to get Anna to eat, but she was being stubborn.

George was quiet for a second, looking out the window at the people walking by. "There is no good way to tell her, sweetheart, so I think I'll just go see her and face the music. She can be an evil woman, so I don't want to ruffle her feathers too much. I am not going to tell her where we are going for a while. I really don't want her bothering my uncle."

"I want us to be a family like everybody else, George." Maria reached across the table and laid her hand on top of his. "We need to have lots of babies and go to church. Join the P.T.A. at school and take our kids to little league and tap and ballet classes, not spend the rest of our life hiding from the police."

George smiled and squeezed her slender hand. He agreed with everything she had said, but the wrinkles in his brow still showed a troubled man. He could leave his past for a better life, but he could not undo the past. One thing would always follow him, and that was the fact that he had been in that car the day Mick and Sarah had been killed. Sure he had been pressured into it, but he could have said no. Instead he bowed to his mother's wishes, and every day for the rest of his life he would wait for that knock on the door. Although Sarah's death was unintended, it bothered him to no end. Every time he looked at Anna he would think of her. But the thing that bothered him the most right now was the behavior of his brothers, and he wondered how long it would be before they were arrested for something else and talked. As long as they stayed in the drug business, that was a good possibility. Or maybe they would be mad at him if he moved out, and would that steer the police his way? What a mess he had made.

The police were tailing Manny Sanchez wherever he went. Last night at Wales an undercover officer had been at the table right next to his for most of the night. She had seen Beth, also, and thought her out of place. What was a young white woman doing alone in a place like that? If she wanted music and entertainment there were much better places a few blocks away. She didn't appear to want drugs or sex, which were the reasons most people went to Wales. But then Manny had started acting up and her attention had gone back to him. She had witnessed him passing drugs to two men but otherwise he didn't tip his hand too much. Maybe next time. She wasn't here to watch for minor drug crimes, and she didn't want to blow her cover.

Diego had stayed out of sight since the court action. He knew they would be watching him, and he was not going to give them much to look at. So he stayed home with his mother, directing most of their business over a cell phone that he knew could not be tapped. Tomorrow he would be going to Chicago to meet the people George had worked with for so long. Diego was also making plans to get rid of the only witness the police had to the killings ... Larry.

Beth slept late on Saturday morning because she had tossed and turned most of the night. She had been within two feet of one of the men who had killed her husband and daughter, and it bothered her that she had not taken out that gun and killed him on the spot. She might never get another chance, and that was what bothered her the most. She was going to go down there again tonight, and this time if she was so lucky as to see him, she was going to make some kind of a move, even if it was wrong.

"Larry, how's it going?" Beth was sitting at the kitchen table with her coffee and a bottle of nail polish. She had the phone trapped between her neck and shoulder trying to dry her fingernails by fanning her hands.

"I called you last night, Bethy, but you were out. Or screening your calls."

Beth laughed. "I might have been outside talking to neighbors, Larry. When I did catch your call it was too late to call back. The contractor is coming Monday to make the modifications to the house, so I would say by Wednesday I should be ready for you if they will let you move."

"Everything's packed and ready. The boys at the police station are going to move my stuff."

Beth moved the phone to her hand. "I'm cleaning out the office today," she said. "Look, Larry, I can't get over today, but I just wanted to check in with you and let you know I'm looking forward to having you here with me."

"Thanks, Beth. You don't know how much this means to me."

She washed some clothes and broke down crying when one of Sarah's socks came out with the load of wash where it must have been stuck in the machine. She put the sock in the dryer and when it came out she put it in the pocket of her jeans.

The rest of the day was spent making the office ready for Larry's furniture. She moved a lot of the office furniture into the basement and covered it with a sheet.

By five thirty when she was finished she was tired and hungry. She would shower and get dressed, and then catch a sandwich on the way down to Wales.

Last night her clothes had not been right, she decided. She had dressed the way she thought most people that went downtown would dress, but had ended up looking more like a whore, in her opinion. Tonight it would be the designer blue jeans she had worn today and the other top she had bought.

Beth got to Wales later than last night and parked closer in a Park-and-Lock lot. She walked faster tonight; maybe she was more confident or just better pre-pared. That, and the fact that she had called her doctor this morning and he had prescribed some Valium for her depression. It seemed to help a lot.

Her only other worry was gone the minute she went in the door and saw Manny was sitting at the bar with a woman hanging on each arm.

There was a different bouncer tonight and that was good. She didn't want to be recognized as someone who had been here last night, if she could help it. Instead of choosing a table, tonight she saddled right up to the bar two stools down from Manny. Beth had a plan, but it would only work if she could talk to him, preferably alone.

For about an hour Manny drank and talked with the two women. Beth saw one of them slip him some bills, and he in turn reached into his pocket and then placed his closed hand in hers. Beth didn't know what he gave her, but she had a pretty good idea.

"I'm going to the watering hole," Manny announced and slid down off his stool and headed for the bathroom. This was the chance Beth was waiting for.

Trying to be as inconspicuous as possible, she walked around the dance floor and went to the women's restroom. She was going to have to time this just right. Looking up, she saw the security camera at the end of the hall so she went and stood under it where she couldn't be photographed. The men's bathroom was to her right and the women's to the left, just off two small hallways that teed off the main hallway.

Two black men who were obviously very drunk came out first and stopped to talk to each other, but just then the band started playing again and they took off. Neither of them gave Beth a second look.

Manny came out a few seconds later wiping his hands on a paper towel which he threw the floor. "Hi, baby," he said, stopping.

Beth started to talk but nothing was making sense. "I need to see you if ... if you have some moment. I mean, a moment."

"Whoa, baby, slow down," Manny said. He reached up and touched the side of her face with his fingers. "You need me for what, baby?" Manny had been peddling dope for a long time and he thought he knew what she wanted. "You need to get high, baby?" Here." He gave her two red pills.

"I need more," Beth said, "lots more."

Manny stared at her for a moment. "What's your name, baby?"

Beth tried to think fast. "Ellen," she said. Ellen had been her mother's name. My God, what was she doing?

"Aw, that's a sweet name, baby. What makes you think I got what you need?" Several people had gone by them on their way to the restrooms.

"A friend told me to see you," she said.

"Who's your friend, baby"?

"Diego," she said. She knew she was taking a big chance using his brother's name.

Manny was drawing an imaginary circle around the tip of her breast with his fore-finger without actually touching her. He was thinking and watching her eyes.

"Tell me what you want," he said.

"A thousand dollars worth of coke," she said.

"Let's go back to the bar and let me buy you a drink," Manny said. "I need to make a call."

Beth was sweating tacks. Was he calling Diego? She tried to hear the conversation but the band was too loud. She did hear the last four words, however, and that was all she needed. "Wales in an hour."

Back at the bar, his other two girls had left. Beth ordered a gin and tonic and Manny ordered a Corona. He threw a twenty on the bar.

Beth was afraid he was going to stay with her and talk, but another girl came over and they headed for the dance floor. Manny yelled back over his shoulder, "Hang tight, baby."

What was coming in an hour, Diego or some drugs for her? Beth had no idea, but if this thing went sour she didn't care. If Diego showed up she would take them both out, and. then herself. She was shaking like a leaf. She reached in her bag for her prescription bottle and shook out another Valium, washing it down with her drink. She was getting dizzy from mixing the booze and the drugs.

Manny ignored her until she saw him talking on his cell phone, looking at her from across the room. The booze, the loud music and the Valium were all combining to make her unstable. She felt like a cat in a room full of dogs. Her eyes darted around the room. She needed to get this over with tonight, if possible, as she doubted she would be able to stand another night like this. In fact, she was about one inch from bolting right now and getting out of here.

She tossed down the last of her drink, her third of the night. No sponge in the baggy tonight ... she had drunk them all. Reaching down on the floor for her bag she looked under her arm toward Manny. He was still on the phone and he was still looking her way. The walls seemed to be closing in on her. It was time to get while the getting was good. Grabbing the straps on her bag and slipping them over her shoulder, she turned to go and ran right into Manny.

"Let's go somewhere and talk, baby," he said.

"I've changed my mind," Beth said

Manny looked at her with defiance etched on his face. "I have the stuff on the way ... there is no changing your mind." He grabbed her arm and walked with her to the front door. She tried to resist but the last thing she wanted was a scene.

The bouncer was not there when they walked out. The only person who noticed them leaving was Kerry Hughes, the undercover officer. She still had a tab to pay and she held up her hand to get the waitress' attention.

Manny walked Beth around the corner of the building to a small parking lot. He clicked the remote door key in his hand and the lights flashed in a black Blazer.

"What are you doing?" Beth asked. "I'm not going with you. I don't even know you."

"Relax," Manny said. "Nobody's going to hurt you. We're going to wait a few minutes for your delivery. This ain't a department store, baby. You bought it and there are no returns."

Opening the driver's door, he said "In," and gave her a push, sliding in behind her and slamming the door behind him.

Beth was terrified, to put it mildly. She had bitten off more than she could chew. Her brilliant plan was being blown out of the water, and the only thing she could think of was getting to the gun in her bag, which now lay on the floor by her feet. He had her pinned, her back to the door, her knees together, and her feet on the bench seat.

She knew now that she was not going to shoot anyone. She didn't have what it took. She just wanted to point it at him and get away fast. She looked out the darkened windows but there was nobody else out here. It was just a small employee's lot. A single light bulb burned above a door in front of the car, reflecting the aged yellow brick of the building. There was a note on the door that said 'Attention' and that was all she could read. The rest of the letters were a blur.

"We're going to sit right here and wait for the stuff to arrive, and then you are going to pay me, and then I never want to see you again." He literally spat the words at her.

She was too scared to talk and just nodded her head.

Manny stared at Beth for moment and then an idiotic smile came over his face. He reached over her knees with his right hand, pushing the hand she had raised for protection aside. "In the meantime, let's you and I get to know each other, baby." Manny turned to face her. His right hand was on her breast as his left hand ripped at the buttons on her jeans. She could smell his rancid breath on her face as he tried to kiss her. Her knees were against his chest but he was stretching over them.

Detective Hughes had run outside, but there was no one in sight. She looked around the building into the employee lot, but the smoked windows in the Blazer made it look empty in the dark. She ran to the other side of the building, and then saw a couple down the street that she was sure was them getting in a green Acura and speeding off, the tires squealing on the asphalt.

Hughes stood helplessly. She kicked a trash can in anger, spilling the contents all over the sidewalk. Both of her fists were clinched at her side. Then she walked across the street to the unmarked Ford sedan next to a fire hydrant, with a parking ticket on its windshield. Throwing the ticket on the dash she drove off. It was time to call it a night.

Beth was afraid to fight too much for fear of what he would do, but she was fast losing the battle to keep her jeans and panties on. She was trying to hold them up with her left hand while her right-hand searched wildly for her bag on the floor. Manny was laughing like it was some kind of a sporting event they were engaged in. He had let go of her breast long enough to unbutton his own pants and for brief second Beth saw his swollen appendage sticking out of the top of his jeans.

"You are going to like this, baby. Maybe Manny will knock off a few dollars if you're good." He laughed hysterically at what he had said. Then grabbing her left arm and spinning her around so she was face down on the seat, he pulled her clothes down to her knees. She tried to scream, but he was pushing her face into the seat and she could hardly breathe, let alone scream. She could feel him probing her, trying to force himself inside her from behind.

Beth was trying to keep her legs together when, turning her head, she was looking at her bag on the floor. Her eyes had now adjusted to the dark and her left hand shot into the bag and grabbed the revolver. "Oh, my God," she groaned as he started to push himself inside of her.

With one super human effort she squirmed and flipped over on the seat. The gun came up and Manny eyes were wide with fear. His hands raised in surprise and surrender as he retreated against the opposite door but only for a second ... the second it took Beth to pull the trigger. The .357 bucked violently in her hand and the recoil sent the gun back into her face, slamming into her forehead. The noise was so loud that she was rendered momentarily deaf.

The bullet went in above the bridge of his nose and came out the top of his head along with a cloud of blood and brain matter and lodged in the roof of the car.

He fell forward on top of her with a loud groan, blood and gore draining onto her chest. Beth pushed him onto the floor and sat up, her feet on top of his back. She could feel his body still trembling through the bottoms of her feet and hear his raspy breathing.

He was lying on top of her bag, but seeing one strap, she yanked it out from under him. Pulling up her jeans, she scanned outside the windows and saw nothing. Beth stepped out the passenger's door and ran between cars to the back of the lot. She finished buttoning up her jeans and then ran as fast as she could down the alley, whimpering like a puppy filled with fear. Beth had one thought and one thought only: to get far away from this car as soon as she could.

The wig was falling over her eyes so she grabbed it and pulled it off, stuffing it in the bag as she ran. Finally she was at the end of the street and under a streetlight. Her white blouse was drenched with blood, and she could smell its coppery odor. She could also taste blood in her mouth and she gagged, sending a stream of vomit into the gutter.

Stepping back between two dumpsters behind a pizza shop, she took a second to gather what wits she had left. *I need to get rid of the blouse,* she thought. *I can't stand having his blood and gore all over me. I can't walk down the street to my car like this, but I can't walk down the street in just my bra either.*

Someone had left the back door open, and inside on a hook in the hall that led to the kitchen were some aprons. She could hear the noise of the café coming out the door. A young girl twirling a pizza crust in her hands walked by the hallway entrance to the kitchen, laughing and talking to someone that Beth couldn't see. A calico cat was sitting on top of the dumpster looking at her. Beth waited for a second and then reached in and grabbed the top apron and ducked back between the dumpsters and pulled her blouse over her head, throwing it in the dumpster and sending the cat scurrying away.

Slipping the red apron on and grabbing a greasy pizza box from the dumpster, Beth then walked around the corner and down the street.

It was four blocks to the lot where her car was parked and it was the longest four blocks she had ever walked. She carried the pizza box in front of her on top of her bag as if it were hot. She passed several couples walking on the sidewalk but no one paid any attention to the pizza delivery lady with some sauce spots on her face.

-22-

When Diego arrived at Wales the place was really rocking. Some of the band members had taken off their shirts and turned the volume up a few notches. It was almost impossible to talk and be heard inside the building. Wild disco lights were flashing like strobes on emergency vehicles, but much more brightly.

He stopped to ask the bouncer if Manny was in there, not wanting to go in himself unless he had to. The bouncer said, "I'll check for you, but I don't think he's here."

Diego stood just inside the door in the vestibule with his hands in his pockets scanning the crowd through the window glass.

"I'm sorry," the bouncer said. "The people he was with said he left about twenty minutes ago, but he said he'd be back. One of the guys said he had a woman with him. He didn't know who she was. Somebody new, I guess."

For Diego it was just another disgusting example of Manny's behavior. One they had come to expect, just another conquest. He wouldn't be happy until he'd laid every woman in town. Normally he wouldn't deliver drugs for Manny, or anybody else, but tonight no one was available and it was a big sale. Business had not been good lately because a lot of people knew the police were watching the Sanchez brothers closely.

He walked back out and stood on the sidewalk. He would wait for a few minutes but that was all. Then peeking around the corner of the building, he saw Manny's car.

He approached the car cautiously because common sense told him if Manny was in there he was getting laid, and he would not be happy with being interrupted. He stood by the driver's door for a second but there was no noise from inside. The locks were up though, and he never left the car unlocked, as he always had some drugs on board. The first thing that told him something was wrong was the shattered window on the driver's side. It was spider webbed but still intact. Also there was a dent in the roof where it looked like something had almost penetrated the metal from the inside. Diego stood back as he swung the door open, his hand on the gun in his pocket.

When Beth had left Manny the stench in the car had been of gunpowder and blood. Now the stench was the smell of death. Diego stared at the carnage in front of him, his mouth gaping. A low moan came from his throat and he moved back another step. "No, No, No," he said. He was looking at the soles of Manny's shoes and the lower half of his body. The dash was splattered with blood and gore. One of his hands was behind his back, the fingers squeezed into a fist. The other one was underneath him. Slowly he closed the door and went to the other side and opened the passenger side door. Manny's black hair shined wet in the light from under the dash but Diego soon saw it was from blood and bits of bone. He also saw that the back half of his head was gone, and that the puddle on the floor that Manny's face was submerged in was blood.

For a second he was overcome with grief and dropped to one knee on the asphalt. Afraid to touch him, his hands hovered over Manny as if he was giving him some kind of blessing. Then he stood up and his shock and grief turned to anger.

Wiping his tears on his sleeve, he reached to close the door, but something on the seat caught his eye. It was a little girl's anklet, with lace around the top and an animal of some kind embroidered on it. Diego reached in and, picking it up, held it to the roof light. The animal caricature on the sock was Mickey Mouse. He put it in his pocket.

He closed the door and looked around. A young couple was copulating in the back of another car across the lot. The back door was open and the man was standing outside the car while the woman lay on the back seat, her legs locked around him. He had his hands on the roof of the car and was thrusting into her and moaning. A bomb going off would not have been heard by either of them right now.

Diego turned and walked away a few steps. He had to think. There might be drugs in Manny's car and the cops would find them, but Manny was dead and there wasn't anything they could do to him. He had to get rid of what he had with him before he called the cops, or at least not be here. He went back to his car which was double parked in the street and pulled away, dialing Wale's number which he knew by heart as he drove.

"Wales," the female voice answered.

"There is a body in a car in the lot next to your building," he said and disconnected.

Beth was crying so hard she could hardly see to drive. She knew she was speeding, but she had to get home and get this mess off of her. If the police stopped her, they stopped her. She was convinced it was just a matter of time until they came after her, anyway, because she had to have been seen or left clues. She didn't know what, but so many things had happened that she couldn't even begin to sort it all out.

Block after block flew by, and twice she blew right through red lights. Luckily, no cross traffic was coming. Her steering wheel was sticky with the mess on her hands and she tried to wipe it off on the pizza shop apron she still had on.

At last she careened around the corner, the jeep's tires screeching, and into her driveway. She started into the garage before the door had even risen far enough and the roof racks on the car scrapped on the bottom of the door.

Beth sat in the car trembling while the door closed slowly behind her. Then she grabbed her bag and walked into the house, hitting the light switch next to the door that bathed the kitchen in bright white fluorescent light. Looking down, she noticed she had left spots of blood on the white floor. Then she looked in the mirror by the door behind her and screamed. She looked like she had been in the worst accident of her life. An ugly cut on her forehead was still oozing blood that was running down her cheek and dripping onto the floor.

Beth kicked off her shoes, and taking off the apron and laying it on the floor, she stripped, putting her clothes on top of the apron until she had only her panties on. Then rolling the whole works into a ball, she walked into the living room and stuffed it into the fireplace.

Next she went into the downstairs bathroom, which had a tub with a shower. She took off her underpants, tossed them in the toilet and flushed it, making sure they went down. Then she stepped into the tub and adjusted the shower spray. The water turned reddish at first and then gradually faded to its natural color as she scrubbed and rescrubbed. When she was convinced she was clean, she wrapped herself in a towel and went out into the kitchen and dug in her bag for the valium.

Beth went back into the bathroom and bandaged her forehead, which had now stopped bleeding, then, adjusting the plug in the tub, she filled it full of hot water and slid in. Before she did anything else she took the top of the bottle of valium and poured the pills out in her hand. She pushed them around with her forefinger counting them. There were twenty-five left. How easy it would be right now to just swallow them all and then she would slide beneath the water when she passed out, and it would be all over. She would be away from this mess and back with Mick and Sarah. *Thou shall not kill* rang out in her head.

"Too late," she giggled. "I already did."

Sobering again, Beth looked at the pills in her hand for a few moments, and then she popped two of them into her mouth and slid down low enough in the tub to get a mouthful of water and swallowed.

She sat back up long enough to put the rest of the pills back in the bottle and set it on the floor, then laid back again. For a while she just enjoyed the warmth of the water, closing her eyes as the valium slowly clouded her mind. She even poured some bath oil in with her. Then she remembered Manny penetrating her for a brief moment in his rape attempt and her fingers explored herself. She did not appear to be sore or injured. He could have had 'AIDS' or some other disease, she thought with a shudder, but the thought of him inside of her made her shudder even more. The valium was making her very sleepy so she pulled the plug and got out. She dried and wrapped herself in the same bath towel and went upstairs, stopping long enough to get her big fluffy white robe off the back of the door, then crawled into bed. Crying softly, she let sleep take over.

Dan Wicks stood back from the scene, watching his detectives work. He had spent a lot of nights like this in his career. Normally he wouldn't have been called to a murder scene when he was off duty, but he had a personal interest in this man, and the detectives knew it. They had called him at home the minute they identified the body. So far there was not a lot of evidence at the scene, other than Manny's registration in the glove compartment and his billfold with his driver's license in his back pocket. But a cop killer was dead. "What goes around comes around," was on the minds of a few of the detectives, but being the professionals that they were, they knew they had to try and solve the crime and apprehend the person who had done it.

The car was dusted for prints and the slug that had traveled through Manny's brain was recovered from between the roof liner and the outside steel of the car, but it was so badly damaged that it was doubtful it could be used by ballistics. The rest of the lot outside was searched, but with the exception of a few used condoms, they found only the normal garbage one would find in any parking lot. One condom in particular was taken and bagged because it seemed to have been recently discarded, although it was a long way from Manny's car. The lot was almost empty, as most of Wales' employees wouldn't park there because so many cars had been damaged or stolen.

Patrons in Wales who had seen the two leave described Beth as a thirty to thirty-five-year-old woman with too much makeup and jewelry, almost to the point of being over-dressed for a place like Wale's. She seemed to be very nervous and had kept to herself. She had black hair and was dressed in designer jeans and a white top with spaghetti straps. After confiscating the security camera films for that evening, the police were finished inside. A chaplain and a supervisor from the police department had been dispatched to the Sanchez house to break the news. One hour after police had arrived at the scene, Manny's body was taken to the coroner's office, the car was towed to a police impound lot for further testing, and Dan Wicks went home to bed. One of the cop killers had been taken care of.... there were two left.

Beth sat straight up in bed. The dream had been so real that for a moment she thought Mick was there in bed with her. In her dream he had come back and told her to get rid of the gun and the wig. "They have nothing else on you," he said. Then he had smiled and said how proud he was of her. He had kissed her so softly that it was as if a cotton ball had pressed against her mouth. Beth rubbed her lips with her fingertips.

He had seemed so real it was eerie, and right now she shivered as if a cold mist had come into the room, despite the fact it was over seventy in the house. She tried to think of what more had happened in her dream. Something told her there was more, but it remained on the edge of her subconscious just out of reach. Beth turned on the lamp, almost expecting to see Mick sitting on the edge of the bed or on the chair in the corner, but all that was there was some wash she hadn't put away.

The clock on the nightstand said 4:45. In an hour it would be daylight. She was wide-awake and feeling more relaxed than she had in a long time. As terrible as the things that had happened last night were, she didn't think about them. She could almost believe they hadn't happened, if not for the bandage on her forehead.

She went downstairs and turned on the lamp in the living room. The clothes she had thrown in the fireplace were still there behind the glass doors. Going out into the garage, Beth gathered kindling and two pieces of oak firewood from the pile Mick kept in the corner. She crumbled some newspaper, put the kindling into the fireplace and lit the fire, then sat on the cold tile floor in front of the fireplace and watched the fire grow on top of the clothing. The flames reflected off her moist eyes as she thought of the times she and Mick had lain in front of that fireplace and snuggled on cold winter nights while Sarah slept in her room at the top of the stairs. Two solitary tears spilled out and slid down her cheeks.

The fire was going good, so she put the two logs on and then went into the kitchen. She was hungry. Beth set out some left over ham and put two slices of bread in the toaster. It was then she saw her shoulder-bag sitting there. The beige bag was spattered with blood.

Being careful to not touch any blood, Beth emptied the bag on the tabletop. The first thing to fall out was the gun and it scared her as it clunked on the formica top. It, too, had blood on it and still smelled like gunpowder. She took it to the sink and wiped it off with a paper towel, then flipped open the cylinder and extracted the one empty shell casing.

She examined the wig for blood, and when she found traces she washed it in hot water and then put it on the top of a kitchen chair to dry. The rest of the things were clean and she left them on the tabletop, while the bag went into the fireplace with the rest of her burning clothes and the paper towels. That done, Beth sat down and ate. She was starved.

When she was finished she went upstairs and dressed, putting on a new pair of white jeans and a red and white checkered blouse she hadn't worn for ages. She pirouetted in front of the dresser mirror. *Not bad for a middle-aged widow,* she thought. She also packed a small bag, as she was going to be gone for a day or two.

Beth took her bag to the car and then remembered the sticky steering wheel. She went back in and put hot water and soap in a pan, and coming back out scrubbed everything, including the seat she had sat on.

She had two stops to make before she went to her dad's, the first being to an all night florist. The sun was just coming up in the cemetery. Beth had not been back here since Sarah's funeral but she drove right to the graves without hesitation. She would never forget where they were. She shut off the car and walked across the lawn tentatively as if she was afraid to approach them. The early morning dew was collecting on her tennis shoes and she could feel her socks getting wet.

Stopping first at Sarah's grave, she prayed that her daughter was in God's arms, away from all pain and suffering. With her hand she brushed away the grass clippings that had accumulated on her marker, then put a solitary rose next to it, after she had first held it too her face and wet it with a tear. Then stepping over to

Mick's grave, Beth said out loud, "I have something for you, too, darling," and pressed the empty 357 casing into the earth next to his marker.

Beth surprised her dad as she was there just in time to take him to church. The drive had been relaxing and she felt refreshed. She told him she was returning his car.

There were no beatitudes in the homily this time. No lectures on killing anyone, just a sermon on being more generous to the church. She obliged the priest with a folded hundred dollar bill.

In the late afternoon while her dad napped on the couch, Beth took the wig upstairs and put it back in the dresser. Then she took Brandy and Rascal and walked down through the familiar woods to the river where she had come so many times before. She carried a small bag over her shoulder much like the one she had burned the night before that held the revolver.

Beth stood and watched the river current for a while. This time she refused to allow herself to be nostalgic. Reaching into the bag, she took the gun out and threw it into the middle of the river. Brandy jumped in to retrieve it but Beth laughed and called her back. Now all had been taken care of. That night she beat her dad in scrabble for the first time.

-23-

It had been a bad night for Rosemary Sanchez to start with. First she and George had argued for two hours about him moving out of the house and leaving the business, and now this police chaplain standing at her door was the final straw.

He told her as sympathetically as possible, "I am sorry to tell you this, Mrs. Sanchez, but your son Manny has been found shot to death in a car outside of Wales night club. We are investigating the death as we speak. Your son's body has been taken to the county coroner's office for an autopsy."

Rosemary had let out a scream loud enough to be heard a block away and then she collapsed. The officer and the chaplain tried to assist her, but she angrily slapped at their hands and rose to her knees hissing, "Get out of my house you filthy bastards. You killed him as surely as you killed Raul, and I hope you all rot in hell. I will make you sorry you ever heard of the Sanchez family." Rosemary stood up and grabbed a plaster statue of a horse from a shelf and flung it in the direction at the retreating officers where it smashed on the sidewalk, and then once again she collapsed sobbing on the floor.

George heard the commotion and started down the stairs, but seeing the police car out the window, he had stayed on the landing until they left. He had heard what the chaplain had said to his mother, but didn't want to be seen. Now he ran to his mother, but she turned on him, her face masked in agony. "Go. Go, you son of a bitch, and never darken my doorstep again. Had you been taking care of your brother, this would have never happened. You are a traitor. You're a traitor to me, to your father, and to the whole family."

George stood with his hands at his sides. This was just as he feared it would be. He walked back up the stairs and faced Maria, who was standing at the top holding Anna.

"Manny?" she asked.

"Yes, Manny, and next it will be us if we don't leave. We go tomorrow."

"But what about your brother's funeral? Aren't you going to stay for that?"

"I am no longer a part of this family. You heard Momma. I never should have listened to her in the first place, Maria. Raul was killed because he was trying to kill police officers. He deserved to die. I don't know why Manny was killed, and I don't care. It was just a matter of time for him. He was no good." George had tears in his eyes and he took Anna from Maria and buried his face in the toddler's hair and cried. Maria hugged both of them.

Diego sat in his car for a long time on a hill that overlooked the river. The car was idling and the radio was playing soft Mexican music from a Latin station in town. He was not crying, but his face showed deep sadness. He dragged deeply on the cigarette he was smoking and then lowered the window, and flicked it out into blackness, where it landed in a shower of sparks.

He had expected retaliation from the police but not from her. What confused him right now was why she would have left that anklet. He flipped on the dome light and looked at the sock, noting again the tiny Mickey Mouse emblem on the side and the Disney tag inside. She wanted him to know it was her, and she was telling him he was next. That could be the only answer.

His cell phone ringing jogged him back to reality. "Diego," his mother wailed. "Come home. Manny is dead."

"I'll be right there, Momma," he said and starting the sleek silver Porsche he drove slowly home.

Round three would be coming up, he thought, *and Motrin's wife would be the loser this time.* She wasn't going to get a chance to kill him, he was convinced of that.

Captain Wicks leaned back in his chair and listened to his chief of detectives. It was Sunday afternoon and they were in his office.

"We have very few things to go on, Captain, but here is what we have. The car was full of prints but the only ones we got a hit on were Manny's and some sleaze ball named Charles Kidd, who we know sells dope for Manny and drives a cab over in the northeast. The slug out of the roof liner was a .357 Magnum but that's all we're going to know about it. Between Manny's skull and the roof of the car it was shattered pretty bad. We have some photos of the woman he was reported to have left with from the security camera in the restroom hallway. It looks like she was aware of the camera, because as she came down the hall she kept her right hand in front of her face. None of the other cameras picked her up. She pretty much stayed at the bar. The bartender swears she was in there the night before, also, but they taped over the security tape so there are no pictures for that night."

He handed Wicks three pictures to look at.

"Look at the ring on her right hand, Ron. That's kind of an unusual ring. Looks like a friendship ring of some kind." Dan pointed to the picture he was talking about. "See if the lab can blow that up for us so we can see it better."

"Sure thing Captain," said the Chief. He put the picture in his shirt pocket. "The other thing we have is a witness who saw a man at Manny's car about the time this would have happened. Now mind you she's not the best witness, because she's a prostitute who was servicing some john in the back seat of his car when she saw this guy. But she is a friend of Manny's and she did come forward. She won't tell us the name of the john, because she says he didn't see anything. He was too busy poking her. The odd thing is, she says she saw the guy at the driver's door first, and then he went around the car and opened the other door. He just stood and looked for while and seemed quite upset. She is sure that he did not shoot anything or anybody. Not while she was there anyway."

"Now listen to this, too," Ron went on. "About an hour ago a guy from a pizza shop called and said he found a bloody white blouse lying in their dumpster. He found it when they brought out some boxes. Normally he wouldn't have paid much attention what was in the dumpster, but they have two dumpsters and that one is reserved for cardboard only. The lab is running some tests on it, but it sure looks like the one that gal was wearing in the pictures we have."

Wicks, who had been listening intently with his hands clasped behind his head, spoke up. "So if she dumped her blouse she must have been running around in her bra or less, if she didn't have one on. Have you checked to see if anyone saw a half naked female running around?"

"We have, and no one we talked to saw anything like that."

"Go back to that pizza shop, Ron, and see if they're missing any jackets or clothes. Maybe she just stayed in the alleys and no one saw her, I don't know, but let's keep checking. It's Sunday and I'm going home." Wicks stood up and grabbed his hat and jacket. "Keep me posted, Ron."

His chief detective nodded his head.

Dan turned at the door and looked at his detective again. "I thought we had an undercover watching Sanchez down at that club."

"We did, Dan. She claims they left the place so fast she couldn't get out the door fast enough to follow them."

Wicks shook his head slowly in dismay and said. "See you tomorrow."

Beth was back by dark on Sunday night. Walt dropped her off at the curb, declining her invitation to stay, saying he had to get right back as he had a doctor's appointment in the morning. She still wasn't sure what to do about the dog. She had planed on bringing Brandy back, but at the last second asked her dad if she could leave her for a few more weeks until things settled down. Walt just smiled and quipped, "You can leave her forever for all I care. She's good company for me and Rascal."

Beth had a contractor coming in the morning so she had some things to get ready for him. The plan was for Larry to move in on Friday morning. Most of Larry's furniture was going into storage and some of his cop friends were coming over to help him out with the move.

Next Monday Larry would start his training at the dispatch center where he would eventually be working. In a way it would be a relief for him to get away from the seamy side of life he had experienced in Homicide. He was really looking forward to a fresh start. Several people in the detective bureau had held Larry's sexual orientation against him. It was always there just under the surface, and he could sense the jokes behind his back. Never blatant, but they were there.

On Tuesday morning a small crowd gathered while Manny Sanchez was laid to rest. Unlike the huge funeral they had held for Raul, only family and a few close friends were there. Rosemary Sanchez hid behind a thick black veil that fell from a wide brimmed hat. For the most part she was silent in her grief and her intense anger. Hiding from the prying eyes of those who attended, she wore a black flowing shawl over a black pant suit. She leaned on Diego from time to time for comfort and support, her hands nervously rolling and unrolling the Order of Service. It was almost as if she could not wait for it to be over so she could get back to her reclusive life. Her anger was not only for those who had taken her son's life; it was also for her oldest son who, true to his word, did not attend.

At the cemetery the heavens opened up and it rained hard … so hard that only those under the canvas shelter stayed, while the others beat a hasty retreat. It mattered little to Rosemary, who could think of only one thing. Vengeance.

On Tuesday afternoon Wicks met once more with his detectives. The autopsy results were in, as were the lab tests. Ron Robertson, the chief of detectives, stood in front of large flip chart on which he had written several sheets with facts and figures. He had a laser pointer in his hand, and stood with his other hand in his pocket jingling some change and keys.

The Deputy Chief of the department and several other detectives from the bureau sat around the conference table.

"As we thought, the cause of death was a massive gunshot wound to the head." Ron flipped a morgue picture on the screen to show what he was talking about.

"The bullet entered just under the left eye and exited out the top of his head in the back along with about twenty five percent of his brain tissue. It hit the roof of the vehicle just above the driver's door and lodged there under the headliner. From that trajectory, it looks like he had been leaning over and whoever shot him had been under him. The window was broken as a result of his head hitting it, so the shot knocked him back pretty far. Powder marks on his face and one hand attest to the fact that the gun had been no more than a foot away from him when fired. There was no casing found in the car or around it, so it must have come from a revolver or it was picked up."

He showed another picture from the morgue. "By the way, the slug was of no use to ballistics. Not much left of it." Ron stopped to take a drink of his coffee and then continued. "There were signs that he had been engaged in sexual activity. His pants were open and his penis was out. There was evidence of vaginal fluids on the end of his penis, but only the very end, which would indicate incomplete penetration. Maybe he was interrupted. There were also traces of blood that were not his and could have come from menstrual flow or forced sex. He had not ejaculated. There was enough vaginal fluid to do a DNA sample, and that's being done. He had traces of cocaine and marijuana in his blood along with enough alcohol to be legally drunk. In his car, the drugs that we found were enough to constitute a felony. More than a casual user would normally have had. "Yes, Cory?" Cory Chamberlain, one of the detectives who had been at the scene raised his hand.

"Ron, was there any other evidence from his sexual partner?"

"Well, I am not sure if 'partner' is a good word but yes, we have three pubic hairs that were found that were not his. Two were on his penis and one was on his hand. They're also being checked. Any other questions before I go on?" He looked around the table. Seeing no other hands raised, he continued. "The blouse that was found behind the pizza shop had Sanchez's blood on it, but it also had blood from someone else. Right now we are betting it was the blood of the person who wore it. The pizza shop is missing an apron from the back of the shop and we're thinking that's what she used to cover up with. Especially since a witness called to say her and her husband had seen a young woman walking down the sidewalk carrying a pizza. She didn't think much of it until they got even with her and she could see there was a cut on her head, and that she had only a bra on under the apron. She also had a shoulder bag, which would have been unusual for a delivery person. But get this ... She was described as having very short red hair. Yes Cory" He had raised his hand again.

"Any prints, Ron?"

"You mean in the car?" Ron asked.

Cory nodded.

"Just Manny Sanchez's and one of his dealers'. There was nothing else that matched anything in the data base." He looked at Cory for a moment as if he was expecting something else, but Cory was silent.

Wicks raised his right forefinger as if he had a question and Ron said, "Go ahead, Captain."

"Did you get those pictures blown up, Ron?"

"I did, Sir." He sorted through some papers and came up with three eight by ten pictures, which he set up on the easel holding the flip chart. The first showed the woman when she first walked into the hallway. It was the only unobstructed shot they had, but she was turned slightly, looking behind her as if she was afraid someone was following her. There was no mistake about the blouse. It was identical to the one found in the dumpster.

The second picture was of the woman's backside. She was standing almost directly under the camera, with her head bent down as if she was looking at her shoes. It showed one incriminating feature ... short hairs on the back of her neck which appeared to be lighter than the rest of her hair.

Cory poked Wicks with his elbow and said, "Gal has a nice ass, don't you think?"

Wicks gave him a sick smile.

"This last picture is the one you wanted, Captain." Ron said, putting it up.

It was a blowup of her right hand showing the ring Dan had commented on. The ring had two tiny cherubs blowing trumpets on either side of a heart. They looked at it for a few seconds and Dan Wicks seemed to be deep in thought, but then he slowly shook his head no, as if he had abandoned the idea, and walked over and put the second picture back up. He pointed to a part of tag hanging out of the bottom of her hairline. "She's got a wig on boys, and you know what, Cory? She does have a nice ass."

They all laughed and the meeting was over.

-24-

For the second time in less than a week Mick had come to her in a dream. Beth sat up in bed clutching her pillow to her chest. Her hands went to her face and found it wet. *My God* she thought, *I have been crying in my sleep.*

Like last time, she could remember only snippets of the dream, but felt that there was so much more just out of the grasp of her waking mind. Mick had seemed more business-like this time. More like a father than her lover. Last time he had kissed her so softly she still could remember it, but this time they seemed to be talking across some distance. There was nothing but a black void between them and try as she may, she just couldn't get any closer. But as unexplainable as that was, it was his concern for her well-being that puzzled her.

Beth remembered something about her rings. She looked down at her hands and the two rings she wore. Her wedding set and the friendship ring Mick had given her on their first date. She was in some kind of danger. She could just feel it. Now she knew how he felt when he had killed Raul. Was the hunter becoming the hunted?

Her arms were covered with goose bumps and she shivered. The clock on the nightstand said 4:45. Wasn't that the same time she had awakened the last time she dreamed of Mick? She switched on the lamp and put on her white bathrobe from the end of the bed.

The construction crew would be here at seven so she thought she might as well get up and make coffee. They had started yesterday morning and gutted the bathroom. Today they were supposed to put it back together, making it more user-friendly for someone in a wheel chair. There would be a lift for the tub and a higher toilet stool, as well as a lower sink and vanity top, and an assortment of grab bars. They had also made a ramp for the back steps that Larry could use from the garage. In time he would be trained to drive again using hand controls.

The sun was just coming up in the east and there wasn't a cloud in the sky. Two humming birds hovered over the empty feeder outside the window. It had not been filled since Mick's death and she felt their disappointment. She made a mental note to get it filled. Staring out the kitchen window and daydreaming as she ran water in the coffee carafe, her gaze fell to her hands and her rings again. The dream? What was it all about?

Shortly after the construction people left later that day, Beth dressed for her dinner with Laurie. They were going to a small bistro that Laurie frequented a lot.

"You are going to love the cuisine," she had told Beth.

The café was small but homey. The owners had first intended it to be a coffee bar but they had added on when the store next door went out of business, and now they did food, also.

Laurie's face lit up the moment she saw her friend come in the door. Beth, too, broke into a wide smile and the two old friends embraced before they sat down and ordered large cups of hot, steaming chicory coffee covered with foam. They had so much to catch up on.

The special that night was poached salmon that was to die for, and it was the best meal Beth had eaten in a long time. They followed it with more coffee until she could feel the caffeine buzz making her already short hair stand up. Then they went for a walk in a nearby park and stood on a stone arched bridge over a quiet pond.

"Laurie, I want you to know how much you comforted me in my hours of need. I still have a lot of healing to do, but it is getting better. Most days now I think of living instead of dying. Something I contemplated and I want you to know that. I know there are rough days yet to come, and I hope that I am enough of a survivor to face them."

Then looking down as if to avert Laurie's concerned gaze, Beth said, "We all need this, Laurie," she said, gesturing to the park and the pond. "We all need a quiet pond from time to time."

Laurie squeezed Beth's hand and through her tears, said, "Thank you. Not for what you said as much as just for being my friend."

Beth went on to talk about Larry moving in and how she wanted to get back to teaching in the fall. They reminisced about old times and all the fun they had

had together. Then Laurie broke the news. "I have another new friend, Beth, and I want you to meet him sometime. He and I are thinking of moving in together."

Beth squealed with delight for her friend.

The rest of the week was spent finishing the preparations for Larry's arrival. Boozer and Dougie, two of Larry's friends, made countless trips bringing in some of his furnishings, and Beth did the decorating. She went shopping for new curtains for the bathroom and the bedroom. His car was brought over and put in the garage.

Larry could not wait to get out of the rehabilitation center. He had been a good student and was becoming quite proficient with his new equipment. A week from Monday he would start training at the dispatch center for his new job, and he was actually looking forward to it.

On Friday morning Beth spent a little extra time in the shower, shaving her legs and getting ready for her appointment with the OBGYN. Her breasts actually had quit hurting for the most part, and she considered canceling the appointment. But then remembering what had happened to her mother, she thought, what the heck.... she needed the peace of mind of knowing that everything is all right.

She had gone to the same doctor for a long time, beginning with her pregnancy with Sarah, but had not seen her now for a few years. Maybe she was getting to the age now where she should go more often, she thought.

There were just a couple women in the office, one young and very pregnant, and one older woman who seemed to be quite nervous. She was flipping through magazines, and then getting up and checking with the receptionist every few minutes to see how much longer it would be.

Dr. Rebecca Tully was in her early fifties, an age where patients start to feel more comfortable with a doctor. They figure they are old and experienced enough to know what they are doing, but not too old to be on top of the latest medical techniques.

A nurse she had not seen here at the office before showed Beth to her examination room. She gave her the traditional paper gown and a container for a urine sample, and led her to the small connecting bathroom, smiling and saying, "The doctor will be with you shortly."

It was cold in the small room and Beth crossed her arms to ward off the chill. A vanity in the corner had a white top and sink. A glass shelf above it holding an array of medical supplies was the only hint that she was in a medical facility. A variety of prints depicting old Saturday Evening Post magazine covers with doctor themes hung on the walls.

Dr. Tully never forgot a patient and smiled enthusiastically as she came in the room. "Beth, good to see you," she said. Then sobering, she took Beth's hand and said, "I am so sorry for your loss."

Beth gave a weak smile. "It has been hard to deal with," she said. "There were times when I didn't think I could."

"Let's hope better times are ahead," Dr. Tully replied. "Now it says here that you've had some tenderness in your right breast for the last few weeks," she said, getting down to business.

"Actually, there has been some soreness in both of them, but the right one was worse. I must admit they seem better now than before. I guess with my mother dying of breast cancer, I always have that in the back of my mind."

"And its something you should worry about," the doctor said. She had dropped the top of Beth's gown and was examining her breasts as she talked.

"You haven't bumped or hurt yourself?" The doctor asked.

Beth shook her head.

"How long has it been since your last period?" The doctor asked.

"Well, it was while we were planning our trip to Disney World...." Time had been a blur to her lately. Beth tried to think of dates. Today it was one month since Mick and Sarah had been shot. Oh, my God ... could it be that she was pregnant? She had never been very regular with her periods, but.... "Yes," she said. "It has been nearly six weeks."

Beth's mind was spinning with thoughts. *The last time she had been pregnant she had been really sick with morning sickness, but she hadn't had any of that. If she had this time it would have tipped her off more than anything. Also, the last time she was pregnant she didn't remember having sore breasts. Oh, maybe later in her pregnancy, but not in the first few months.*

Dr. Tully had picked up the phone and dialed the lab, asking for the results of Beth's urine sample. A moment later she turned and said with a smile, "Just as I thought, Beth, you're pregnant. It's early, that's for sure, but I think your sore breasts are the result of your pregnancy."

Beth said nothing for a moment. Then the tears came when she realized what had happened. Her husband and daughter had been ripped away from her, but now she was getting something back.

Dr. Tully had tears in her eyes, also, and the two women held each other for a few minutes.

Finally Dr. Tully held Beth out at arms length and said, "Congratulations, Beth. You're going to be a mother, once more."

The rest of the visit was a blur. Beth remembered getting dressed and making another appointment for a month later. She would have a more complete examination then, including an ultrasound. She vaguely remembered the doctor cautioning her about her diet and getting enough rest.

Then she wandered back through the office. The older woman was still there, looking more irritated than before. There were a couple of new women who had not been there when she went in, and one of them had a small child with her who was throwing a fit while the woman tried to talk to the receptionist. They all saw Beth's tears and wondered if it was tears of joy or sadness that were running down her cheeks.

For Beth it was a little of both.

Diego had watched the house for two nights now. He had to be sure she was alone. If he parked one street over, he could watch the kitchen and the living room from between the houses. The driveway of the house he was parking at had a tall hedge on one side and was partially obscured by a tree on the other, so people coming down the street could not see his car until they were even with the end of the driveway. The house was up for sale and empty. Last night a real estate agent had shown up while he was parked there and he pretended that he was looking at the property, even going so far as to make an appointment to see it the next week ... an appointment he had no intention of keeping.

He had shown the anklet he had taken from Manny's car to his mother the day after the funeral. They were on the same page in thinking that Beth had done it, especially since his snitch at the police department confirmed that Mick and his family had been at Disney World on vacation.

Diego was on a power kick now that he and his mother ran the drug business and George was gone. He had gone to Wales and talked to people who were there the night Manny was killed. No one had ever seen this woman before. They said she didn't look right. She surely didn't look like she belonged in Wales.

The thing that cinched in his mind that it was Motrin's wife was the wedding rings she had forgotten to take off and the anklet. The waitress at Wales had told him about the rings. It all added up. Diego was doing a better job of investigating this case then the police department, he thought. But then, the people at Wales would talk to him, and they hated the cops. And the woman certainly had a motive, that was for sure. He had felt bad about the little girl when he first heard about her, but those stupid cops who take their kids to work with them should know better. Right now he was not thinking so much about revenge, although there would be some. This was a case of survival.... he had to take her out before she took him out. Saturday night was the plan, but if not, he would work something out.

Beth drove around for a while after leaving the doctor's office, trying to sort out her thoughts. In the last month her daughter and husband had been murdered, their friend shot and paralyzed, and she had been driven by grief and depression to coming ever so close to taking her own life. Also, last Saturday night she had been raped ... well, she had not actually been raped, but it had been too close for comfort ... and had killed a man, and now, she was sure, the police were hunting her for that crime. What else could happen to her? All in all, she had been pushed well past the breaking point.

But now things were suddenly different. Something good had come her way. Something positive had happened in her life. In a way she had been living for Larry and her dad, but now she had something more important to live for ... her and Mick's baby. She smiled nervously at the thought.

Beth reached into her purse and took out the bottle of valium she had been saving for her demise. Taking the cap off, she poured them into her hand. Then lowering the car window she let them filter through her fingers one by one to the pavement below.

-25-

It was uncanny … another dream involving Mick and the clock, once more, said 4:45. As before, she didn't remember much, but he had brought up the rings again and sounded happy about the baby. This time Beth had not seen an image of Mick at all, just heard a voice in the darkness that seemed to come across a deep, dark abyss that she could not cross. She felt sad because something told her that this was the last time he would be able to come to her. She turned on the lamp and stared at her hands. Her rings were gone. Beth turned the covers back and there they were, lying in the sheets. She had removed them in her sleep. Picking them up, Beth put them in her jewelry box on top of her dresser. For the time being she would leave them off.

Two things were happening today that Beth had looked forward to. Larry was moving in this morning, and Dan Wicks had called last night and told her he would be stopping by early with Mick's life insurance check.

She made coffee and put a bagel in the toaster. The sun was just coming up and it looked like a bright sunny day. Just a few wispy clouds filtered the early morning rays.

A jogger ran by and through the open window she could hear his tennis shoes squeaking on the street out front and his labored breathing. Mick had loved to run in the early morning, and when they were first married they would run together and then shower together afterwards. Sometimes it would lead to love-making, but more often than not they would just hold each other and enjoy the warm wet embrace.

A tear ran from the corner of her eye and down her cheek. She was happy about the baby, but sad that Mick was not here to share her joy. The smell of her burning bagel brought her back to reality. "Shit," she said, and threw the two black bagel halves in the garbage. She would have some yogurt instead.

Dan Wicks had been to the house before, but it had been a while and he had gotten off on the wrong exit. Quickly he realized his mistake, corrected it, and was now pulling up to the house. He was nervous because he really didn't know Beth that well. *I hope she's up,* he thought. It was just about 8 a.m., and normally he would not have come this early, but it was Saturday and he, like so many others, wanted to get out of town and go up north to the cabin.

Beth heard the car in the driveway and was at the door when Dan rang the bell. She was wearing her faded blue Levis and one of Mick's old blue shirts. She was painting the bathroom for Larry.

Beth spoke first. "Good morning, Dan. Come on in. I would shake your hand but mine are full of paint," she smiled. "I don't know if you heard or not, but Larry Sorenson is going to be staying here for a while until he finds something manageable. His apartment was not handicapped accessible, and I can use the company."

"I can only stay a minute, Beth." Wicks made no comment about Larry. "I wanted to get this check to you, and you need to sign these papers." He was staring at her hair. "You cut off your beautiful long hair."

"Yes, well, it is summer, and this is so much cooler. Most years I've had it cut before the weather gets warm, but just not this short. I thought I'd try it." She brushed her hand over her head. "Do you like it?" She was talking over her shoulder while she washed her hands in the kitchen sink.

She seemed to be in a much better mood than when he had last seen her, but that was understandable. Dan set the papers on the table and was holding a pen in his hand when Beth turned to face him, wiping her hands on a paper towel. The check for one hundred thousand dollars lay on top of the pile of papers. Beth picked it up and studied it for a second.

"This is the state money, Beth. There is another one hundred thousand coming from the federal policy, but it will be a while, yet." He was trying to see her hands but she still had them wrapped in the paper towel. At last she threw the towel into the wastebasket and reached for the pen with her right hand. *No rings,* he thought. *Just a white ring on her skin where they once had been. I wonder how she got that cut in her eyebrow.*

"I know this is a small amount for Mick's life, but I hope it helps you get back to a normal life." Dan saw the tears forming in her eyes. There was an awkward silence for a moment.

Then Beth said simply, "Thank you," and signed the papers.

"I really have to get going, Beth. As soon as I get that other check I'll get in touch with you. Take care." He reached up and touched her shoulder and she touched his hand.

Smiling weakly, she watched him walk out the door and down the driveway. Beth gave him a small finger wave as he backed out.

In all of his years as a detective, Dan Wicks greatest successes had come about because he had acted on a hunch, an inner voice that told him that something was not right, and in this case that inner voice was, unbeknownst to him, amazingly accurate. He knew that the person who killed Manny Sanchez had to be someone with a motive, something Beth certainly had. She would have had access to a weapon and quite possible knew how to use it. The gun in this case was a .357 caliber. Mick's service weapon, which he had delivered to her, was a nine-millimeter, so that didn't check out. But Mick could have had other guns. Most cops do. Her hair cut was suspicious, also. He was almost certain that the woman in the photos was wearing a wig and the long hair that she had had the last time he saw her would not fit under a wig. Not that wig, anyway.

When he met with her after Mick's death, and at the funeral, she had had a wedding ring on. He had noticed that. He hadn't noticed the other ring on her right hand, but the white mark on her finger said there had been one there. Then, there was the cut on her head and the blood on the blouse. That could be checked out. In fact, it was being checked out. Dan smiled as he thought about it all. He had been frustrated by the lack of evidence in Mick and Sarah's killings, and his inability to make a case out it. He, too, had seen the smirk on the Sanchez's attorney's face as the judge refused to make a case out of what they had. She had not believed Larry's eyewitness testimony. Now the shoe was on the other foot and he wasn't sure what he was going to do about it. He was sure about one thing though, and that was that he was going fishing.

Larry's friends brought him to the house around noon with most of the stuff he had picked out at his apartment. They spent the afternoon in the back yard, drinking beer and joking around. Around three they all left and it was just Larry and Beth for the first time. He had not eaten all day, so Beth made an early supper for them while he unpacked and put his stuff away.

After supper while she stacked the dishes in the dishwasher, Beth asked Larry if he would be all right if she went up to her dad's for the night. "I want to pick Brandy back up before she overstays her welcome. I just might stay the night, if you think you'll be all right alone."

"Look, Beth, I appreciate so much what you're doing for me, but right now my goal is to be as self-sufficient as I can be. I learned a lot at the rehab center and I'll be just fine. Please don't let my being here make you change your life style."

Beth smiled and said thanks. "I need to tell you something that I haven't told anybody else. It's hard for me to do because I dreamed about the day I would have been telling Mick, not a friend. I'm pregnant Larry. I just found out yesterday."

She sat in her chair and the tears came again. Larry wheeled himself next to her, and taking her dinner napkin, wiped her face. "I have never been happier for anybody, Beth. It's a new beginning for you." Then changing the subject to something lighter, he said, "Do me a favor, would you? Take my car. It needs to be driven. Outside of being driven over here, it's just been sitting for over a month, and it'll be a while before I can get it rigged so I can drive it."

"Sure, Larry."

She didn't leave for the farm until almost dark. She called her dad and told him she was coming and he said he would wait up for her. Larry's sports car made her feel young again. The car had a deep throaty roar whenever she punched the accelerator and was much more responsive than her jeep.

The evening air was cool and the further she got from the metropolitan area the fresher it smelled and the quieter it was after the traffic thinned out. She rode with the car window down, her arm out the window. There was a clearer view of the moon and the stars, and everything just seemed more vivid. Maybe her enhanced senses had something to do with her more positive state of mind, but whatever it was, it was soothing.

His first night on his own gave Larry a feeling of independence that he needed badly. He thought he would try the shower stool that had been placed in the bathtub for him. At the rehab canter he had always had help getting in and out of the tub. Now it was time for him to do it by himself.

He went into the bedroom and managed to get his clothes off, then gathering a clean set of underclothes, rolled into the bathroom. He parked his wheelchair next to the tub and got ready to make the switch from his chair to the tub. The tile was slippery and every time he tried to get the leverage to move from his wheelchair, he would slide away from the tub. It took five attempts and left him weak and perspiring but at last he sat in the plastic chair staring at his thin useless legs. The same legs that had once climbed mountains and swum across rivers were now just dead weight appendages that were more trouble than they were worth.

Controls for the water flow were built into the sidewall of the tub enclosure, so he could easily turn them on and adjust the water. There were two nozzles, one on each end of the tub, so he washed front and back at the same time. The warm water felt wonderful, but the thing that warmed him the most was that he was doing this for himself.

Getting out of the tub was difficult, too, but it went much more smoothly than getting in the tub, using the knowledge he had gained. He dressed in clean underwear and a short robe and went to the kitchen and made coffee. Then he wheeled himself into the living room and sat beside the fireplace. Beth had left paper, kindling and a few logs where he could reach them. He took a shovel from the fireplace accessories and smoothed out the ashes in the bottom of the firebox to build his fire.

There were some copper-colored items in the ashes that caught his eye and he retrieved them with the shovel and held them in the palm of his hand. They were buttons, copper buttons, the kind used on denim jeans. He dug some more and found some u-shaped metal pieces that looked like they might have come from an under-wire bra.

Why would Beth burn her clothes here in the fireplace? Why not just throw them in the trash if she didn't want them? Larry put the buttons in his robe pocket and threw the metal strips back in the firebox. For some reason having a fire no longer interested him.

Larry made himself a drink and watched television until eleven p.m., and then decided to call it a night. As inviting as his bed looked, he thought maybe he would just sit here in his chair for a while and watch out the window. The back yard was well illuminated tonight by the full moon in the cloudless sky.

Beth was bringing Brandy back tomorrow and it would be nice to have the pup around for companionship. He had grown found of the dog when he cared for her when Beth and Mick had been on vacation. He thought about Beth being pregnant and how maybe that was what she needed … to have a purpose in her life once more. He was genuinely happy for her, even though he knew it would be the end of their living arrangement.

Diego was on edge. He had killed before without much emotion, but this one was going to feel good. This bitch and her husband had ruined his family. With two of his brothers dead and George bailing out, he was struggling to hold it all together. Even his mother had talked about selling the house and moving to Chicago.

When he drove by Beth's house about four-thirty in the afternoon the garage door had been open and he had seen Beth's car parked inside. He went to Wales for supper and a few drinks to pass some time. He was still looking for clues in Manny's death, but nobody was saying anything he didn't already know.

When the band took a break at ten thirty, he left. He drove around for a while, going over his plan once more. Diego had a manufactured alibi that he had paid handsomely for. It was from ten to midnight, so he had two hours to get in, get the job done and get out. The weapon of choice this time would be a knife. He had a 9-millimeter automatic in the back of his pants, if it came to that.

At eleven, he parked his car a few blocks away in front of a darkened house and started jogging back to Beth's house. When he was even with her driveway, he ducked quickly around the back of the garage. He was preoccupied with the garage service door and getting in, or he would have noticed the handicapped ramp built next to the new deck. It had not been there the last time he was, but he missed it. He also missed seeing Larry, sitting in the dark and watching him from his wheelchair.

Larry could not believe his eyes. One minute he was looking at the trees gently moving in the evening breeze and then this intrusion came into view. He had been dozing, but something told him to open his eyes, and there it was. He had to lean forward, his forehead almost against the glass, to see that the person who had come into his field of vision was fumbling with the door on the back of the garage. For a moment the lock was holding, but at last the knife the intruder was using held the strike back and the door opened.

Larry pushed his chair back to his room, and reaching under a pile of clothes on the dresser, took out his service pistol. It was loaded but not cocked.

The man was in the house now, and Larry could hear him walking across the kitchen floor. He saw the shadow cross his doorway and heard him breathing as he headed upstairs. Whoever it was knew where he was going. Burglars were just not this brazen.

Using a pillow from his bed to muffle the noise Larry pulled back the slide on his automatic. Then sliding from his chair to the carpet, he inched his way to the doorway on his elbows, pulling his useless lower body along behind him. He was still a couple of feet from his open door when he heard Diego yell, "Now it's my turn, you fucking bitch! Now it's my turn to kill," and Beth's bedroom door slammed open. Diego had turned on the bedroom light and Larry could imagine he was confused by the made up bed and the empty room. He heard the bathroom door slam open next, and then heard the man come out of the bathroom, go across the hall and open the door to Sarah's room.

Diego was confused and now stood for a moment between the two rooms at the top of the stairs, thinking of his next move.

Larry's right hand holding the pistol, and his head, were all that showed around the corner of the door as Diego came down the stairs. He was halfway down when Larry's voice stopped him in his tracks.

"Looking for someone, Sanchez?"

It was dark downstairs and Diego didn't see Larry lying there for a few seconds. When he did, he dropped the knife from his right hand and reached behind him for the gun in the back of his jeans as he retreated backwards up the stairs.

As soon as Diego's gun appeared from behind him, Larry fired, and the .45 caliber slug tore through Diego's chest and shattered a picture on the wall behind him. It fell off the wall and spun down the stairs with a tinkling of shattered glass as Diego moaned loudly.

He fell backward, landing on the steps. His right hand holding the gun came up again, but before he could pull the trigger Larry fired once more. The bullet went in under Diego's chin, hit bone and went out the back of his head. Diego's lifeless body slid partway down the stairs and then somersaulted the rest of the way, landing right in front of Larry. A pool of blood started to spread out under his head.

Larry stared at the dead man not more than a foot from him. He was totally unemotional. This was the man who had killed his best friend and his daughter. This was the man who had made him a cripple for the rest of his life. He had come to kill again and ended up dead himself.

Larry crawled back to his chair and pulled himself into it. He then went to his bedside and dialed the phone.

"Police and fire, 911."

"This is a city police officer," Larry said. "I have just killed a man who broke into the house and who was trying to kill me. Send a squad, please."

-26-

Dan Wicks sat on a kitchen chair listening as Larry explained what had happened. Lights had been set up in the room as the forensic people went about collecting evidence. Diego's car had been recovered from down the block along with a letter that had been taken from the Motrin's mailbox in early April and a young girl's anklet.

"Do you think he was here to get Beth or to get you?" Wicks sat across the table questioning Larry.

Larry pondered the question for a moment, knowing full well that the man had been after Beth, and then said. "I am not sure who he was after. All I know is he pointed his gun at me."

"Do you think Beth Motrin would have been capable of killing Manny Sanchez? I guess you know her better than me." Wicks was half heartedly trying to make sense of things.

"I don't know how she could have, Captain. She was with me that night."

Dan walked around the house and into Beth's bedroom. He flipped open the top of her jewelry box and sorted through the assortment of earrings, bracelets and necklaces. There was one ring in the box. Her wedding set.

He sorted through the closet looking for a .357 caliber gun, but there was only Mick's service revolver. He also found no wigs.

Dan went across the hall into the other bedroom but there was nothing there for him, either. Before he closed the door he gazed at Sarah's belongings which were just as they had been the day she was shot. He tried to imagine what it must have been like for Beth to lose both Sarah and Mick the way she did.

Back downstairs the detectives had finished their work. "Let's pick up and get out of here," Dan said. "This looks to me like a case of justifiable homicide but the grand jury will have to decide that."

Larry called Beth shortly after six to tell her what had happened.

"I'll be coming right back," she said. "Are you okay?"

"Yes, I am fine," Larry answered. "Or as fine as you can be after killing some-one."

Beth did not answer him but she wanted to say. "I know what you're going through, big guy. "

When Beth returned home, everyone was gone except Larry. He had called a friend who came over and helped clean up the mess, and outside of a bullet hole in the wall at the top of the stairs and the broken picture, the house looked pretty good.

She made lunch for the two of them. Brandy seemed glad to be back home, although she seemed to be looking for someone, and Beth knew it was Sarah. After lunch she and Larry took their coffee and went out on the deck to talk.

After Beth sat down, Larry said, "I have some things I want to ask you, and if you don't want to answer, you don't have to." She looked at him through her lashes while blowing on her hot coffee.

"Diego Sanchez came here looking for you last night, Beth, not me. Just before he kicked your bedroom door open he screamed something about it being his turn to kill. What do you think he meant?"

"Why does it matter?" she asked. "He's dead now."

"Why did you burn your clothing in the fireplace, Beth?"

She still didn't answer him but kept blowing on her coffee.

"Did you kill Manny Sanchez?" Larry asked.

She set her coffee down and lowered her eyes to her lap, but she didn't answer him. She didn't have to, Larry knew the answer.

"Let's go inside," he said, "its starting to rain. Hey, can I take you out to sup-per? We could go someplace nice, if you like."

"I would like that," Beth answered.

On the following Wednesday afternoon there was a staff meeting of the homi-cide detectives, presided over by Dan Wicks. It wasn't a special meeting, just one that they had from time to time to go over things. Several names were written under a subtitle on a white board behind him including Mick and Sarah Motrin and Manny and Diego Sanchez.

Dan pointed at the names and said, "These are the names of four people who were murdered in the last six weeks. Cases you all have been working on. All of these cases are being dropped. Mick and his daughter were murdered by Diego and Manny Sanchez. We knew that, even if the courts didn't. Since Manny and Diego are both dead, I'm calling this case solved.

Manny Sanches was killed by an unknown assailant who most likely was defending herself from being raped. We have no new evidence in this case, and considering the nature of the crime, we are dropping it. We could reopen it if something comes up. Diego Sanchez was killed by Officer Larry Sorenson in self defense, and this morning the court found it to be a justifiable homicide. George Sanchez, who was rumored to have been in the drive-by shooting has left the state. We are not going to actively pursue him. Are there any questions?"

A tall, skinny red-headed detective raised his hand. "Yeah, I have a question. Who ate all the damn doughnuts?" They all laughed.

A couple of weeks later Beth Motrin received a call from Dan Wicks saying he had her other insurance check, but that she would have to stop by and pick it up. She was going to the doctor that morning, anyway, so she said, "I'll stop by on my way home."

"Sounds good to me," Wicks replied.

Beth left the doctor's office feeling good. The baby was growing rapidly and she had sat in awe as she watched the tiny heart beating on the ultrasound. Dr. Tully gave Beth some pre-natal vitamins to take, but otherwise, in the doctor's words, Beth was the perfect place in which to grow a baby.

Tomorrow would be the first of July, and the hot summer sun beat down on her as she left the doctor's office to head downtown to see Dan Wicks. She was squinting her eyes until she realized her sunglasses were still on top of her head. She put them on as she pulled out of the parking lot.

Beth had done a lot of thinking in the last week, and she was going to go back to teaching, but not at the school where she had been. There were just too many memories there. She had applied for a job in a small town closer to her dad's place.

She talked it over with Larry and he was willing to buy her house now that it was all fixed up for him. His job as a dispatcher was going well and he was becoming more self-sufficient every day. He had a new van with a chair lift and all the hand controls he needed.

When Beth arrived at the police station Dan Wicks was in a meeting, but his secretary told her to have a seat as he would be done in a minute. As she sat in the waiting room she noticed a plaque that had been hung to honor the police officers from the department who had died in the line of duty.

She walked over to the plaque and could see that the last name was freshly etched in a row of about twenty names. She first read the statement at the top that dedicated the plaque to the officers who had made the ultimate sacrifice in protecting the citizens of the city. The last line came from the Bible. **Greater love hath no man than this. That he would lay down his life for his fellow man**.

Beth reached up and touched Mick's name with her finger tips, her eyes filling with tears. Just then inside of her the baby's heartbeat quickened, and for the first time she was aware of two hearts beating in one body. It was as if she could feel them both for a brief moment.

Dan's hand on her shoulder startled her.

"I just got the plaque back yesterday from the jeweler. I hope it's a long time before we have to take it down again."

She nodded her head, and wiped her eyes.

She signed for the check, just as she had before, and then Dan tore off the top part and handed her the bottom half with the check. His eyes left hers for a moment to look at her hands. There were no rings on the left hand but on the right hand was the friendship ring she had put back on.

"That's an interesting ring," Dan said holding her fingertips.

"Mick gave it to me before we were married. I've always worn it ever since."

Dan smiled but did not answer her except to say, "God bless you, Beth. Stay in touch."

In September Beth was packing to move to her new home in her new town. Next week she would start her new job. Her baby boy was growing rapidly inside of her and last week she had felt movement. Yes, she knew it was a boy, the ultrasound picture confirmed it.

She was looking around the house one last time when the phone rang. Beth decided to let it go to the machine, as it was probably for Larry anyway.

The sound of the female voice startled her. "Mrs. Motrin. This is Maria Sanchez, George Sanchez's wife. I'm calling you from Chicago and I was wondering if I could meet with you for a few minutes next week when I'm in your city. It would mean so much to me just to meet you. Please call me back." Then she gave the number.

For a moment Beth didn't know what to think, but at last she copied the number down and erased the call.

She walked around with the number in her pocket for most of the day and then realized she was moving and would not be available anymore at this number after today. Larry was changing the number. She could ignore it and try to forget about it, or maybe if she called, it would close the last chapter of this horrible story for her.

Beth called Dan Wicks and asked his advice. "I would ignore it, Beth," he said. "We still have a warrant out for George Sanchez, but we haven't asked that he be picked up. If he comes back here he'll be arrested. The reason we are not pursuing him is that we have nothing to charge him with that we could make stick. We know he was in that car, but outside of Larry's testimony that the courts won't buy, we have nothing."

Beth thanked him and hung up the phone. She left her keys for the house on the kitchen table and closed the door behind her. Larry and Beth had said their goodbyes last night and he was at work right now. Brandy was waiting in the car for her, and she drove away for the last time.

It was sad leaving this little house on Elm Street, and a flood of memories washed over her. She remembered coming home from their honeymoon to it and setting up housekeeping. There was the memory of bringing Sarah home from the hospital two days after her birth and feeling that for the first time they were a real family. She remembered all of the birthdays and anniversaries. There were Christmas holidays and the cold winter nights in front of the fireplace. All of the remodeling and fixing up they had planned and done. She thought of Sarah riding her bicycle for the first time in the street out front with-out training wheels, and Mick running along beside her, gasping for breath and hanging onto the back of the bike. But what she remembered the most was the undying love they had had for each other and for Sarah,

She was crying again but it was a controlled cry. The kind you need to have from time to time, and end up feeling so peaceful when it is over.

It was the next day when she called Maria from her cell phone. She was sitting on her new bed, in her new house that smelled like plaster and fresh carpeting.

The voice was so faint at first that she thought they had a bad connection. "Hello, this is Maria."

"Maria, this is Beth Motrin. You called and left message for me to call you back?"

There was an eerie silence for a few moments and then Maria's trembling voice. "Mrs. Motrin." She was crying now. Beth could sense it.

"I don't know where to begin. I want to meet with you and tell you my part of the story." She blew her nose quietly and then continued. "I have asked my husband to meet with you, also, but he us afraid of being arrested. He prays everyday that you can forgive him. He says he will spend every day until he dies living in shame for what happened. When he heard about your daughter he wanted to kill himself."

"I wanted to kill myself too," Beth said. "I will spend the rest of my life in pain for what happened. We don't need to meet, Maria, and I thank you for calling me. Please tell your husband that no one is after him any longer."

A small voice in the background said "Mommy," and then something Beth could not understand.

"You have a child?" Beth asked.

"Yes. A little girl named Anna. She will be three on her next birthday. I am pregnant now with her brother."

Beth was crying now, but she sucked in her breath and tried to calm down. "I'm pregnant, too, with Sarah's brother," she said. "Maria, as a mother and a wife you know all to well what it would be like to lose your family, and I think that's why you called me The pain and heartbreak I went though, well I couldn't wish that on anybody. Tell your husband I forgive him, and I wish you both all of the happiness in the world. Goodbye and God bless."

"Thank you, Beth. I will tell him, and God bless you, too." It was punctuated with a sob that was cut off as Beth broke the connection.

She was glad she had called, but it was time to put it all behind her and get on with her life. She went into the other bedroom and looked at the crib and baby furniture, the wallpaper with yellow ducks swimming in a blue background. Her hands touched her swollen abdomen and she smiled as she felt the tiny kick. He approved.

It was April and Beth had made her way back to the city for a visit. Mickey Motrin lay in the back seat in his infant seat watching the scenery go by, his little fist stuffed in his mouth. The jeep had been replaced with a white minivan that still had that new car smell.

Beth met Larry at a café for lunch and a visit. She could never go back to that house, but it was good to see him and see him looking so healthy. Laurie showed up later with her new husband and she was fascinated with Mickey. "Maybe someday," she said touching her husband's hand and they all laughed.

It was a cold blustery Minnesota day, and Beth had bundled Mickey up before taking him with her across the frozen ground in the cemetery. This was her last stop before heading home. Today was one year from the day that Mick and Sarah had been taken from her. Things had gone from unbelievable pain and grief to a soft tolerable ache in her chest. Everyday in her life was becoming more pain-free, and like the coming of spring, everyday showed more promise. It had been weeks since she had cried.

Beth stood and looked down at the brown grass around the monument. She emptied the vase and put fresh flowers in it. Digging around in the turf with her fingers, she found the bullet casing she had put there on that day long ago, and clutched it in her fist. There was no need for this anymore.

She took the blanket from the little boy's face, and, holding him over the grave, said softly, "This is your son, Mick. This is your brother, Sarah. I just wanted you to see him." She kissed her fingertips and touched each monument. On the way back to the car she dropped the casing in a trashcan. There had been a time a year ago when she had had nothing to lose, nothing to live for. But that all had changed.

The End

978-0-595-51432-8
0-595-51432-4

CPSIA information can be obtained at www.ICGtesting.com
Printed in the USA
LVOW052123120712

289829LV00008BB/55/P

9 780595 514328